The Co
(Relic Hunters #11)

By
David Leadbeater

Copyright © David Leadbeater 2024
ISBN: 9798878088633

All rights reserved.
No part of this publication may be reproduced, distributed, or transmitted in any form or by any means, including photocopying, recording, or other electronic or mechanical methods, without the prior written permission of the publisher/author except in the case of brief quotations embodied in critical reviews and certain other non-commercial uses permitted by copyright law.

All characters in this book are fictitious, and any resemblance to actual persons living or dead is purely coincidental.

Classification: Thriller, adventure, action, mystery, suspense, archaeological, military, historical, assassination, terrorism, assassin, spy.

Other Books by David Leadbeater:

The Matt Drake Series

A constantly evolving, action-packed romp based in the escapist action-adventure genre:

The Bones of Odin (Matt Drake #1)
The Blood King Conspiracy (Matt Drake #2)
The Gates of Hell (Matt Drake 3)
The Tomb of the Gods (Matt Drake #4)
Brothers in Arms (Matt Drake #5)
The Swords of Babylon (Matt Drake #6)
Blood Vengeance (Matt Drake #7)
Last Man Standing (Matt Drake #8)
The Plagues of Pandora (Matt Drake #9)
The Lost Kingdom (Matt Drake #10)
The Ghost Ships of Arizona (Matt Drake #11)
The Last Bazaar (Matt Drake #12)
The Edge of Armageddon (Matt Drake #13)
The Treasures of Saint Germain (Matt Drake #14)
Inca Kings (Matt Drake #15)
The Four Corners of the Earth (Matt Drake #16)
The Seven Seals of Egypt (Matt Drake #17)
Weapons of the Gods (Matt Drake #18)
The Blood King Legacy (Matt Drake #19)
Devil's Island (Matt Drake #20)
The Fabergé Heist (Matt Drake #21)
Four Sacred Treasures (Matt Drake #22)
The Sea Rats (Matt Drake #23)
Blood King Takedown (Matt Drake #24)
Devil's Junction (Matt Drake #25)
Voodoo soldiers (Matt Drake #26)

The Carnival of Curiosities (Matt Drake #27)
Theatre of War (Matt Drake #28)
Shattered Spear (Matt Drake #29)
Ghost Squadron (Matt Drake #30)
A Cold Day in Hell (Matt Drake #31)
The Winged Dagger (Matt Drake #32)
Two Minutes to Midnight (Matt Drake #33)
The Devil's Reaper (Matt Drake #34)

The Alicia Myles Series
Aztec Gold (Alicia Myles #1)
Crusader's Gold (Alicia Myles #2)
Caribbean Gold (Alicia Myles #3)
Chasing Gold (Alicia Myles #4)
Galleon's Gold (Alicia Myles #5)
Hawaiian Gold (Alicia Myles #6)

The Torsten Dahl Thriller Series
Stand Your Ground (Dahl Thriller #1)

The Relic Hunters Series
The Relic Hunters (Relic Hunters #1)
The Atlantis Cipher (Relic Hunters #2)
The Amber Secret (Relic Hunters #3)
The Hostage Diamond (Relic Hunters #4)
The Rocks of Albion (Relic Hunters #5)
The Illuminati Sanctum (Relic Hunters #6)
The Illuminati Endgame (Relic Hunters #7)
The Atlantis Heist (Relic Hunters #8)

The City of a Thousand Ghosts (Relic Hunters #9)
Hierarchy of Madness (Relic Hunters #10)

The Joe Mason Series

The Vatican Secret (Joe Mason #1)
The Demon Code (Joe Mason #2)
The Midnight Conspiracy (Joe Mason #3)
The Babylon Plot (Joe Mason #4)

The Rogue Series

Rogue (Book One)

The Disavowed Series:

The Razor's Edge (Disavowed #1)
In Harm's Way (Disavowed #2)
Threat Level: Red (Disavowed #3)

The Chosen Few Series

Chosen (The Chosen Trilogy #1)
Guardians (The Chosen Trilogy #2)
Heroes (The Chosen Trilogy #3)

Short Stories

Walking with Ghosts (A short story)
A Whispering of Ghosts (A short story)

All genuine comments are very welcome at:

davidleadbeater2011@hotmail.co.uk

Twitter: @dleadbeater2011

Visit David's website for the latest news and information:
davidleadbeater.com

The Contest

The Contest

CHAPTER ONE

The sun beat down. The man named Phoenix shielded his eyes, even though he wore designer sunglasses. He was a tall man, broad, with long, dark hair and carefully trimmed facial stubble. The man was dressed all in white. Around him hung an air of authority.

He was seated on a set of bleacher-like stands, but his area was opulent. He was surrounded by tapestries, draperies and lavish fixings. Beneath him, there was a throne. Around him were guards and two other sovereigns. There were always several sovereigns present at the games, though generally never the full quota of ten. Phoenix, of course, was always present.

A sovereign leaned in to him, head bowed respectfully. 'A fine show today, sir.'

Phoenix nodded without speaking. He looked over at a guard, a man dressed in a black suit, black sunglasses, and sporting an automatic weapon. 'Raise the sunshade a little, would you?'

The guard complied. There were several other guards arrayed around the bleachers, all alert and watching their perimeters.

Phoenix turned to the sovereign who had spoken. 'Who do you fancy to win today?'

'Oh, the blonde. She is far more skilful.'

Phoenix pursed his lips. 'Then a wager,' he said. 'I will back the redhead.'

'And what would you care to bet, sir?'

Phoenix shrugged. 'Does it matter what we bet? These are our days now. This is our time. Does it get any better?' He spread his arms, laughing. The sovereign looked a little confused at first, but then laughed along with him.

'We are all sovereigns,' Phoenix continued. 'And we hold the power of life or death, literally, in our hands. If the redhead wins, we still have the power to end her life. It is that simple. Now... let us watch the action.'

His gaze fixed on the scene down below. At the base of the bleachers was a round arena, a dirt-floored battleground. There were currently two women in the arena, both carrying swords. The blonde was muscly, fit, and held the sword proficiently, whereas the redhead was a touch too skinny for combat and had little strength in her wiry frame. She also looked as if she was already defeated, standing limply and offering little in the way of a challenge.

Phoenix rose to his feet. 'Do not forget what rests on your compliance,' he yelled. 'The fate of all your friends.'

This perked the redhead up a bit, made her face harden. The blonde came in with a half-hearted swing. Phoenix felt his breath catch in his throat. The redhead flitted aside quickly, showing she had some defiance in her at least. She raised her sword.

'Fight!' Phoenix yelled.

The women, galvanised by his voice, raised their swords and attacked. There was the clash of steel ringing out across the land. Phoenix smirked to himself. He could make them do anything. The women pushed each other away. The blonde struck downwards with her sword, barely missing the other woman's head. The redhead looked shocked. Her mouth fell open. She raised her sword and thrust forward. The blonde skipped out of the way.

'Now they're getting in to it,' Phoenix said happily.

The action ramped up a little, broadening his smile. He looked around. The bleachers were dotted with many guards, making him feel safe. The two sovereigns present were enjoying themselves. Beyond the bleachers stood the other buildings, the barracks, the jail, the mess hall. Various other structures that dotted the savannah in this far corner of the world.

A corner that he was utilising most nicely.

The two women again grabbed his attention. It seemed they had both come to terms with what had to be done. Neither of them looked happy about it, but at least they were getting into the spirit of things. Phoenix always hated it when they had to be physically forced to fight, or even shot. It took away the magnificent spectacle of the blood sport.

The blonde swung her sword. The redhead blocked it with her own. Again, there was the sound of metal clashing, a satisfying sound that made Phoenix shiver despite the heat. He watched more closely, leaning forward, eager.

The blonde swung. The redhead leaned away, then used her sword like a knife, stabbing. The thrust nicked the blonde's ribs, made her scream. Blood soaked her shirt. She staggered and pulled away, almost dropped her sword. If the redhead had pushed her advantage then, she would have won.

But she didn't. She wasn't a fighter. She hesitated, aghast at what she had done. One of the sovereigns laughed at her expression. Whilst the blonde bled, the redhead looked up at the bleachers.

'Please don't do this,' she said. 'We've done nothing to you. Please let us go.'

Phoenix didn't like her attitude. He nodded to a guard. The man drew out a handgun, pointed it at the woman and fired. The bullet kicked up dirt between her feet. She screamed, did a little dance. The guard fired again, this time coming within an inch of her right foot. The woman sobbed.

'Fight,' Phoenix said simply. 'This is now a timed event. If one of you has not killed the other in five minutes, one of your friends will die... .and so forth, and so forth.'

The redhead fell to her knees, apparently broken. The blonde, clutching her bleeding stomach, took a step towards her, raising her sword.

'That's it...' Phoenix breathed.

The blonde aimed her sword at the redhead's ribs, looking as if she was going to run the woman through. Sweat dripped off her forehead, spattering the ground. Her limbs were dusty, dirty, her entire frame trembling. Phoenix could hear her hyperventilating. He swallowed drily, practically able to taste the blood in his own mouth.

The redhead looked up, caught the blonde's eyes. The blonde hesitated, but then thrust forward with her weapon. The redhead rolled away, but the point of the sword nicked her. She, too, was now bleeding.

Both women were then on their feet, circling each other.

'That's better,' Phoenix said.

There was now a look in both their eyes, a look that said 'I don't want to die.' Their gaze was frosty, narrow, focused. They held their swords lightly. Phoenix had

The Contest

seen the heat of battle settle over people before, countless times, and it had happened to both these women now.

Perfect.

He reached out towards a low table to his right. On it sat a goblet of red wine. Next to that sat a plate of nibbles. Phoenix sipped the wine and ate the cheeses, watching raptly, an enormous grin on his face.

The women were in hell. They circled and thrust and skipped aside. They bled. Their faces were dirty, streaked with sweat and dust and blood. They cried out to give themselves courage despite their shaking limbs.

'We push them to their absolute limits,' Phoenix said softly. 'I love it.'

Phoenix's lead guard, a man named Rahim, came up alongside him. 'Five minutes have passed, sir.'

Phoenix waved him away. 'It has got better. We don't interrupt them now. They are ready to kill each other.'

'Of course, sir.'

He watched. The women jabbed, cut each other, backed away. They were both dead tired. The blonde still looked the strongest. Phoenix stood by his wager, though. He drank and ate fruit and watched as the women got closer and closer to committing murder.

The blonde lifted her sword above her head, ready for a downward swing. The redhead saw it and, on some kind of animal instinct, leapt forward, thrusting hard, forcing the sharpened blade all the way through the blonde's body. There was blood and there was screaming and the redhead stood back, hands to her mouth, terrified at what she'd done.

Phoenix rose out of his chair, clapping. 'Bravo,' he said. 'You win. You have done me proud.'

The woman looked up at him, hatred and terror etched into her face.

The guards came forward into the arena, grabbed hold of the still dying blonde and started dragging her away. Two more cuffed the redhead and led her back to her quarters. Phoenix finished his wine and then looked over at the other two sovereigns.

'Some wonderful sport,' he said. 'I wonder what's up next.'

They nodded, an eager light in their eyes. Their bloodlust was far from slaked. From his vantage point atop the bleachers, Phoenix could make out most of their immediate surroundings. He could see the various buildings and the other contraptions of pain and madness that stood scattered about the compound, waiting for the contestants.

The others were following his gaze, also looking at the challenges.

'I saw a superb attempt at the gauntlet yesterday,' one sovereign said. 'The man got over half way before the swords hacked him apart.'

Phoenix laughed. 'I saw that, too. Such entertainment. And the really good part... it's just another day for us. There's a lot more where that came from.'

The sovereigns seemed content, which pleased Phoenix. After all, they were a big part of the complex and he couldn't do it without them. Keeping them mollified was all part of the deal.

He looked from the enormous, wicked looking gauntlet to the vast plain beyond, to the misty mountains and the dense forest, all of which played a part in the games.

The Contest

'What do you see for the future?' a sovereign asked.

Phoenix thought about the question, unprepared for it. 'I see nothing wrong with the way things are,' he said finally, simply. 'So... more of the same.'

'I like that,' the man said.

As they sat there, chatting, two figures were led into the arena. They were cuffed, their heads hanging low, their backs bent. Two males this time, both walking on trembling legs. They shuffled, clearly not wanting to be there. Phoenix licked his lips. The next bout of entertainment was about to begin.

'More of this?' he said, smiling at the other sovereigns. 'I can handle that.'

This time, daggers were handed out, and the men told that one of them had to die. They already knew what would happen if they refused to fight. Never were contestants brought here who didn't have something to lose. Something huge. It was how Phoenix made them fight to the death.

He beckoned Rahim over. 'Do we have a full day's entertainment?'

Rahim nodded. 'Yes, sir. We have two more in the arena and then two on the gauntlet. Following that, we have a bout in the killing pit and then a hunt.'

'Very good,' Phoenix said. 'A full day. I do like the sound of that. So tell me, Rahim,' he leaned forward. 'Who do we have coming next month?'

CHAPTER TWO

It had been an odd few weeks, Reilly reflected. The relic hunter team he was now a part of had found a wealth of diamonds and was due a substantial cut of the proceeds. They were all currently living out of hotels in New York, separately because they didn't want to get on top of each other. It was an odd kind of stasis in which they found themselves with nothing to do and money due to them. Heidi and Lucie were handling all the details and passing information along to the team.

Reilly had joined the relic hunters just a few months ago when they were fighting their way through the Amazon. He had a shock of long, blonde hair, electric blue eyes, was fit and finely chiselled. He was a well-made man and had once worked for the Bratva. Not liking the life, Reilly walked away from them without consulting them and was now not sure if they were hunting him, or had accepted the split. He had gone down to the Amazon to disappear and do the least criminal-minded thing he could actually do. Facilitating. A bit of smuggling. He lived constantly with a sense of being hunted. But Reilly had found a way of living with himself. On the side, he'd reported the really bad things he'd seen, the properly evil bastards. Reilly hadn't exactly been an informer, but he'd definitely and happily turned out to be an anonymous caller. He worked like that for years, plying his trade, staying under the radar, until Guy Bodie and his team came along.

And with them, of course, his old girlfriend – Yasmine.

Reilly had never lost his feelings for Yasmine. Seeing her, years after they split, in the Amazon had only rekindled the flame. Of course, he wasn't sure how she felt, and still wasn't, but for him, the emotions were still there.

And add to that a strange affection he felt for Heidi and things were well and truly confusing. As well as being exciting.

Reilly wasn't sure where Bodie and Heidi stood together. It was clear they liked each other, and they'd been out on at least one date. But they were taking it real slow. Maybe they'd both been burned before.

Reilly sat in the hotel restaurant alone. He'd eaten alone for the past two nights. The days were long and boring. As a team, all they were doing was waiting, waiting for something to happen with their financial disbursement. They couldn't start a new job even if they wanted to, because they needed to be on hand to handle any complications that might arise with the new upcoming arrangements.

He waited for his meal, sipping a beer. Sitting in a New York restaurant was a far more civilised life than what he was used to, and Reilly wasn't exactly sure he liked it. He was used to the rough lifestyle, the meagre choices, the hard living. To him, it was normality. This was all completely different. Truth be told, he didn't know what the future held.

He'd quit the Amazon to run with the relic hunters. They offered excitement and camaraderie, and the chance to be part of a team. Maybe even a family. Did Reilly want that? He wasn't entirely sure, wasn't entirely sure about anything.

In truth, Reilly was confused.

Did Yasmine want him back? Was Heidi available? Did he really fancy either of them? When he got his share of the money, what should he do?

The questions barrelled around his head like well-hit snooker balls. He'd been struggling with them for days now.

Reilly ate his meal and drank his beer. The restaurant was quiet, sparsely peopled. It was nighttime, and the dark was pressed up against the glass as if seeking entry. He wondered what the others were doing tonight, Yasmine in particular. He knew vaguely that Bodie and Heidi might be going out on their next date. Second or third, he wasn't sure. He didn't know what the others were up to or when they might meet again. Basically, he was sitting around waiting for a message, a heads up.

Reilly's mind flickered over his reckless past. It had been a rough old life, he reflected. Running missions for the Bratva, climbing the food-chain. Steering clear of the worst crimes whilst gradually realising he wasn't cut out for any of that kind of work. It took him years to come to terms with that, and then just a day to decide to run away from it all. Back then, he knew the danger of it, knew the Bratva wouldn't let him just leave. You didn't just quit an outfit like that. In fact, once you were in, you were in for life. At first, Reilly hadn't been able to see a way out.

And then he just left.

Ran away. Pocketed all of his cash and left the country. Just disappeared. Maybe they thought he'd died, come to grief at the hands of some faceless enemy. Reilly decided it was better to vanish without a trace than anything else. That way, nobody would ever know. Through the years, he'd often met people who worked around the Amazon basin. It was anonymous, shadowy, nameless work, they told him. If you worked there for too long, a man could forget his own name.

Right then, it sounded perfect to Reilly.

When he arrived, he found people leading a thriving, muddy, basic existence. If you could put up with the environment, the hazards, the danger, then you could make a decent living. Reilly set about doing just that.

His years in the Amazon were good ones. He met some pleasant, honest folk, and yes, some incredibly evil ones. But mostly, he kept to himself, cultivated a small circle of friends, and worked hard. He got to know the area, which, essentially, was how he ended up meeting with the relic hunters.

Would he stick with them?

It was a loaded question. He liked all of them, liked their set up. He also enjoyed the danger they seemed to attract. And working with a globe-trotting team would keep him on the move, out of the way. They had something good going. What was it Bodie said? *Family is a sense of belonging?* Something like that. Reilly understood it and even thought he might want some of it.

But what was the alternative? He guessed that depended on what kind of cut they might get from all those gemstones they'd found. Would it make him comfortable for life? He hoped so. The damned gemstone search had nearly cost him everything.

Reilly stopped thinking for a while as he finished his

meal and paid the bill. He tipped, left the restaurant, and headed up to his room. With energy to burn, he knew it was going to be a long night. Maybe he should go for a walk, but he didn't know New York well enough by now. But the trails of the Amazon... that was a different story.

Reilly had a bottle of bourbon stashed. He started on it now and sat on the bed, watched something banal on the TV. He couldn't stop his mind flitting back and forth. Funnily enough, he always ended up on Yasmine.

What to do about her?

That's her decision.

Of course it was, but it didn't stop Reilly from wondering...

... and hoping.

CHAPTER THREE

Guy Bodie grew up fast and hard, an orphan. After his parents were killed, Bodie bounced around from home to home and found it increasingly hard to socialise and make friends. It was a trait that had stayed with him his entire life. He'd got into trouble early, committed burglary, and then fell in with a man named Jack Pantera who made sure Bodie only stole from those who could afford to lose what he took. Pantera took Bodie under his wing, and Bodie never looked back.

But he still found it hard to make friends. That was why the relic hunters were so dear to him, so special. In them, he'd found a family, something he'd lost at an early age. In them, he'd found trust and friendship and acceptance.

Bodie had short hair, a rash of stubble, a strong build and a standoffish manner to anyone but his friends. He didn't like easily.

Right now, though, he liked life a lot.

He and Heidi were on their second official date. This time, they had decided to go see a movie. They had found a cinema with the right film showing in the midafternoon, and had then made their way inside to the plush seating, drinks and snacks in hand. They sat next to each other and sat through the adverts, the trailers, and then settled in to watch their movie. Bodie was happy just sitting next to her.

Heidi seemed comfortable too.

She was a tall woman, with long legs and curly blonde hair and a lived-in face. Heidi had seen a lot during her time with the CIA. It had left her jaded, but still driven to help people. When her time at the CIA ended because she chose to run with the relic hunters, she had found different ways to help people.

Now she turned to Bodie and whispered, 'The committee contacted me today.'

The body that had been chosen to oversee the entire gemstone scenario comprised experts, a gemologist, lawyers, a CEO and a leading cop and, collectively, were known to the relic hunters as the committee.

'Any proper news?' Bodie asked quietly.

Heidi leaned in closer so that he could feel her breath on his ear. 'Some small progress. They've catalogued all the gems, identified them, valued them, and are ready to move forward with their recommendations. We should hear something next week.'

'Sounds good. At least we'll have some liquidity then.'

'I've missed handling hard cash. Plastic just isn't the same.'

'The first thing I'm gonna do is pay that plastic off.'

Heidi's lips brushed his lobe, sending a tingle through him. He had to wonder if she'd done it on purpose. 'And what else?'

'Depends on how much we get. Look for a home?'

'Guy Bodie setting down roots,' she said with a smile. 'I can't see it.'

Bodie had to admit that she might be right. 'Set up a business then,' he said. 'Relic hunting.'

'Services across the globe,' Heidi said. 'Sounds good to me.'

The Contest

'Think we'll have any competition?' Bodie asked.

'There's always competition. We'll just have to hope it's not too cutthroat.'

Bodie nodded and settled back. They watched their movie, not saying much more. Two hours later, they were shifting in their seats as the credits rolled, ready to stand up and exit. Bodie didn't want the night to end.

'What do you say to trying out Gray's Papaya?'

Heidi also didn't appear in a hurry to end their evening. 'It's on Broadway. That's a subway ride.'

'That's okay. I'll treat you.'

'Does it count as a third date?'

'It can be anything you want it to be.'

'That's a bit vague. If I smell of fried onions, will you still kiss me?'

Bodie blinked and then met her eyes with a deep intensity. 'I'd kiss you anytime.'

In the cinema, standing almost alone now, they embraced and then kissed. Bodie felt it from his brain all the way to his toes. His eyes were as close to Heidi's as they'd ever been and he noticed light blue flecks in there.

'Gray's,' he said huskily.

'And then?' She left it hanging.

Bodie wanted to take her back to his hotel room. He wanted to do it right now, but felt compelled to keep the decorum. Besides, a quick trip to Broadway wouldn't take long and he was starving for the kind of food they served up.

The couple linked arms and then left the theatre, walked through the cinema to the exit doors. They left the cinema behind, stepping out into a cold, cloudless day. It was early evening, the light still in the sky but dimmed, dying. The streets were packed with people, six deep, just on their side of the road. Bodie and Heidi joined the flow.

They headed for the nearest subway and joined the masses heading down the concrete steps. It was a free-for-all, a horde of humanity pounding every which way. The couple made their way through the station, down escalators, and found the right train.

Luckily, their carriage was a quiet one, and they could sit down. Heidi put her hand in Bodie's and laid her head on his shoulder. This was turning into a great night with the promise of more to come.

The train rattled down the lines, and it was then that Bodie noticed four other men in the carriage. He'd been distracted by Heidi and their spectacular night until now. The men were well built, shaven headed and all wearing leather jackets as if it was a uniform. The reason Bodie noticed the men was because they were all staring at him.

And then they rose to their feet.

Bodie sensed trouble coming. He nudged Heidi, made her aware. What the hell did these guys want?

'Three minutes until the next stop,' one of them said in a British accent. 'That's where you're getting off, pal.'

Bodie rose to his feet. 'Is there a problem, guys?'

The men exploded into action. They came forward fast, fists lunging. Because of the restrictions of the carriage, only two men could attack at a time. Bodie and Heidi stepped forward to meet them.

Bodie raised his arms, caught a blow, punched back. His fist connected with his opponent's skull, bruising his knuckles. The man ducked and came in low, driving a fist at Bodie's body. Bodie half turned, deflecting it again. He was close to the man, the two of them too restricted to make their blows count.

The Contest

The men behind were pushing in hard. Bodie backed down the train carriage, creating space. He took hold of his opponent's head, smashed it into a metal pole with a loud clang. The man fell away, replaced by another. This one backed Bodie up to the seats where the backs of his knees folded and he abruptly sat down.

The main rained down blows.

Heidi also used a standing pole to smash her enemy's head into. The man hit nose first. Blood coated the metal and ran down it. The man fell to his knees, and a second took his place. This man fought furiously, throwing out punch after punch without letting up and despite the fact that very few of them landed. Heidi had to cover up. She waited for the man to step just a little closer.

When he did, she kicked him in the groin, making him fold. By now, the first man was back in her face with his bloodied nose. He punched her in the gut, threw a haymaker at the side of her head. It connected. Heidi saw stars and wilted.

Bodie was in a difficult position, one he wasn't sure he could get out of. The train rattled on. There were three other occupants of the car and all of them were on their feet by now, one with a phone to his ear. They looked scared and shocked. Bodie yelled at them to call the cops. The man assaulting him was doing so from above, throwing punches down at Bodie's head so fast he couldn't stand. He was stuck. He tried kicking out, but his strikes were ineffectual.

A very brave man came up to them, shouting, demanding that they stop. One of the attackers turned to him and punched him in the gut. Bodie used the distraction to thrust himself to his feet, and now he was face to face with his enemy, their noses practically touching.

Together, they both went for the headbutt, cracked heads. Bodie bent down and used his shoulder to push the man back. He then lashed out at the man's face, connecting and splitting skin. The man didn't seem to feel any pain. He didn't cover up either. He was reaching into his jacket.

And now came up with a knife.

Heidi staggered, holding on to the pole to stay upright. The two men in front of her rained blows down now, making her see double. Her hair hung over her eyes. She couldn't think straight. Everything was blurry.

Suddenly, she felt the cold press of steel against her throat.

She focused, looked up, knew the knife was pressing deep into her skin. She met the eyes of the man holding it.

'You're coming with us,' he said.

The train screeched as it approached the next station, slowing gradually. Heidi didn't dare move. The blade was pressed in hard. She met the eyes of the man in front of her.

'Why not use the knife to start off with?'

He grinned and now produced a gun, which he pushed into her gut. 'Because we like to get down and dirty,' he said. 'Have a little fun first.' He was bleeding profusely, and licked at a red runnel with his tongue.

She straightened. The other occupants of the car were standing frozen with fear. The train neared the station. Heidi turned to check on Bodie.

She saw him covered by a Glock too, this one held against his head.

'Do as we say,' one man said. 'And nobody dies.'

'Or gets stabbed for fun,' the man she'd kicked between the legs growled.

The Contest

The train slowed rapidly. The new station platform flashed past the windows. Finally, the train stopped, and the doors opened. The attackers, now abductors, spent a few seconds warning the other passengers to remain on the train and stay quiet... or else they'd die too. Then they ushered both Bodie and Heidi off the train.

And onto the platform. Bodie counted about eight people waiting to board the train and a few disembarking further down. Now, the gun was nestled into the small of his back. The knife had disappeared. Heidi was being treated the same way. Walking like that, the four men escorted Heidi and Bodie off the platform, up the escalators and into the main station.

This was Bodie's chance. The place was packed. If they made a scene here, they might just get away, make a break for it. He readied himself, confident that his enemy wouldn't fire a shot in the busy environment. Besides that, they surely wanted him alive. Otherwise, why go to all this trouble? They could have shot him point blank on the train.

He primed his muscles, prepared to break free and run. It was right then that the man holding him turned him slightly, made him focus on Heidi.

Even here, in this chaos, they were holding a knife to her throat.

'We don't need her,' the man whispered in Bodie's ear.

There was no way to tell if he was being truthful. There was only the terrifying sight of sharp metal being pressed against Heidi's throat. His eyes locked on to her through dozens of passing figures. He couldn't understand why no one else could see it, but then they were all going about their business.

And it was only for a few seconds.

Bodie held out his hands, let his muscles relax. The man holding him leaned in.

'Good man,' he said.

Bodie felt the gun jam harder into his spine. 'Now walk,' the man continued.

They crossed the station and came up against a set of wide steps. The men brought Heidi closer until they were practically walking together. They climbed the steps steadily, all the way to the top and out into the bracing early evening air.

Up here, it was even busier, crowds thronging the streets. Bodie saw several cars idling at the kerb. His captor urged him towards one of them.

'Get in,' he growled.

Bodie saw freedom narrowing. Once he was in the car, they could do anything to either of them, capture them entirely. He contemplated escape once more but, again, his enemy sensed it coming.

They forced him to look at Heidi, at the fear in her eyes, and then quickly showed him the knife that was nestled into her ribs, just pricking through the clothing.

'Don't be an idiot,' the man said. 'Let her live a while longer.'

'What do you want with us?'

'Oh, I assure you. It's gonna be exciting.'

CHAPTER FOUR

Jemma Blunt sat in her hotel room, sipping wine. She was the cat burglar of the team. Her long, dark hair, as usual, was tied up in a bun. When she was working, it was her trademark, but when she relaxed she usually let her hair down. Not tonight. She couldn't be bothered. The wine was going down rather well. It was warm, red, and perfectly gluggable.

Jemma was an outstanding planner of jobs. She wasn't shy, just quiet, and usually responded to more outgoing people. Like Cassidy, for instance. She and Cassidy got on incredibly well, and Jemma often let the redhead lead her into situations she might otherwise have avoided. Situations that often turned out rather well.

Take a few nights ago, for instance. Cassidy had insisted they visit a new nightclub and see if there was anything worth dancing with. They found a couple of guys, danced the night away, and ended up snogging with them in a booth. Ordinarily, Jemma would never have gone near a situation like that. But Cassidy led her on with excellent results. She had swopped numbers with her man, and was looking forward to seeing him again in a few days' time.

She was content with her own company. She thought of the relic hunters, of Cassidy, Bodie, Heidi, Lucie and

Reilly, and of where they were right now with their lives. In a moment of immobility, she thought, and maybe balance. It was tough not knowing what was coming next, but she hoped the committee would come up with an offer soon and solve a few headaches for the team.

Jemma had been a cat burglar for as long as she could remember. Her young life had been hard; her parents worked long hours but barely had enough money left at the end of the week to rub a few pennies together. To supplement her meals, she used to steal, first from the corner shop and then the supermarket, and then advanced to more lucrative establishments. She fell in with the right – or *wrong* – crowd and learned her trade. She worked for shady men and women, bringing them pieces they could never own. Jemma learned her trade on the go, by making mistakes, and always owned up to them, always overcame them. It was a dangerous existence, though, and she never knew where her next penny was coming from.

Kind of like her previous existence.

Then she met Guy Bodie, and they joined together to rob from the rich only, from those who could afford to lose it. They made a decent living, developed a reputation for themselves. For Jemma, meeting Bodie had become a sweet deal.

And now, ever since he'd been broken out of that Mexican prison, they'd become relic hunters. First working for the CIA, and then getting out, now working for themselves. Again though, *yet again,* she'd found that money was the problem.

The problem being they had none of it.

They'd managed for a while, but now they really were living on their last few dimes. If the committee screwed them, they'd be up shit creek for sure.

The Contest

Jemma leaned her head back against the headboard, sipping even more wine. Tonight, the entire bottle was going to go down, and just because she could. She wasn't a heavy drinker, and would probably wake with a huge hangover tomorrow, but... occasionally... it was worth it.

Her phone buzzed. Jemma reached across the bedside table and grabbed it, looked at the screen. It was a text from Heidi, saying: *meet me in the lobby.*

Jemma stared. *Now?* She was sitting in her underwear, enjoying the wine, chilled out for the evening. And Heidi wanted to meet *now*. It couldn't be good news. She texted back.

Can't we just call?

No. I need to see you in the lobby.

Jemma sighed. She placed her glass on the nightstand, swung her legs off the bed, and stood up. She dressed, slipped into her shoes and took a last, longing look at her wine.

I'll be back, she thought.

Just in case, Jemma took her coat and headed towards the elevator. She waited for the car to arrive, heard the low ding, and watched the doors slide apart. She was alone in the car as it sank five floors to the lobby.

The doors opened to a blanket of noise. The lobby was busy, people traipsing through the front doors and crossing over to the reception desk, others zigzagging their way to the restaurant or the bar. Jemma missed her room already. Being an introvert, these hectic scenarios tended to daunt her.

She stepped out and looked around. No sign of Heidi, but then it was very busy. She decided the best idea would be to walk straight across the lobby, standing out, see if she could spot Heidi that way. She started out, looking left and right, hoping to set eyes on her frizzy-headed friend.

She crossed the lobby once, all the way to the far windows. Still no sign of Heidi. Maybe it was time to text her. Jemma found a quiet alcove and fished her phone out.

She looked up. A man stood before her. He was bald and broad and wore a black leather jacket. In the alcove, she couldn't see past him. She frowned.

'Can I help you?'

'You can come with me. Quietly.'

Jemma couldn't believe her ears. She readied herself, knowing she could fight off the man and attract attention.

'Get the hell away from me, you asshole.'

The man reached out and grabbed her shoulders. Jemma couldn't quite believe what was happening and struck out, catching him across the throat. He coughed. She threw a punch at his solar plexus, made him back away.

'What the hell?' She was still in shock.

'Come with me,' he grunted, and now he smiled.

Jemma didn't like the look of that. Not at all. He was entirely too confident. She tried to look around him, still couldn't properly weigh up the situation.

'We're in a crowded lobby,' she said. 'All I have to do is-'

He reached out fast like a striking viper, grabbed her throat. She found she couldn't speak, couldn't breathe. Now she struck out, kicking his shins and then aiming for his groin, but missing. She punched at his face, but he blocked her attack with his free arm. He squeezed

The Contest

harder. She found him incredibly strong, but the hand around her throat was making her weaker.

Still, what the hell was he planning to do in the lobby?

She continued to fight. She kicked at him and threw punches. One got past his defence, struck him across the cheek. His head jerked violently. She got another one through, again striking his face. They were locked in a harsh struggle, there in the dim alcove of the lobby, each struggling to contain the other.

Jemma was past her shock. Now she just wanted to get the hell out of there. In addition, she was worried about Heidi. Had she been lured down here? She swung out left and right and broke through her opponent's defences.

But the man held on, his grip like iron. Jemma was seeing darkness in front of her eyes. Her blows were still strong, but she could feel a weakness invading her body. The man pressed into her.

Struggling wildly, she finally saw around him. Her heart sank. There were two other men just like him stood behind him, blocking people's view of the struggle. The alcove was small, and she was trapped in it, unable to move. It was surreal, unbelievable. It couldn't be happening to her.

But it was.

She turned into a dervish, fighting wildly. She wrenched herself out of his grip, struggled for air. Jemma didn't have enough even to scream, and he was already reaching for her again.

But this time, in his left hand, he held a knife. He pressed it into her stomach.

'Stop,' he said simply.

She gasped for air, drew in a few lungfuls. 'You can't force me out of here,' she snarled.

The man plucked something out of his other pocket. It was a black phone and now he fiddled with the screen.

'Look,' he said.

She didn't tear her gaze away from his eyes, his face, memorising them. She was furious. Her throat ached. It gratified her to see she'd scratched his cheeks in her struggle. But he didn't look phased. In truth, he looked pleased with himself.

'Look,' he said again.

Jemma could hear the noise in the lobby, peoples raised voices and laughter. The sound of a man calling out for a friend. A woman's voice, asking someone for the correct time. She heard the front doors opening, the hum of traffic on the street outside. But none of it was real for her. Only this tight, terrible situation was real.

She switched her gaze from the man's face to his phone. There was a picture on the screen. She squinted and did a double take.

It was Bodie and Heidi, sat together. And they both had guns pressed to their heads.

Jemma felt her world tilt at an angle.

'No,' she said.

'Do you understand?' the man said. 'You come with me now.'

CHAPTER FIVE

Lucie Boom, the researcher of the relic hunters team, was wandering nonchalantly around New York's National History Museum. She loved it. The endless rooms, the sometimes well-lit, sometimes gloomy passageways. The crowds drifting from spectacle to spectacle. It was warm in here, and the atmosphere was quietly full of excitement and respect and awe. She'd just passed a display of insects and was moving on to the quieter rooms where ancient artefacts awaited. It never failed to inspire and amuse her she'd also contributed to the location of certain artefacts along the way. None of them were here, but that wasn't the point. She was, in fact, a relic hunter.

Shouldn't she get special treatment?

Lucie smiled as she wandered down the latest corridor. Special treatment was one thing she really didn't want. She was blonde, with her hair currently hanging down and bright blue eyes. As often as she could, Lucie wore a woolly jumper, and today was no different. Today's offering was green and baggy and kept her warm even though, in here, she didn't need it.

In fact, she was sweating. They kept the temperature high, all right. She also had on a coat, which didn't help, and had brought along a hat and gloves. Lucie liked to be prepared. She often lectured the team on preparedness in her crisp military manner when she was explaining all about the latest artefact.

She missed the quest.

The last mission had been fun, though, searching for the gemstones. *Fun?* Well, there had been a lot of danger, too. These days, though, Lucie wasn't bothered about the danger half as much as she used to be. It was as if she'd accepted that it was there as a necessary evil. That, to make progress, they needed to go through a few people along the way.

She paused now, staring at a glass cabinet where a few old meteorites sat. They weren't large, but they were old and fascinating. Lucie bent over, staring down at the most colourful one. Around her, a multitude swarmed. The dense flood of people was affecting her enjoyment. She looked around. Maybe there were quieter passageways...

She saw face after face, figure after figure. She recalled the map she'd seen earlier, tried to think of a way through the throng. Lucie decided on a strategy and fought her way through the crowds, eventually ending up in another room where it was much quieter. Here, there were no meteorites, but there were a few stuffed animals and the stunning jawbone of a T-Rex.

Lucie crossed the space to study it, getting as close as she could. She checked her watch. It was getting on towards closing time. She would have to hurry. This afternoon had been a great distraction. The team was currently mired in red tape, waiting for some kind of payout. Who knew what would happen after that? She didn't like it. Didn't like the thought of not knowing what came next. The last thing she wanted was for the team to disband. Ever since she'd joined the relic hunters, Lucie had been living her best life.

The Contest

She checked her watch again. Around her, nothing moved. She had well and truly found a quiet place, and congratulated herself. Yes, these old places were dusty and creaky and spooky, especially at night, but it didn't really bother her. Maybe she'd apply for a job if the team broke up. Maybe she'd get it.

She looked around. Silence reigned. She saw nobody, except...

... except a figure peering around a far door, staring at her.

Lucie narrowed her eyes. Was someone watching her? Now, she felt alone, vulnerable. Where was a gaggle of civilians when you wanted them? She looked at the man, who pretended to be studying some wooden cabinet in the far corner. She then noticed he wasn't alone. Two other men were with him.

Lucie walked away. If she walked far and fast enough, she was bound to come across some people. Was she being paranoid? Probably. But it was far better to be paranoid than to be a victim. She left the T-Rex jawbone and headed for the far exit. The men didn't follow.

Now she was in a wide corridor, this one dimly lit. It ran for quite a way and was empty. Lucie listened as she walked. There were no other sounds. She turned around. Nobody was there. Could she hear something, though? The faint whispering of forced air circulating through the vents? Or was it quiet footfalls?

She walked faster, not caring where she was going. The map in her head didn't matter. She reached the end of the corridor, turning right into another room. At the door frame, she lingered, turned.

Three men were walking up the corridor towards her.

Now her heart started to hammer. They wore dark

clothing, jackets, and jeans. They were well built, clean shaven and striding towards her with a purpose. Lucie span and hurried away, crossed the room noticing nothing in it, entered another, crossed that one. She could hear them now. They were hurrying too, practically chasing her. She saw someone at last, four people ahead. But it was a family – mum and dad and the two kids. She couldn't drag them into this.

Whatever *this* was.

She went past, carried on into another section. The footfalls seemed to come closer. She longed to see a guard – there had been several earlier in the busier parts – but saw none. Her whole body was taut, tensed up. Her mouth was dry.

Without slowing, she hastened through the next section.

As luck would have it, this part of the museum was dark and dingy. The further she penetrated, it seemed, the gloomier it became. She rushed on, thought she heard a grunt behind her, this time quite close. She didn't dare turn, and now considered running. Her feet slammed the polished floor. Her bag suddenly snagged on a low cabinet and hauled her back, the strap wrapping around her throat. Lucie almost screamed. She unsnagged herself, took a moment to draw breath, looked back.

Three shadows lurked at the entrance to the room.

She heard their breathing, saw their movements towards her. They were coming. She turned and ran, throwing caution to the wind now, sweating profusely. She came across another family, and then another, couldn't bring herself to involve them, looked back. The men were chasing now, malevolent shadows in the

The Contest

bleakly lit rooms. They slowed as they passed the families. She didn't. She drew ahead.

But there seemed to be no end to the corridors and rooms. She went from one to the other, totally lost, wondering where the hell she was and, through panic, unable to structure the museum map in her mind. If anything, the rooms got darker. Behind her came running footsteps and grunting and loud shuffling.

A figure walked out in front of her. Lucie almost screamed. She saw a face looming, thin arms tucked into pockets, and then... a uniform. *She'd found a guard!* Lucie ran up to him now, panting, slowing as she reached him.

'There are men,' she said. 'Chasing me.' It sounded lame now, here, as she faced the startled guard. 'You have to help.'

His hands went immediately to the radio attached to his chest. But he didn't speak into it. He stared at her and then past her.

'You're being chased?' he questioned.

'I know it's unusual, but I-'

They came flying out of the shadows. Three men running hard. One of them hit Lucie, tackling her around the waist. The other two took out the guard, hitting him head on with their fists flying. One enormous fist smashed into the guard's head, knocking him into the wall where he left a large dent in the plaster. Another buried itself in his abdomen. The man's eyes instantly closed, and he slithered to the floor.

Lucie was being clasped around the chest, her arms pinned. The man holding her had a grip of iron. She struggled, wrenching this way and that. She could feel his breath close to her ear, feel his body against her. As she watched, one of the other men kicked the unconscious guard in the head.

Then he turned to her.

'Stop fighting.'

She struggled relentlessly, knowing that was what other members of her team would do. She slammed her heel back into her captor's shin, tried to wriggle out from his iron grasp. Then she threw her head back in an effort to headbutt him, succeeded, heard a pained grunt. But his grip never let up.

Maybe she could bend over, somehow pull him over her head. Was she strong enough?

Then everything exploded. The man facing her punched her in the face. Lucie couldn't see, couldn't think. She slumped in the man's grip.

'Now,' she heard. 'Stop your struggling.'

She opened her eyes. A man was leaning in, staring, eyes just a few inches from her own. 'You will come with us,' he said.

She shook her head, regretted it as the world started spinning. She could feel blood trickling from the corner of her mouth and the taste of it inside. The man holding her grunted and then slightly loosened his grip.

She acted on impulse, instantly. Maybe it was being around the team for so long, seeing how they reacted to every situation. When the man's grip lessened, she wrenched her arms clear and kicked out. Her right foot smashed into the guy in front of her, making him grunt. She flung an elbow into the face of the man behind her. She wriggled free, saw the space ahead, prepared to run for it.

The third man stepped into her eyeline. He had a knife.

The Contest

She paused, thought *fuck it,* and ran anyway. She kicked out first, again striking the man in front of her. She started moving, came up against a flying fist that doubled her over. Lucie tried not to fall, but the punch took all the wind out of her. She staggered, swayed, couldn't go any further.

The knife was suddenly pressed to her stomach, its point pressing through her clothing.

'You want me to gut you?' a voice asked. 'Right here, right now. You're an extra in this game, not the star.'

Game? The word, for unknown reasons, stood out to her.

She stopped moving. There was no getting away. She couldn't outrun them. It was all a game of chance. Maybe though... maybe there would be more guards further on, more people, a way out. She would never give up.

She gathered herself once more.

The man facing her nodded, his face impressed. 'I like your grit,' he said.

Another man got in her face then, the man she'd been kicking. His eyes seemed pained, a look she enjoyed.

'You fight for nothing,' he said. 'We already have you.'

And he showed her his phone. The picture. Lucie stared at it. She saw Bodie and Heidi sitting in a room, their backs to a white wall. Two men had guns pressed to their heads.

'Come with us or watch them die,' the man said. 'Your choice.'

Lucie stopped struggling.

CHAPTER SIX

Cassidy Coleman was sweating from every pore, and she loved it. At the moment, this was the best way to stay active, to keep her body fit. She came to the gym sometimes twice a day, worked for a couple of hours, and then hit the shower. She had become a fixture, the staff nodding at her, the regulars smiling. Cassidy wasn't sure she liked it. This wasn't her world, nowhere near it.

Cassidy was a striking redhead, over six feet tall. She was the muscle of the relic hunter team and had often been called upon. Every mission, actually, and she'd never come up against an opponent she couldn't handle. She'd grown up fast and hard in LA, spent a stint on the streets, worked for a Hollywood movie studio, participated successfully in underground street fighting, and had come out at the top of that game for four years.

Joining Guy Bodie's team changed her, focused her. Once she accepted his hand in friendship, she never looked back. She became a better person. Cassidy loved the relic hunter team with all her heart. Truly, she thought, it had saved her life.

She prayed it would never disband. What the hell would she do if it did? She, Guy and Jemma were the oldest surviving members. They had seen everything and been together for over a decade. There simply was nothing else in her life.

The Contest

Lately, she had become worried. They had had no direction, no motivation. It seemed they were immobile, unable to operate without new funding, which, hopefully, would come from the recent unearthing of the gemstones.

But their momentum had stalled. The team seemed restless. Was it falling apart? Cassidy sincerely hoped not. She enjoyed seeing Bodie and Heidi becoming closer. It had been on the cards for a long time. But even that... even that might change things.

Cassidy finished on the treadmill and moved to the rowing machine. She did a few extra stretches, stared out the mid-level window that ran right across the gym. Outside, it was dark and getting darker, the busy streets swept by wind and a little light drizzle. In here, it was bright and warm and inviting, and she tried to shrug off her melancholy. It wasn't easy, though. She was deeply worried.

Cassidy needed the stability of a team. It was how she'd escaped the hard life before, and she agonised about being pulled back into it. After all, if the team fell apart, what would she do for money, for action, for enjoyment? Cassidy needed all three.

She worked hard on the rower, felt the sweat flying off her brow. She managed to ignore her anxieties for a while. After the rower, she walked over to the weights area and started with the dumbbells, light to start off with. The surrounding gym was lively. Workers coming in after they'd finished their day jobs, she imagined. Music played through loudspeakers. Several TV screens were tuned to various shows, and almost everyone had a pair of earbuds in. Cassidy didn't bother with that stuff. Even though her inner thoughts weren't wholesome at the moment, she preferred to work through them rather than bury them under a barrage of music and pictures.

She curled the dumbbells, unable to get on any machines right then. That would come. She was patient. She wondered if the boxing ring might be free. It was way over the other side and around a corner. She hadn't punched anyone in weeks and wanted a good fighting workout.

With that thought, she was looking towards the entrance to the gym. Two men wearing bandannas had just come in, but clad in suits and headed for the changing rooms. Next, she saw a crowd push through the entrance. Eight of them. Five men and three women. She noticed them chiefly because they didn't carry gym bags, didn't appear to be interested in anything except scanning the gym.

Clearly, they were looking for someone.

The eight newcomers spread into the gym, looking all around the room. Cassidy curled her weights and watched them, curious. The men and women looked serious, their eyes and faces harsh. They meant business. Others were looking at them too, clearly wondering what was happening.

Cassidy saw one of the gazes fall upon her and widen with recognition. This person gave a shout. Suddenly, all eight pairs of eyes fastened upon her. Cassidy blinked, uncharacteristically unnerved.

What the..?

She held on to her dumbbells as all eight people started towards her. They made an odd procession walking through the gym, dressed in jeans and jackets, all with their focus firmly on her. People stared. The newcomers ignored the attention.

The Contest

One man spearheaded the approach. He was tall, broad and had a hook nose. Eyes blacker than obsidian. He came right up to Cassidy and stopped before her. The others fanned out around him.

'Hey,' he said.

Cassidy narrowed her eyes, saying nothing.

'We could make you come with us,' he said. 'But we've been told how good you are and want to test that out. What do you say?'

Cassidy heard him, knew she should react hard and aggressive, but didn't want to be the one throwing the first punch in the busy gym.

'What the hell are you taking about?' she played for time, still trying to get her head around the strange turn in events.

'We're here to kidnap you,' the man said clearly. 'That's our job. But we want to fight you first. Does that make sense?'

Cassidy wasn't one to hold back. She struck out with the right dumbbell, clouting the hook-nosed man across the face with it. She struck out with the second, hitting another man. Everything then went to shit. The remaining people, six of them, all stepped in towards her. Cassidy threw both dumbbells at the same time, hitting two more people, and then flung elbows and knees out, striking more. Faced with overwhelming numbers, she sought items in her environment to help.

She ducked behind a weights machine, used it as a barrier between her and two opponents. A woman came running around the side. Cassidy stepped in a tripped her, sent her sprawling. A gym-goer leapt out of the way. Others were backing up, moving towards the edges of the room. Several were staring in shock.

Cassidy threw left and right punches. She connected solidly with a woman and a man. They staggered to their knees, but still more were coming. There were too many. She took one out and two more took their place. The hook nose man was back in it, nose bleeding, but face as severe as cut glass. He came at her now, running, lifting his knee and trying to smash into her. Cassidy spun and sent him hurtling past into a treadmill where he fell face first, grunting hard. She kept spinning, led with an elbow, smashed a man's nose. Blood flew everywhere. She'd hit them all now, sent some of them to the ground, but at least four still surrounded her.

They started to land punches and kicks. Cassidy felt a fist connect with her ribs, another smash into the back of her neck. She shrugged the pain off, kept moving, kept kicking and punching out. Another blow struck another rib, made her grimace. She grabbed hold of a man, threw him into the cables of a weights machine, saw him get tangled there. She clasped a woman around the throat, smashed her head into the handles of a treadmill. Once again at the rack of dumbbells, she grabbed two and started swinging.

But still they assaulted her, every blow a debilitating attack. She felt impacts on her thighs, her stomach, her chest, her skull. She blocked dozens of hits. This was getting downright desperate, dirty fighting now, and she knew exactly what to do.

She bent low, struck out, aimed at the most vulnerable places. Pressure points. Groins. Temples. Knees. Fingers. Elbows. She worked hard, twisting and turning, never presenting a static target. She broke bones, saw two men fall in agony, clutching their limbs. Cassidy sought eyes with stiffened fingers, saw a woman twist away.

The Contest

A man fell at her knees. She broke his nose and cheekbone. They were thinning, at least four of them out of commission. But that still left four, and the battle had already taken its toll on Cassidy. She was hurting, bruised and battered. She staggered now, barely able to keep up the pace.

Hook nose was suddenly right next to her, throwing short sharp punches. She felt them impact her chest; her face. She covered up, but another man stepped in from the side, concentrating on her ribs. A blow struck the top of her head. Someone tried to take her legs out, hitting the backs of her knees. They clearly didn't want to harm her too much – they didn't want to break anything – but weren't holding an awful lot back.

Cassidy's fraught eyes swept the gym. She saw a couple of people had tried to help her, but had been driven away by her attackers. Now people lined the edges or were leaving, not wanting to get involved. Some were on their phones.

She slumped a little. More blows rained down on her. She rallied, kicked out at a knee and made its owner fall flat on his face. Now there were three. Cassidy was close to victory, but still so far away. Hook nose was suddenly close to her ear, whispering.

'Not bad,' he said. 'You're better than I thought. But we have to end this before the cops make an appearance. Now, stand up.'

Cassidy straightened. The attack had stopped. Her eight opponents were picking themselves up, some limping, others groaning, all bloody. She wondered what the hell was going on here.

'See this,' Hook nose held out a phone.

Cassidy stared at the picture. Bodie and Heidi, both with guns to their heads.

'If you want them to live, you will come with us,' Hook nose said.

Cassidy nodded. 'Couldn't you have just said that at the start?'

'Are you kidding? This way was much more fun.'

CHAPTER SEVEN

Yasmine was alone, thinking about Reilly. It was poignant that he had come back into her life. Poignant indeed. She wondered if he was interested in her still, and was she still interested in him?

She was currently in a record store, browsing through a load of dusty LPs. Yasmine loved the old classics, and the old vinyl, loved how it sounded. Back home in Morocco, she had an ancient record player, but obviously hadn't been there in a long time. Now, she played LPs in store booths. That was as good as it got. Nevertheless, it helped relax her, made her narrow her thoughts to a sharper angle.

Reilly. Did she want to go there again? And their current situation... what would happen once the committee had paid them out? She didn't actually think Bodie would put an end to the relic hunters, but it was possible. She'd fallen in with them quite by chance a while ago now but had embraced their comradeship, their sense of belonging together. She worked well with them. It was far better than working for the Bratva. Although she missed her old friend Eli Cross. They all did.

Yasmine chose a record and took it over to a booth, slipped on a pair of headphones, and started listening. She enjoyed the music, the sound, made a purchase. No, she didn't have a record player in her hotel room, but this was very much for a future that hadn't even been envisioned yet.

She listened to a few more records, enjoyed the music playing over the store's speakers. It was a lovely, calm atmosphere inside the shop, and it instilled within her a deep sense of peace. After a while, though, it was time to return to the hotel. She could revisit the store another day. She had plenty of time.

Yasmine left the shop and started walking down the street. It was dark and cold and she tightened her coat around her, putting her head down. She fought her way through the crowds, only about five blocks from her hotel. A chill gust of wind washed past her face. A man jostled her from the left and muttered an apology. She passed shops with open doors, the smell of food leaking out, making her stomach rumble. Two blocks passed and she could almost sense the approach of the hotel. It's warmth. It's restaurant. It's cosy little room. Maybe she would call Reilly tonight, start a conversation. It was innocent enough. But who knew where it might lead? It wasn't as if she had any other prospects on the table at the moment.

She almost laughed aloud at that. She looked up. It was almost time to cross the road. At first, she didn't compute that there were four men standing around her. It took a moment. Then she realised they had herded her to the side of the street whilst she walked and were now hemming her in up against a brick wall.

But there were still plenty of people around, flooding past them. Yasmine looked from face to face, saw severe expressions and hard eyes, broad shoulders and a military bearing. These men meant business.

The Contest

'What do you want?' she asked. She felt uncertain. This was a strange situation to be in.

A man stepped forward. This one had a scar from his left eye to the corner of his curled lip. 'We want you to come with us,' he said. 'Quietly. No screaming or shouting. No fighting. We just want you to capitulate.'

'Do you even know what that means, or did your boss explain it to you?'

The man's eyes hardened ever more. 'No protests,' he said. 'Just come with us.'

'Now why the hell would I do that?'

Carefully, he held up a finger, asking her to pause for a moment. Then he pulled a phone from his pocket, swiped at the screen, and showed it to her. Yasmine was looking at a photo of Bodie and Heidi, both with a gun pointed at their heads.

'That's why,' the man with the scar said.

Yasmine felt ice flood her veins. She suddenly felt isolated, alone, despite being at the centre of the busy street. Of course, the feeling had a lot to do with the situation her family was in. How were the others doing?

'You have everyone?' She fished.

'Almost,' he answered. 'You're the last.'

The last? She hated the sound of that and worried about the plight of the others. After a moment, she came back to the present. It was time to start worrying about her own situation.

'You're never going to get me out on the street,' she said. 'And your threat's hollow. No way will you shoot them. You want all of us.'

And she kicked out, caught a man on the thigh. Her elbow smashed another man in the throat. The way they were surrounding her hid the action from the people on the street, so no one noticed; no one paused as they passed by. Yasmine looked for a way out.

She noticed the alley to her left, just a few yards further up. She lowered her head and ran, barging into one man, striking his solar plexus, making him fold. He reached out to grab her as she slipped past.

Yasmine made it into the alley. Just as she was about to run hell for leather, she felt a contact from behind. Someone had stuck out a foot and tripped her. She fell headlong, sprawling onto the concrete. Without thinking, Yasmine tucked up and rolled and was almost instantly back on her feet.

She whirled. The men were following her into the alley, crowding after her. The man with the scar came first, looking none too happy. He had been hoping for an easy catch, but that would never be the case with Yasmine. She wasn't built to be taken meekly, without a fight.

She stood her ground, knowing she couldn't turn her back on them. Luckily, it was a tight alley and they could only come at her one at a time. Darkness was an issue – she couldn't see them very well – but she could strike at shadows just as easily as she could strike at flesh.

She delivered a front kick, driving her opponent back. He caught it, tried to twist her, but she yanked the leg away and stepped in to him. Now she fired in her punches. One, two, three, into his stomach. The guy took them and grunted. She felt his legs give way, but he rallied, held his ground. She jabbed stiffened fingers at his throat. This time he gargled and threw his head back. His knees folded.

Someone pushed past him. Yasmine met this man too, not backing down. She punched at his face, striking

The Contest

cheekbones, jabbing at eyes. Her attacks struck true, and soon he was crouched over with his head in his hands.

Yasmine had a brief moment to decide what to do. Her thoughts swirled. If all the relic hunters were being targeted and captured, they needed someone to remain free. To act on the outside. If they were all caught, they were in big trouble. She turned to flee. The only option here was to run away.

Spinning, she was caught again. Scarface had lunged, grabbed her jeans and tugged her back. He fell. She went down too, unbalanced, falling to her knees. That allowed another man to squeeze his way through and confront her.

She tried to rise. The man didn't let her, raining blows down at her head and temples. Yasmine saw stars, felt the force of his blows inside her head, rattling her brain. There were dark spots forming at the edge of her vision. She couldn't last much longer.

She scrambled away, trying to evade the onslaught. The concrete scraped her hands. She was aching and bloody on her exposed skin. She thrust herself to her feet.

Just in time. The man was already on her. She surprised him with her speed, made him take a step back.

Yasmine knew she was fighting a losing battle. There were too many of them. She'd debilitated two, but even now they were recovering, and she faced two fresh adversaries. She blocked the first man's flurry of attacks, tiring, walking backwards. He didn't let up, just kept coming, striking at her. Yasmine had no chance to counterattack.

That way, they retreated down the alley, step by step.

It was hard going. Yasmine gritted her teeth and took the pain. They hadn't beaten her yet. All she needed was a chance.

And then it came. The man driving her back stumbled. His right foot slipped on a random can and he fell forward. Yasmine was ready. She made sure he stumbled into a face plant that broke his nose. Made sure she bruised his eyes and that two of his teeth were knocked out. He went straight down to his knees, groaning heavily.

She'd acted instantly. And now there was just one more fresh attacker, with the others picking themselves up. Yasmine faced the last man, not moving, waiting for him to act.

When he did, she didn't like it. He drew a long curved blade from his waistband, waved it around in front of his face.

'You aren't going to kill me,' she said defiantly.

'No rules against sticking you a little, though,' he muttered.

'Your betters wouldn't like that.'

He snarled. 'Betters?'

She'd said it on purpose to distract him. It worked. As he snarled, she leapt in, grabbed the knife hand and twisted. The man yelped and dropped the knife. Yasmine heard it clatter to the floor. She led with an elbow, and then another, bloodying his face.

Just then, Scarface came flying past the man. He barged into her, knocking her back at a tremendous rate. Yasmine knew what would happen next but couldn't control herself. She flew backwards, backpedalling hard, and fell over the man she'd felled earlier. Now she crashed to the ground, slamming her head into the

The Contest

concrete. Instantly, she saw stars and gasped, her breath coming out painfully and fast. Scarface was immediately on her.

He held a knife to her ribs, smashed her in the face with his free hand. She groaned and almost blacked out. The impact with the ground had hit hard.

'Haul her up,' Scarface rose and turned to his men. 'Drag her out of the alley. The van's waiting.'

'Think she broke my cheek,' a man moaned. Another was holding his ribs and still another staring at his bloody, lost teeth.

'Don't worry,' Scarface said with satisfaction in his voice. 'We'll all be there to watch when she enters the Killing Pit.'

At that, everyone smiled.

The four men formed in front of Yasmine. One hauled her to her feet and held her under her arms, then started dragging her towards the alley exit. Yasmine's head swam. She wanted to fight, but her body wouldn't listen. She demanded that it act, but nothing happened. Thoughts battered at her. Terrible thoughts. She was helpless, being dragged away against her will and unable to do anything about it.

Even as she went, she tried to summon her will. But the blows to her head, the fall, it had incapacitated her badly.

'Please...' she muttered.

'You're ours now,' Scarface said with satisfaction. 'Along with the rest of your team.'

'Where... where are you... taking us?'

'Don't worry,' came the answer. 'You'll love the killing compound.'

CHAPTER EIGHT

Guy Bodie was fully awake and aware. He was cuffed and gagged and had been forced to sit on the floor inside a huge, cold, draughty old hangar. The place was vast, with a high ceiling and wide doors that would admit any plane he could think of. The floor was hard and dirty, the gag wet in his mouth, the cuffs cutting at his wrists. Armed guards stood about the place. Bodie had counted twelve of them, most smoking and talking, shooting the shit with their teammates. They glanced at Bodie only briefly, confident that he was secure.

Bodie hadn't been there long when Jemma arrived. She was also cuffed and gagged. More guards prodded her into the room and then sat her down next to Bodie. They could only communicate through their eyes, and both were wide. Neither of them, Bodie knew, had any idea what was happening here.

Twenty minutes later, Lucie appeared, also similarly secured. She too was placed on the floor, the three of them now forming a sorry-looking line. Still, the men and women watched them infrequently as they talked and smoked and stamped their feet to stay warm.

Bodie shivered. He tried to talk around the gag. It didn't work. He fought to wriggle his hands free of the cuffs. The action only brought him pain. An hour had passed since he'd been deposited here. Already, he was sure what would come next.

The Contest

Another relic hunter.

And so it happened. They shoved in Heidi next, forced her down to the floor. Heidi looked at Bodie with haunted eyes.

'Please,' Bodie could actually make her muffled words out. 'What do you want with us?'

The guards ignored them. Just made sure they stayed sitting in a line on the cold floor. Bodie could feel the cold sliding its way up through his body. The bracing wind whipped through the draughty warehouse, practically slapping him in the face. There were only two of them left, he thought. Cassidy and the newcomer, Reilly.

Maybe they hadn't caught everyone.

He could only hope. But as he waited, his hopes were dashed. They dragged Cassidy in next, fighting even as she was shoved and prodded in the right direction. Cassidy, he knew, would never be subdued.

Finally, she was deposited next to them. The guards started gathering around them. One man stepped forward and kicked Cassidy's ankles.

'Is this all of them?' he asked.

'The complete team,' another man said. 'They call themselves the relic hunters.'

'Can they fight?'

'They've been around a bit.'

'Well, they ain't seen nothing like this before,' the first man said. 'Let's get 'em on board.'

Bodie and the others were shoved to their feet and then marched across the hangar. Bodie's arms and legs ached from the captivity, but the exercise did him good. They headed for the hangar's massive doors, into the face of the wind.

Bodie could hear it as he approached. The massive engines of a plane idling. Outside the hangar, they saw a large black aeroplane with its rear ramp down. The team, unable to even look at each other now, were shoved onto the ramp and then made to climb into the belly of the plane. Once there, they were pushed down onto hard benches and told to remain still. Slowly, surely, with a groan of gears, the rear ramp raised. The team could only glance sideways at each other.

Where on earth were they going?

Bodie knew they were in hell here. All captured, they could be taken anywhere, made to do anything. They could use any one of them against the other. *Of course,* he thought, *they didn't get Reilly.*

There could only be one reason for that, he knew. Reilly was a recent member of their team. Whoever abducted the relic hunters didn't know he had become a part of them.

It was the only ray of light in this new darkness. But would Reilly realise they'd been taken? How long would it take him to do so? What, realistically, could he even do? Bodie knew it was pointless to speculate. Reilly would do everything that he could.

But they couldn't rely on him for a rescue. They had to do that for themselves.

Already thinking of escape, Bodie braced himself as the plane rumbled down the runway and then lifted off. There were over twenty guards inside the plane, all seemingly at ease and paying little attention to their captors. Bodie hated to admit that they'd done their job well. He couldn't move his hands without pain, couldn't speak. There would be no quick escape, he knew.

The others, alongside him on the hard bench, were in

THE CONTEST

the same dire straits. He met their gazes, saw the anger and fear in their eyes. Wherever these people wanted to take them, they were going.

It was a long flight and full of turbulence. Bodie closed his eyes for some of it, fought to relax. He hated turbulence. Being bounced around, back and forth, whilst being thirty thousand feet up in the air just wasn't right. He held on tightly to the bench with his knees clenched, determined not to show his fear as the guards occasionally turned to stare at them. To be fair, he saw some guards sitting down, looking anxious and afraid. In the meantime, the plane shook and vibrated and swayed from side to side.

It fell suddenly, making Bodie's heart hammer. One guard laughed and whooped. Another grabbed the bulkhead, looking sick. Bodie was glad when he heard a voice come through the loudspeaker.

'Twenty minutes to landing,'

He'd lost count of the time they were in the air. He had no way of measuring it. Many hours, he knew. But he was actually glad they were landing. It would get them out of the plane and enable them to assess what came next.

The plane came in for a mercifully smooth landing. It taxied a long way, then turned and stopped. The guards were already on their feet, guns in hand, which clearly meant they weren't landing at any normal airport. Bodie wondered where on earth they could be. Then, the rear ramp started to lower and a blaze of sunshine blasted in.

Bodie felt the scorching heat almost immediately. It was insanely bright, too. They were forced to their feet and then marched down the ramp. Bodie got a glimpse of a wide plain, several stands of trees and lots of brush. The sky was blue from horizon to horizon, the sun an angry, fiery ball. In a line, they walked down the ramp off the back of the plane and then formed a line to wait for their guards. Soon, there were many people milling around.

They waited in the blazing sun. The guards weren't happy, but Bodie overheard someone saying that the Jeeps were late. After a while, he heard engines approaching and then quite a few sports utility vehicles made an appearance. They bounced up a dry, rutted track, leaving a smoke trail behind, and came to a stop near the guards. Several drivers jumped out, some staying behind the wheel.

Bodie waited. Soon, they were all forced into the back seats of several vehicles and told to sit still. Bodie wondered how the hell they were supposed to do that when you saw the state of the roads and they had their hands cuffed behind their backs. The vehicles then turned around and set off. It was stifling hot inside.

Bodie was sweating profusely. Suddenly, the cold airplane hangar seemed pleasant. It was so hot he found it hard to breathe at first as his body struggled to get used to it.

They bounced down a rutted track away from the airfield. Bodie saw trees on both sides for a while and then a wide open plain. The scorching sun beat off it and dust spouts spiralled towards the skies. He saw a wide running stream next that meandered to the right, and then a massive lake. In the far distance, there were mountain peaks.

The jolting ride seemed to go on forever. Bodie felt decidedly car sick, but pushed through. It was like fighting a battle. They flew down the rickety road, surrounded on all sides by thick vegetation.

Through the grimy windscreen ahead, Bodie then saw

The Contest

a set of high wooden gates. The road evened out. The vehicle aimed for the centre of the gates, which opened as it approached. Bodie saw several sets of antlers hanging above the gate, but no name. It felt as if they were driving into a ranch.

They drove under the gate and into a vast compound. Bodie could see little through the windscreen except a bunch of outbuildings, some contraptions made of wood and several stands of trees. The vehicle made a wide approach to the front of a building and then stopped in a line with all the others. Soon, the engine was turned off, and they were told to move.

Bodie struggled to get out of the vehicle, but made it without falling. Once outside, he breathed in the hot air and looked around. They were standing in a semi-circle of buildings. Through the gaps between, he could see many large wooden devices, but did not know what they meant. He could also see the top of a set of bleachers not too far away. Beyond the immediate area, open plains ran straight towards distant forests and, even further, a range of mountains blurred with the distance.

Bodie turned to his friends as they all lined up. They were all taking in the various sights, eyes wide.

Bodie focused on the nearby buildings. What could he make out? One of them, four storeys high, looked like an upmarket hotel with balconies and wide revolving doors and golden furniture. Others were office buildings and those further away looked perfunctory, so might house the guards or provide a mess hall.

Finally, they were forced to move. They passed all the buildings and found themselves being prodded toward a long, squat structure. Beyond the structure, they saw open space for miles. Clearly, they had been brought to a massive compound.

Their captors took them to the main front door, opened it, and urged them inside. Bodie was ready for anything but, on first look, he was a little surprised.

They had been led to a prison.

CHAPTER NINE

The squat building was made up of narrow corridors with prison cells on either side. Bodie and his team were led along a corridor until their guards stopped them and pushed them into a cell each. After that, their gags and cuffs were removed. Without another word, the doors were locked, and the guards walked away. Bodie noticed a jug of water in one corner of the room, a toilet, and a low bed with a stained mattress and a once-white sheet.

There was nothing else.

With little choice, Bodie sat down on the bed. He felt exhausted after the flight of the night before, the travelling, the mental challenge of what was happening. His cell was compact and looked across the corridor onto another cell, this one empty. As he sat there, he heard the low whisper of conversation. There were other prisoners here, too. Of course there were. But to what purpose?

Hearing Cassidy's voice, he rose to his feet, went over to the bars and took hold of them. He gave them a good shake, found that they were solid, and then investigated the walls. Pure block. It was well made, solid. He went back to the bars and gave them another shake for good measure, inspected the lock. They hadn't been searched. He wondered if Jemma might still have her lock-picking tools.

He asked the question.

It took a while for Jemma to answer, but when she did, it was in the negative.

'You okay?' Bodie asked through the bars.

'Not really. Why the hell are we here, Guy?'

'I wish I knew. But they've had every chance to hurt us, so it's not that.'

'They're professional,' Cassidy said. 'Good at their job. They took us down. They run this place. We're gonna have to be every inch as good as they are.'

'And remember,' Lucie said. 'They might be listening to every word we say.'

It sobered Bodie a little. He looked immediately for the hidden speaker, the concealed CCTV camera. Found nothing. He gripped the bars again, tried to think of a way out of their situation. 'Anyone got an idea of where we are?'

'I'm guessing Africa,' Cassidy said. 'It's huge, and the plane journey was a long one.'

Bodie could almost hear Lucie shrug. 'Doesn't matter,' she said. 'We're stuck here until they let us go.'

That didn't seem likely. Bodie wondered what the bleachers and the other wooden devices were for. He rubbed his wrists where the cuffs had gripped tight, took a swallow of water to rinse out the nasty aftertaste of the gag. The water was tepid and tasted metallic.

'Could sure do with some air con in these cells,' Cassidy said.

'You should mention it,' Heidi said. 'Next time we see someone.'

'Maybe I will.'

They talked for a while, each of them settling in to their new environment in their own way. Bodie felt anxious, tense and unsure. There really was no way of finding out what would happen next. After a while, and despite their misgivings, they grew tired and went to their beds. There were no windows that he could see, but Bodie guessed it had grown dark outside as night fell. The other murmurings in the cell block went quiet, and despite his calling out, nobody answered. Maybe there was some rule regarding newcomers. He didn't know, but he did know that he was worn out and, soon, his eyes closed.

He woke with a start. At first, staring up at a strange ceiling, he had no idea where he was, and then the light dawned on him. The uncertainties and questions came rushing back. Hundreds of them. He swung his legs off the bed, rose to his feet, did a couple of laps of the cell to stretch. It didn't take long. He went back to the bars, called out for someone.

Cassidy answered. 'They haven't delivered room service yet.'

'You should complain.'

'I just might. Fancied some hot buttered toast this morning.'

'And coffee,' Bodie said. 'Tell them to bring coffee.'

The others were awake, and soon joined in, trying to take their minds off their predicament. About an hour passed. They were interrupted by the arrival of a group of guards, all armed, all looking purposeful. A man stepped forward.

'We will take you for breakfast,' he said. 'At a place we call the Core. It is there that you gather, eat, and drink. You are newcomers. We ask that you eat, drink and talk to no one yet. Everything will be explained to you after you have been to the Core. You have been uncuffed and are not currently required to wear a gag. Behave, and you stay that way. Do you understand?'

Without waiting for an answer, the guards stepped forward and unlocked their cells. They were ushered out. Bodie saw his friends, gauged how they looked. Lucie appeared nervous, staring from the guards to the ground. Cassidy challenged each guard with her eyes, but remained passive. There were too many of them to start a fight, and all of them were armed. Nobody wanted a gun fight just yet. Jemma and Heidi did as they were asked, standing easily and looking as if they were unphased. Yasmine observed the guards as if to learn how each of them acted, as if learning their patterns.

It wasn't a bad idea.

Bodie allowed himself to be led down the corridor, away from their cells, and out of the front door into a blazing heat. He gauged it was early morning, but it was hotter than hell already and he was forced to shade his eyes. The guards seemed used to it and just slipped sunglasses on.

They marched across a dry, dusty square towards a central hub area where another squat building stood. It was made of block and brick and had a sloping roof. Windows marched along the front, through which Bodie could see several figures wandering around.

They went through the front door into a large mess hall. Bodie saw dozens of tables and chairs placed around a large floor area, behind which sat quite a few men and women, eating and drinking, looking subdued. Around the edges of the room, a buffet had been laid out and there was a line of people grazing at it from one side to the next. Drinks' machines were in a far corner.

'Remember,' the guard said to them. 'This is your first time. Talk to no one.'

The Contest

With that, the guards left them alone, presumably to grab some food and drinks. Bodie sighed, not sure what to do. On the one hand, he didn't want to follow orders. On the other, they had been told reasonably what would happen. And he was hungry. He could smell the freshly brewed coffee. He shrugged at the others, took his line in the buffet, and piled food on his plate. When he was done, he deposited it on a table and then went for coffee, getting himself two mugs. Soon, the team were seated, eating and drinking and trying to take in this place called the Core.

Bodie stared at the guards first. They were arranged around the perimeter, watching carefully. All of them were armed. They wore a uniform of a black shirt and jeans and all had the obligatory pair of sunglasses. Their weapons were currently pointed at the floor, but all were extremely watchful, Bodie noted. They didn't move much, just remained in their positions. For the amount of people in the room, Bodie counted four people to a guard. Interesting.

He kept eating, swallowed some coffee and sat back. He turned his attention to the other people who, like them, were eating and drinking around the room. Bodie counted twelve of them. Men and women. Today they spoke to each other, but the conversations were muted, lacklustre. There was no laughter, not even half smiles. The people ate perfunctorily, steadily, as if it was a necessary chore. The guards didn't rush them and, it seemed, they could eat and drink as much as they were able. Bodie saw two people go up for seconds and thirds.

The team ate their fill and then sat back. Bodie grabbed another coffee, took his time with it. They weren't rushed. Finally, he decided it was time and signalled to the guards who'd spoken to them.

'We're done,' he said simply.

The guard gave him a grim smile. 'And now you get to experience the best part,' he said. 'To find out the reason you are here.'

The team rose, followed their guards out of the Core, back out into the hot day. A gust of wind caught Bodie in the face, bringing with it a cloud of dust. He coughed. The others stayed close. They were led across the compound to another building, this one fancier looking with leaded PVC windows and a high double front door. As soon as Bodie stepped inside, he felt the blessed waft of air conditioning.

'Oh, that's nice,' Lucie said.

It certainly made an agreeable change, but Bodie knew they shouldn't get used to it. They were led through an outer lobby and then across a wide room with high bookshelves on both sides. The guards stopped outside a carved wooden door made of dark polished oak.

'Wait here,' one said.

One man made a phone call. They waited for ten and then fifteen minutes. Bodie didn't really mind standing in the air con. It was a relief.

Finally, the door opened. Bodie took a deep breath and wondered what he was about to walk into.

CHAPTER TEN

Bodie was surprised to see a man wearing a butler's uniform step through and nod at them. He didn't speak, just waved them through the door. Bodie, not quite knowing what to expect, walked through first.

On the other side, he hesitated. It was a large room. Floor to ceiling windows stood to both sides, looking out over the property. Ahead was a raised dais and, on it, seated on a carved throne, was a figure dressed in white. He was tall, broad, with long, dark hair and carefully trimmed facial stubble. He carried an air of authority even, Bodie thought, without the ridiculous throne he sat on.

The man didn't get up, but waved them all inside. The team walked to the foot of the raised dais, and the guards followed. Now, Bodie saw, their guns were raised, pointed at the team.

'I am Phoenix,' the man said.

He stopped after that. Bodie wasn't sure if he was meant to respond, so didn't. He stared at the man without expression, waiting for him to speak further. To his left and right, the relic hunters stood in line with him.

'I am God in this little place,' Phoenix eventually went on. 'You live or die at my hand, sometimes quite literally,' he allowed himself a chuckle. 'Of course, I understand. You will be wondering why you are here.'

Bodie made to step forward, to the very edge of the dais, but a guard waved him back with his gun. He cleared his throat. 'What do you want with us? Our help?'

Phoenix laughed. 'Not exactly. So listen good, whilst I explain. Your time here will last three weeks. During that three weeks you will face a number of contests. Your skill will determine if you live or die. If you survive the three weeks, you will be set free.'

He paused to study them, gauging their reactions. Bodie tried to remain expressionless, but inside he was reeling.

Contests? Death? Three weeks?

Phoenix went on. 'Purposely, you don't know your location, so that should reassure you that, if you do survive the three weeks, you will indeed be set free. You can't lead anyone to us. You have been carefully chosen because you are skilled and you are survivors. The relic hunter team is famous.'

Again, Bodie remembered this wasn't the full team. They had missed Reilly, most likely because he'd only just come on board. He swallowed. 'Famous among which people?'

'Ah, that would be telling. Suffice to say I have many friends around the world who recommend certain parties to me. It makes the contests, the *games,* more interesting. I and my fellow sovereigns only want to see the best of the best.'

'Sovereigns?' Yasmine asked.

'There are ten of us. This place, this oasis, is set up entirely for our pleasure. A sovereign can visit whenever he or she pleases, but there are usually around two or three present at any one time because of personal constraints.'

'But you live here?' Heidi asked.

'I am the principal sovereign. I own this sanctuary.'

'It's hardly a sanctuary,' Cassidy said. 'Feels like more of a graveyard.'

Phoenix inclined his head. 'And it might be for you. That depends how strong you are. For me, however, it is heaven.'

'Another prick with too much damn money,' Cassidy said.

Phoenix didn't react. 'You will engage in contests together and apart. You will be victorious or you will die. You may have to kill to win. In the end, *I* might decide your fate. Or one of the other sovereigns, if I deem fit. All this for the viewing pleasure of the sovereigns. Do you understand?'

Bodie said nothing. He glanced askance at the guards, gauged where their weapons were, saw Cassidy doing the same. Was it worth the risk right now?

Phoenix guessed their intentions. 'This compound is well guarded,' he said. 'By highly trained, well-motivated men and women. They will shoot to wound if they have to and you will *still* be required to perform. I urge you not to test us.'

'What you are doing is barbaric,' Lucie said, and it was Lucie that Bodie was chiefly worried about. She was the non-fighter on their team.

'Barbaric?' Phoenix smiled. 'How quaint a term. I look forward to seeing you perform. I would wish you good luck, but I don't like to favour any side.' He now grinned. 'So... the compound is vast and well patrolled. Now, listen. It is imperative you understand. When called upon to perform, to fight or die, I realise you might be reluctant. You might wish not to take part...'

He sat forward.

'You *must* perform. You will perform. If you refuse, one member of your team will die. We will choose that person before the contest. Do you understand?'

Bodie stared open-mouthed at the madman. What had they been dragged into? He couldn't quite believe his eyes and ears. Of all the schemes, of all the wild scenarios he had been in or could even think of... this was far and away the worst.

And there was no way out of it.

He stared at Phoenix with hatred in his eyes, and Phoenix stared straight back at him, a little smile playing about his lips. There was intelligence there. Guile. Madness. Bodie didn't like to think of what the next few hours might bring.

It was a sentence to three weeks in Hell, and, despite what Phoenix said, Bodie didn't believe they'd just be allowed to leave. Maybe they didn't know where they were... but it didn't feel right. Bodie already knew that Phoenix was the worst kind of megalomaniac.

And the relic hunters were under his thrall.

CHAPTER ELEVEN

Reilly woke in darkness to the sound of an alarm. He started, sat up, looked at the bedstand. His head was fuzzy, and he was shocked. He only used the alarm as an emergency in case he overslept, which he never did.

Until today, that was.

Reilly turned off the alarm, but didn't sit up. Maybe he'd had a little too much of the bourbon last night. But thoughts of Yasmine had twisted and turned him, and the night had got away. Pretty soon, he wasn't sure how much he'd drank and didn't want to stop. Well, he'd certainly slept well.

He checked the time. Ten a.m. Breakfast would be done at the hotel restaurant, but that didn't matter. He could eat brunch. Reilly wondered if today was going to be yet another tedious twenty-four hours of killing time. Maybe they would hear from the committee today. He certainly hoped so.

Reilly climbed out of bed, realised he was fully dressed, and shook his head ruefully. He was used to drinking – you did little else in the heart of the Amazon – but last night must have been extra special.

Yasmine.

Damn, he was going to have to contact her. He couldn't go on without knowing if their relationship stood a chance. He checked his watch, knowing where all his team were last night. They kept each other abreast via group chats on social media. He checked back through the messages, seeing Yasmine had been chatting about the record shop she'd visited and had posted nothing since. She'd probably just gone back to her room and chilled for the night.

Reilly thought about going down for brunch and calling her later. Then his head started pounding, and he realised why he was in this state. He should call her and stop being an idiot.

Reilly picked up his phone, hit speed dial. Yasmine's phone started to ring. Reilly had a little speech memorised, but decided he would just tell her he wanted to see her today. These things were always better done face to face.

No answer. Reilly made a face. After plucking up the courage, nothing had come of it. He knew she'd eventually see the missed call, though, and ring him back. He debated putting out a group message, but decided against it. Maybe it would seem a little desperate after the phone call.

Reilly went down to the restaurant. By the time he'd finished eating, Yasmine still hadn't returned his call or messaged him. It wasn't like her, wasn't like any of them, in fact. They all liked to keep in touch and always responded efficiently. Reilly risked another phone call, hoping it wouldn't signify him as needy.

Again, Yasmine didn't answer. It had been two hours now.

Maybe she'd gone to watch a movie. Reilly checked the group chat once again. Funnily enough, *nobody* had posted since last night. Cassidy had been at the gym, Jemma in her hotel. Bodie and Heidi had gone to see a movie. Yasmine, of course, had taken a trip to the record store. But after all that... nothing.

It suddenly seemed a little odd to Reilly.

He hesitated. In reality, he wasn't used to this group chat kind of thing. Was it normal to stay out of touch for so long? Would it seem odd if he rang one of the others just to check up on them? He did it, anyway.

Reilly left the restaurant, went to the lobby, and found a seat. Immediately, he called Bodie. No answer. Next, he called Heidi. Again, no answer. Reilly went through everyone and received not a single answer.

A shiver ran from his head to his toes.

What the..?

He didn't think for one minute they were ghosting him or playing a practical joke. He believed they could be in trouble. But he needed some kind of proof. There might even be a plausible explanation for it all.

Reilly wondered what to do next. Go to where they were last seen. Reilly went in descending order of when the messages appeared in the chat. He started with Jemma first, went to her hotel and then her lobby. Tried her room first. No answer. He went back down to the lobby and started asking questions about his friend. One woman told him something had happened the night before. She believed a woman had been abducted straight out of the hotel's lobby.

Reilly knew it was thin. He tried Cassidy next, walking a few blocks to her gym and asking similar questions. He was informed of the fight, of the fact that a woman might have been abducted, a redhead. Now Reilly was starting to feel odd, as if his world were shifting. He went to the National History Museum, learned that there had been a significant disturbance the night before. Nothing obvious had happened at Yasmine's record shop, not at the cinema Bodie and Heidi visited. But, in context, he was finding a pattern.

Had his entire team been abducted?

Reilly walked back to his hotel. On the way, he tried them again. Still no replies. Nothing in the chat. Reilly suddenly felt very alone.

It was an odd sensation. He'd been alone in the Amazon for years, working alongside colleagues, but basically alone. He'd got used to it. But ever since meeting Bodie and the team, he'd really started feeling as if he belonged somewhere. It was odd to think that now he was on his own again. What could he do next?

Get involved. He couldn't just let this happen. And there was one way to be certain that it really was his friends who had been abducted.

He went back to the gym first, found the guy in charge of security, and bribed him. Ten minutes later, he was watching the security feed that covered the gym. Sure enough, the night before, Cassidy had fought several men and women, made an excellent account of herself, but still ended up getting abducted. Reilly watched the feed closely, paying particular attention to Cassidy's abductors. Reilly had been around a lot, from the Bratva to the Amazon jungle, and he knew a lot of enforcers, an awful lot of mercenaries.

There was something familiar about one of the faces. A tall thin man, all wiry muscle and sinew. Reilly recognised him but, for now, stored the knowledge away. He didn't want to be presumptuous.

He moved on to the National History Museum next. There was no chance of getting a look at the CCTV feed there. Too many guards and bosses around. So he went to the lobby where Jemma had been abducted, played the close friend card and again greased a palm. Soon, he was watching footage of the abduction.

It was definitely Jemma. And again, he saw the tall, wiry man.

Reilly left the hotel with a lot on his mind. The tall, thin, wiry man was named Jacko White. Reilly had met him in the Amazon when a few drug dealers breezed through, bringing their entourage with them. Jacko was loud, brash, always the centre of attention. For the few nights they'd hung around, Reilly had stayed on the fringes, being nice but not too nice. It always paid to remember faces.

Now, he went over everything he knew about Jacko White. The mercenary outfit who had breezed through the Amazon, guarding the drug dealers, was named Blackoak One and Jacko worked exclusively for them.

Reilly knew his friends weren't coming back. It left a hollow feeling in his heart, and a need to help them. A burning desire.

Reilly turned his mind to what came next.

CHAPTER TWELVE

It was a long, sultry afternoon. Bodie and the others had been made to change clothes. They now wore loose fitting grey tops and comfortable trousers, like jogging bottoms, also grey. Every hour they were brought fresh water and fruit. Clearly, someone wanted them kept in the best shape possible. They lounged on their bunks and chatted and, with nothing else to do, the subject soon turned to Reilly.

'He has resources,' Bodie said. 'The man has been around.'

'Let's hope so,' Lucie said. 'Or we get three weeks of this shit.'

Bodie didn't like to tell her he didn't think they'd be out of here in three weeks. In any case, they had a lot to go through before then. He wondered when the guards would come to take one of them away for their first contest. He didn't think it would be long.

'Reilly will come through for us,' Yasmine assured them. 'I've known him for long enough to know he's a clever, resourceful, good guy.'

Cassidy spoke up. 'Why didn't you two reconnect?'

Yasmine was quiet for a while. 'It all seems trivial in the wake of what has happened to us,' she said. 'I guess we were both waiting for the other one to make a move.'

Bodie had been like that with Heidi for a long time.

The Contest

He was glad they'd finally got past their misgivings. Their relationship had been growing closer every day.

Now it was on hold again.

Bloody typical, he thought. He decided all the inactivity wasn't helping, got down on the floor and cracked out a few pushups. In the distance, he could hear voices coming from other cells, but there was no one except themselves on their own little block. He wondered if that was done on purpose.

One thing he was starting to dread was the approaching footsteps of the guards. It normally meant trouble. His heart sank as he heard them now, several sets of steps belonging to quite a few people.

Bodie went to the bars, looked down the corridor. Sure enough, several black-clad guards appeared and then stopped outside Cassidy's cell.

'They're starting with you,' one man said. 'I hope you're ready.'

Cassidy rose to her feet, saying nothing.

'If you don't fight, *she* dies,' the guard pointed at Jemma. 'You'll hear all this again once you get out in the arena.'

'The arena?' Bodie asked. 'What's that?'

'It's where she's gonna fight,' a woman said with a grin. 'And where we're gonna watch. It's always a spectacle.'

Cassidy didn't back away. She stood straight as they unlocked her cell and led her away. Bodie could only watch her go and hope for the best. The big problem would come, he imagined, when she met her opponent. They were two innocents being made to fight. How would that work?

He watched as Cassidy disappeared. Some guards

were still here. It surprised him when they started unlocking all the doors.

'What's going on?' he asked.

'You're gonna watch too,' the woman told him with an evil smile.

'Remember,' a man said. 'We're armed to the teeth and cleared to shoot to wound you. Wounded, you will still have to complete your contests. Don't risk it.'

Bodie remained docile, letting himself be led out of the cell and down the corridor, back into the blazing heat. He paused for a moment, letting his eyes and body adjust. The guards kept walking, confident. His friends were all around him. Way ahead, he could see Cassidy being led to her fate.

They walked across the hard ground between buildings and then approached the arena. It was a wide, circular area surrounded by bleachers. People were already sitting on those bleachers – guards on their day off perhaps, invited guests, other contestants. The bleachers were about ten steps high and circled the entire arena.

Bodie and his friends passed through a narrow entryway and then climbed the steps up the bleachers. The sun blazed down relentlessly above them. His eyes hurt and his head pounded. They took their seats along the third row, looking out over the fighting arena. For now, it was empty.

Bodie sat in place and looked around. As expected, he saw the place where the sovereigns sat high above, on the top row of bleachers. It had been decked out lavishly, with hanging drapes and gold architecture. There was a small deck before each sovereign upon which goblets of wine and grapes and cheese sat. Bodie counted seven of

The Contest

them, including Phoenix. Quite a turnout for Cassidy's contest.

The noise level was rising. Guards started to fill the arena and then spread out so that they formed a well-armed circle on the outer perimeter. More guards wandered up the bleachers, taking seats. Still more prisoners were led in under guard and then allowed to sit down. Bodie studied them, wondering if he'd come up against one in the near future. They were quite the assortments – men and woman, young and old, fit and unhealthy.

Bodie had been to a few football matches in his time, and this was like that. Sitting in the crowd and waiting for your favourite team to come out.

Only this time it was a fight to the death.

At least, he assumed so. He didn't know what the contestants had been told. He sweated, and he waited and he tried to take everything in.

From his elevated position, he could see a little more of the area beyond the bleachers. He now saw a terrible, infernal machine, made of wood and steel, that looked like an obstacle course. It was currently empty and unused, but Bodie saw several people working on it as if maintaining it. Beyond it, he saw a series of poles set into the ground and then a wide open plain. He thought he saw some men and women moving across the plain, but the distance and the blistering sun made it all hazy. He couldn't be sure.

He looked back up at the sovereigns. They were all dressed well, none of them trying to hide their identities. It reinforced Bodie's feelings about them being let loose in three weeks. What would happen if he recognised one of them? There were five men and two women all chatting amongst each other and eating their nibbles, drinking their wine. Fresh bottles were being brought out by men dressed as waiters. Bodie blinked and shook his head, wondering if he was dreaming. It all felt so surreal. Everything had happened so fast it was all just a blur, and he hadn't had a chance to come to terms with it yet.

One sovereign caught his eye and smiled, gave him a little wave. Bodie, blinking, wasn't sure what to do in return. The word *surreal* again came into his mind.

But everything was up in the air. Cassidy's future. Their future. What happened in the next few minutes would never be forgotten, not by any of them. It was something Bodie didn't want to see because he knew he'd never be able to rid himself of it.

Time passed. Nothing happened except the filling of the bleachers. People chatted, laughed, leaned back, as if they were watching some everyday sporting event. To them, Bodie guessed, that's exactly what it was.

Bodie felt tension ride in, travelling the length of his body, filling his head with fear and distress.

And that was when Cassidy walked out into the arena.

CHAPTER THIRTEEN

Cassidy wasn't in a good place. She was a fighter. This was what she did. She had been in plenty of rings before, plenty of fights where she could have died. This didn't phase her. It wasn't even that different from the norm.

But it was what she was going to have to do to win that jabbed her brain with poisoned claws.

They had led her to a tiny waiting room. She had sat down on a small bench, sweating profusely. The room had no windows and was stifling hot. A man had appeared, a man dressed in a long flowing robe and a headscarf. He had greeted her warmly.

'Cassidy,' he had said. 'How lovely to meet you. I will be your second for this contest. If there's anything you need, don't hesitate to ask. I am at your service. First, may I explain to you the rules?'

Cassidy nodded, at a loss for words.

'Today, it is swords. You will fight your opponent to the death. If you refuse, your friend Jemma will get her throat cut in front of you.' The robed man said all of his with a gentle smile on his face, as if reeling off a shopping list, as if the words actually meant nothing to him.

Cassidy felt her face drop. 'One of us has to die?' she said.

'That's the idea. Oh, I hope it isn't you. I like you

already. You should prepare yourself. Now, is there anything I can get you?'

Cassidy looked up. 'Yeah, half a glass of vodka.'

The man left the room. Cassidy was astounded when, two minutes later, he returned with half a glass of clear liquid and a beverage of cola on the side. He offered her the glass, asked if she would like to top it up with cola.

She nodded. She drank. The alcohol soothed her a little. She sat, and she waited and wondered what the hell she was doing here and what would happen next. It didn't feel real. She could hear the general din coming from outside and imagined the bleachers were getting full. So many people, so much expectation.

Cassidy didn't want to think about her opponent, didn't want to imagine what she was going to have to do.

'When you go out, you will wait and defer to the Principal Sovereign,' the robed man told her. 'He may wish to do a speech, he may not. Either way, you will give him time to decide. After that, I will hand you your sword and, on the clash of the gong, you will fight.'

Cassidy said nothing, just took a long swallow of her drink. The waiting was interminable. She hated it, but she didn't want to move forward either, knowing what was to come next. The robed man left again, came back with a golden basin full of grapes and cheese.

'Nibbles?' he asked.

She wanted to scream at him. Wanted to punch him. But she knew it wouldn't do her any good. It would, in fact, make things a lot worse. It wasn't his fault, to be fair. He was just carrying out orders.

What were the others making of all this? She wondered. Were they in hell too? She imagined they would be. The big problem was – there was no way out

THE CONTEST

and they were all going to have to go through this.

The robed man checked his watch, popped a grape in his mouth and chewed it. He offered to refresh Cassidy's vodka, but she refused, wanting to stay alert. Minutes passed as though they were trapped in molasses.

'It is time,' the man said.

The dreaded words. Cassidy swallowed, drained the vodka, and rose to her feet. She wiped her brow. The robed man opened the door and stepped out into the heat. Cassidy followed, feeling as if she was having an out-of-body experience. She wasn't really there, wasn't really walking across the dry, dusty ground towards the towering bleachers, couldn't really hear all that noise, see all those people waiting.

It wasn't real.

She passed under the bleachers and then came out into the arena. It was a wide circle, all dry earth and stones. It could probably hold hundreds of people, but there would only be two performing there today. She walked until the robed man stopped, taking her to the centre of the circle.

The surrounding conversation died off. Cassidy looked around, not intimidated, just distraught about what was going to happen. She didn't expect to lose, didn't know if she could do what needed to be done, but was fully aware of what would happen to Jemma if she didn't. She might be about to engage in a sword fight, but there was another sword hanging over her head.

Cassidy waited. She saw Phoenix making his way down the stands and to the arena floor. Someone gave him a microphone. Phoenix raised his hands and greeted everyone.

'I hope you're ready for a spectacle,' he cried.

There were several shouts, a few whoops. Phoenix raised his hand for quiet.

'Today, I give you Cassidy and Natalie. They will fight to the death!'

Cassidy tuned him out, not wanting to listen to the rest of his speech. Her head was spinning; she didn't know where to look.

A figure was making its way towards her. Two figures actually. That would be Natalie and her second.

Natalie was an average-sized brunette with long legs. She wore the ubiquitous grey uniform and had her hair scraped back in a bun. Her arms looked powerful and her face was set in a severe expression. By the way she moved, Cassidy could tell she was both fit and confident in her abilities.

Of course, they wouldn't have matched her up with just anyone. They wanted a proper fight.

Natalie came closer and closer until the two were about three metres apart. Cassidy didn't know whether to look at her or ignore her. Soon, they – both innocent here – would fight to the death. How did you greet a person with that in mind?

Cassidy looked anywhere but at Natalie. The other woman seemed to do the same. Their seconds came up to them and now, Cassidy saw, they both held a sword in their hands.

Cassidy stared at it. The weapon was long, narrow, and deadly. It had a polished bronze hilt. Her second held it out to her. The blade flashed in the sunlight and left an impression on Cassidy's eyes. Something to be aware of. She didn't reach out for it, wanted nothing to do with it.

Her second patiently stepped closer. 'Take it,' he said. 'Remember what happens if you refuse.'

The Contest

Cassidy looked up into the crowd. Now she spotted Bodie and the others. Guards were standing behind them, weapons drawn. Was this really how it was going to be? Cassidy felt nothing but impotent rage. Without looking at her second, she reached out for the sword, felt the metal thrust into her hand. She held it without looking at her opponent. She was watching her friends up in the stand.

Now Phoenix rose to his feet.

'Let the contest begin!' he yelled.

CHAPTER FOURTEEN

Cassidy felt her training kick in.

She hefted the sword and looked immediately at her opponent. Natalie had also positioned her sword in a defensive movement and was staring at Cassidy. Neither woman moved. The hot sun blazed down on them.

The seconds backed away, finally leaving the arena. Cassidy would not be the one to strike the first blow, and it appeared that Natalie had no stomach for it either. For show, the two women circled each other, puffs of dry dust mushrooming up from under their feet.

Out of the corner of her eye, Cassidy could see the sovereigns sitting up in the stand. They were lounging back, eating their grapes, sipping their wine, chatting amongst each other. Clearly, they had seen this sort of thing before and were used to it. They knew that the ending would always be the same. Someone would die. Maybe they enjoyed the slow starts since it prolonged the spectacle.

Cassidy pointed her sword at Natalie and made no move to engage. She was sweating, droplets dripping off her cheeks and chin. The watching crowd had silenced when the contest began, but now broke out in a series of jeers and catcalls and just general conversation. Some were cheering her, shouting her name. Others called out for Natalie to make a move. Of course, Cassidy imagined, they'd have placed bets on the outcome.

The Contest

They circled each other slowly. The intensity of the crowd rose. The sovereigns sipped and ate and leaned forward, some not even watching. Cassidy noted Bodie and the rest of the team on the edges of their seats, saying nothing. She noticed the guard standing behind Jemma had his knife out.

Did she even know?

Cassidy raised her sword, eyed her opponent. Natalie watched her warily. There was a shout from Phoenix, a kind of call to arms, and Natalie's body suddenly jerked as she swung her sword. So she was the first to attack, Cassidy thought, holding her sword in such a way that it deflected the weak blow.

Natalie came at her again, this time a little stronger.

Cassidy blocked the thrust of the sword. The clang of steel echoed around the arena, igniting the bloodlust of the crowd. The swords flashed as the sunshine caught their edges. Cassidy didn't attack. She blocked another strike, this one a little stronger. Natalie was slowly getting into the idea of a sword fight.

Cassidy jumped out of the way of the next attack. Natalie's sword flew ineffectually by. Cassidy could have stepped in at that point and stabbed her opponent through, but she didn't. She refrained and the entire crowd knew it. They booed and catcalled and shook their fists at her. If she hadn't realised by now, Cassidy understood there was going to be no easy way out of this.

Natalie covered up quickly, aware of what had just happened. She licked her lips, wiped her face. Cassidy coughed as dust got into the back of her throat. Natalie used the distraction to launch her hardest attack yet, swinging her sword from left to right. Again, Cassidy stepped back, letting the weapon pass harmlessly by.

This time, Natalie arrested its flight and didn't expose herself. She had now attacked Cassidy four times. Cassidy could see the strain on her face.

Neither of them wanted this. She continued circling, wondering how best to proceed. Natalie came in again, and this time, their swords clashed. A cheer went up around the arena. Two of the sovereigns rose to their feet. Cassidy saw a flash of sparks and a plume of dust as Natalie's back foot slipped. Unbalanced, she fell to the side. Cassidy struck for the first time, just missing the woman's head, nicking the side of her left ear.

She drew first blood.

The crowd roared. The liquid dripped from Natalie's ear and painted the hard, unforgiving ground.

Cassidy backed off warily. Natalie's eyes had taken on a wild glaze, as if she was starting to believe the hype that surrounded her, that filled her brain. She raised her sword and pointed it at Cassidy.

'You know this has to happen,' she said in an English accent.

'I can't see a way around it,' Cassidy admitted.

'Then fight me.'

'I'd rather not. I don't want your death on my conscience.' Even as she said it, Cassidy knew it was Natalie or Jemma. Which death would hurt less?

'Fight me,' Natalie said again.

Cassidy had considered all the other options. She was a fighter – some might say she was a killer – but this wasn't the arena she usually battled in. She fought to help her friends, to save their lives. It clicked then... she was doing precisely that now.

Natalie came at her, this time as hard as she could. Her sword flew in a downward arc, slicing through the air. Cassidy threw her own weapon up and deflected the blow to the side. She could have pursued her attack, but didn't. Natalie didn't let up. She swung again, this time from the side, aiming for Cassidy's ribs. She was deft with the sword, fast. The swing passed less than an inch from Cassidy's flesh.

She hadn't had time to move.

Now, instinct took over. That had been close. When Natalie struck again, Cassidy redirected the attack and then punched Natalie square in the face. The woman, shocked, stumbled back and landed on her ass in the dust.

She sat there, staring. The crowd urged Cassidy to attack, but she held back, choosing not to. Most of the sovereigns were on their feet, shouting.

'You punched me,' Natalie said, as if in shock.

'I'm a street fighter,' Cassidy said. 'Anything goes.'

Natalie climbed warily to her feet, holding the sword point out as if that would ward Cassidy off. She suddenly looked even less sure of herself.

'I will kill you,' the woman said.

And here they were, Cassidy thought. From normal, civilised people thrust against one another to the ultimate threat. The crowd, the sovereigns, the spectacle – it had all overwhelmed Natalie and transformed her into something else entirely. A killer. She swung the sword left and right now with a degree of confidence. Cassidy saw the new hardness in her, the need to win.

Natalie came again, swinging left and right. Cassidy backed away across the hard ground, using the size of the arena to her advantage. She evaded all Natalie's swings and came in with one of her own. Natalie deflected it with ease, but it got the crowd going again.

Finally, they had seen a proper attack from Cassidy.

The sovereigns were swilling their wine, eating at their trough. They were laughing up there, on high, enjoying the plight of the two women, revelling in it. They cheered, and they slathered and they chewed their meat, bloodlust steadily taking over. This was what they were here for.

Cassidy defended once more as Natalie came forward. The swords swung and clanged. More sparks flew off into the bright day. Cassidy arrested Natalie's momentum and threw her back, but this time Natalie didn't let up.

She kept coming.

Maybe she'd seen her chance. Maybe she'd had enough. Whatever the reason, Natalie didn't back away anymore. She kept swinging the sword, blow after blow, apparently feeling no tiredness.

Cassidy blocked time and again, letting the blades of the sword grind together and then slide apart. Her arms were already tired, her muscles aching. She was being forced back towards the bleacher where Bodie and the team sat; her back to them. Natalie powered forward, swinging repeatedly, and now there was no let up to the clanging metal and the sparks. Cassidy found her back bowing, her arms weakening.

This wasn't going well. She still didn't want to act, didn't want to turn into the aggressor. Her back hit the bleachers now, and she suddenly heard a raucous laugh, and then someone kicked her in the spine.

'Get back in there, bitch,' a growl reached her ears.

It shocked her, made her cry out and stagger forward... right into Natalie's sword.

Cassidy angled her body to the side at the last possible

The Contest

instant, but the blade still cut through her shirt, grazed her ribs and drew blood. Soon, it was soaking through and the crowd was shouting, laughing, pointing. Cassidy fell to one knee, sensed Natalie raising the sword behind her.

She would take her head off with that blow.

Cassidy spun, still on the ground, and thrust up. She was aware she was about to die, and instinct took over. She watched as her sword penetrated her opponent's stomach. Natalie's eyes went wide as her own momentum forced her on to the point of the sword, forced her body to press on to it. She gasped. She dropped her sword.

Slumped.

Cassidy let her own sword fall to the ground and Natalie's body went with it. She was vaguely aware of the cheering of the crowd, of the applause of the sovereigns, of the grins of the surrounding guards.

But she was even more aware of her own team's shocked, severe faces, as they no doubt faced up to what would soon come their way too.

CHAPTER FIFTEEN

Reilly sat in a dark hotel room. The curtains were drawn, and he could hear rain spattering the glass. It was warm in here, too warm. He'd already stripped his shirt off and was sitting in his boxer shorts. Before him, open on the bed, sat a laptop.

Reilly had scoured the internet for mentions of Blackoak One. When this didn't work, he had decided to use his own real world contacts. They might be out of touch being stationed deep in the Amazon, but they certainly knew their shit. Blackoak One, as he knew, was a private security firm. They employed ex-soldiers, mercenaries, and usually ended up in some of the worst war-torn places in the world. The mercs were well paid, the company more so. Their corporate image was pretty good for what they were, and, on the surface, they were impenetrable.

Reilly knew he needed to dig beneath the surface.

And there was only one way to do that. Get people involved, people who knew how Blackoak operated, and *where* they operated. Reilly really needed to track down the face he'd seen, the man he knew as Jacko White.

Reilly found a few old contacts, speaking at length to two of them. He told them he really needed to talk to Blackoak, but not through normal channels. He was looking for information on one of their employees and they wouldn't give it easily. What was his best approach?

'There is a way to contact Blackoak privately,' a friend told him. 'They're big users of the Dark Web.'

'I thought that was just for criminals,' Reilly said, a bit naively.

'It is.'

Of course. Reilly should have known a secretive private security firm like Blackoak would have its fingers in all the pies. It worked against – and no doubt with – some of the worst criminals in the world, perhaps even protecting many of them. With Blackoak, it was all about the money.

'Talk to them through the Dark Web,' the man reiterated.

'How do I access it?' Reilly looked at his laptop.

'Well, you can't access it through a normal computer,' the man told him. 'But there are other ways.'

The man asked for some time and, two hours later, called Reilly back. 'Ok,' he said. 'I have a friend in New York. You see, there a certain backroom places you can go to access the Dark Web. They're kind of like a dark internet café. Establishments set up clandestinely for just that sort of thing. I have an address for you in New York but, Reilly, you must know, this is extremely dangerous.'

Right now, danger didn't matter. Reilly was desperate to help his new friends. 'Give me the address.'

Ten minutes later, Reilly was dressed and ready to go. It was ten-thirty p.m., but he didn't want to waste any time. The address they had given him was a few stops along the Metro and he was pretty sure it'd be open late.

Reilly shrugged on a coat and left the room, exited the hotel, and went down to the nearest Metro. He caught a train along with hundreds of other people, all wet, all looking miserable to be out at this time of night, in this weather. He hung on to the pole, waited for his stop to come around.

When it did, he got off the train and made his way back up to the surface. He followed the sodden streets, his hood turned up against the rain. His face was wet, his hands soaked as he checked the piece of paper he'd written the address on. He followed Google maps until the right street came along and then started down it.

It was a dark street; the lampposts having little effect. There were just a few shopfronts, none of them lit up. Reilly saw a jeweller, a craft shop, and a laundry place that looked like it had only just closed up. He carried on by. Soon, he came to a dimly lit window through which he could see a shape sat at a counter. He pushed through the smeared glass door.

A bell tinkled. A man with long, lank hair looked up. 'Help you?'

Reilly didn't think the sentence 'I've come to use the Dark Web' would work. Instead, he said, 'I need access to one of your computers.'

'How did you hear about us?' the youth asked nonchalantly. Both his hands were under the counter and Reilly wondered if they hovered near a gun.

'A good friend gave me your address. I need to talk to someone.'

The youth studied him for a while. Reilly stood as easily as he could, trying not to look nervous. 'Your name?'

'Why do you need that?'

The youth laughed. 'We don't allow just anyone to use our computers, friend. You need a referral.'

The Contest

Reilly recalled his friend had told him he'd made a call. Maybe that was what he'd meant. 'Jon Reilly.'

The youth nodded. 'I know the name. The charge is a hundred bucks for every half hour.'

That seemed kind of steep, but Reilly knew the nature of what he was being offered. He said nothing, just handed the money over. The youth then came around the counter and approached a door with a set of keys in his hand.

'Find a spare table,' he said. 'Talk to no one.'

Reilly nodded. He got it. This was a criminal enterprise, and nobody wanted to be recognised or spoken to. The door opened. Reilly went through into a dim room that smelled of fried food and sweat. About two dozen tables stood around, each one with a computer on top and each one cubicled off. Reilly could see the tops of several heads, but no faces. All he heard was the incessant sound of keys being tapped. He found a table and sat down. There was the computer in front of him, a set of headphones, and that was it. The room was warm and compact. Reilly removed his coat, shedding water onto the floor.

He sat there for a moment, collecting himself. He had an hour and hadn't really thought about what he was going to do. Nobody would help him. He couldn't even approach the other patrons. The computer before him was connected to the Dark Web, something which was highly illegal. Reilly knew government agencies like the CIA and the FBI used the Dark Web too, but for entirely different purposes than he was about to.

He woke the computer, got on to the network. The screen filled with a browser that sure as hell wasn't Google. Reilly typed in 'contact Blackoak One' and waited for the results. Soon, he was through to what appeared to be a robot chat and then started asking questions. He wanted information about a certain man and he would pay for it. That man was Jacko White.

Soon, the robot chat ended and a real person started messaging him back. Reilly was happy just to have made contact. Clearly, the Dark Web was a great way for Blackoak to operate, and they kept it manned all the time.

'I want to speak to Jacko White,' Reilly typed. He knew that his credentials as a criminal equal had already been assured by the contact through the Dark Web. This wasn't like contacting a company out of the blue and asking to speak to an employee. This had already gone several steps beyond that. He was, essentially, inside the security protocols.

'Why?' the man from Blackoak typed.

'I need to ask the man a few questions and I need to know where he has been working.'

'That's impossible.'

'Please. This is of the utmost importance.'

'We don't give out our employee information. Or ways of contacting them.'

Reilly sensed he was being blocked by corporate bullshit, or just being made to squirm. Either way, he needed a new angle, something that sounded appealing.

'I will pay for the information.'

Nothing happened for a while, which told him the other person was thinking hard.

'And all you have are a few questions?'

'That's it. He's just an employee of yours, after all.'

'Jacko White is a busy man.'

Reilly took a deep breath. This was his only lead, and

The Contest

he could feel the high tension of the moment. 'Please. It's important to me.'

Reilly was under no illusions. If this was a formal contact through normal means, he'd get nowhere. That it was covert, through the Dark Web, meant that he'd got through to a shady operative, someone who might help him on the quiet. This was the whole point of what he was doing.

'What's your name? I'm gonna check you out.'

Luckily, Reilly had been expecting this. He knew that any check would reveal at worst that he'd been a shifty operative in the Amazon. It would work for him. He reeled off his name and waited as the guy went quiet. All Reilly could hear was the tapping of the keyboard and the whine of a computer fan.

'All right, you check out. But I wasn't kidding. Jacko is in high demand. I'm not sure when I can get you an audience with him.'

'The pay will be worth it. If you tell me where he is, I can always go to him.'

At this, the man on the other end went very quiet. Reilly knew he'd pushed it a little too far.

'You're in New York, right?' the man asked.

'Yes,' Reilly replied, wondering what was coming.

'I can arrange a face to face with someone. Not your man. I want to see you first.'

Reilly cursed silently. It wasn't what he wanted, and he was conscious of the lost time. 'Really?'

'Face to face,' the man typed. 'Or nothing. This conversation is about done.'

'All right,' Reilly answered quickly. He couldn't risk losing the contact. 'I'll meet. What's your name?'

'You can call me Sten.'

'All right, Sten.'

'The meet's gonna cost you, too.'

Reilly sighed. He had money, but not an endless supply. 'Agreed,' he typed with little choice.

CHAPTER SIXTEEN

Bodie sat quietly in his cell, wondering what would happen next. It had been rough out there with Cassidy. He didn't know how she had found the strength to do what she did. In the end, he guessed, it had come down to a survival instinct.

Cassidy herself had been quiet ever since they were returned to their cells. He couldn't see her, but guessed she was sitting on her bed with her head down. He dreaded to think about her state of mind. But she was strong, he knew. She would get through it.

Lucie and Jemma were talking, but their cells were too far away for him to hear their quiet conversation. He knew Heidi was in the cell to his right, Cassidy to his left, and Yasmine was the next one along. He felt drained, used, weak.

How the hell were they going to get out of this one?

The darkness of despair weaved its tendrils through his brain. It wasn't as though they could hope to survive the three weeks. He had every certainty that they wouldn't be let loose after three weeks. Maybe he was wrong – maybe they *would* go free. But... surely... not.

No, he couldn't identify the place. He couldn't identify the sovereigns or even the guards. How he longed for a good old-fashioned relic hunt where the path in front of you was pre-determined by history and going forward depended on your team skills.

Of course, going forward here also depended on skill.

He didn't like that thought, berating himself for it. They hadn't put themselves in this situation, and he could see no way out of it. Cassidy had already risked her life. What was coming next?

As if in answer to his silent question, he heard the dreaded approach of the guards. At first, he wondered if they might branch off, head down another corridor, but it soon became obvious they were headed for their set of cells.

The usual guard came up to them, glanced from cell to cell. 'You're up,' he said.

Bodie was losing track of time. He knew Cassidy's ordeal had been yesterday. It looked like there was one ordeal per day.

'You,' the guard said.

Bodie looked to where he was pointing. With a sinking heart, he realised it was Jemma's cell. That wasn't good. He knew Jemma was in a bad head state. They all were, to be fair.

'Me?' Jemma asked in a small voice.

'Actually, all of you are taking part in this one,' the guard said. 'But you,' he pointed at Jemma. 'Will have the starring role.'

With a laugh, he directed the other guards to open their cells. They were carefully covered by weapons, aimed not at their chests or stomachs, but at their legs, their thighs. Bodie well remembered that if they tried anything, they'd be wounded, and forced to carry on with the contest.

He exited his cell, following the lead guard down the now familiar corridor and out the door into the blinding sun. He guessed it was around midday from its position

THE CONTEST

and, as he walked, saw that nobody was anywhere near the bleachers.

What fresh hell would they face today?

The guards marched them past the bleachers and away from the buildings to a wide, clear space. The ground was hard and dusty, the space rectangular and bordered by a concrete edging. Bodie was told to halt at the very edge of it.

He stared, wondering what was happening. Inside the space, twelve wooden poles had been driven into the ground. The poles were about three metres high and sturdy, thick. There was no obvious use for them.

Bodie looked from left to right. The sovereigns were there, nine of them this time, including Phoenix. They were seated incongruously on leather armchairs that had been placed around the new arena, spaced out so that they were all alone. There were tables to either side of them arrayed with the now usual assortment of food and drink. Bodie shook his head to see a server positioned behind every chair, a person dressed in a black and white outfit and holding a folded napkin over his arm. It was one of the oddest sights he'd ever seen, but quite in tune with this godforsaken place. Rising above the server was a wide sunshade. All the sovereigns were sitting comfortably and partaking of their nibbles, looking immensely relaxed. It made Bodie want to grab a gun and really put some fear into them.

They waited. A man dressed in a flowing robe came over to the lead guard and spoke. Next, the guard beckoned to Jemma, motioned for her to follow him. The guards waved their weapons. Jemma broke away from the group and walked until she was standing alone in front of the poles. The men left her there. Bodie closed his eyes when he saw the strain on her face. It was all he could do not to act, to attack, to throw his life away in a senseless charge.

They were being forced to watch their friends literally live or die. He'd done it yesterday with Cassidy and it had hurt like hell. He felt impotent, powerless. They didn't even have a plan to get the hell out of here. He moved closer to Cassidy now so that they might better be able to converse on the quiet.

'Hey,' he muttered. 'Any ideas?'

She glanced at him, and her face was desolate. 'I've already gone through it a thousand times,' she replied. 'There are too many guards, and they're well armed. The cells are locked tight every night and checked. We're watched constantly. We have no idea where we are, of the terrain outside this compound. We wouldn't last a few days without water. My only idea is to converse with the other inmates, see what they know. See if they have any bright ideas. You can't fight overwhelming force.'

It wasn't what he wanted to hear, but it was accurate. Even if you grabbed one gun, or six, there were still a hundred others to contend with and very little cover. Her idea about chatting with the other inmates was a good one. They'd be visiting the Core again soon, and that offered a decent opportunity. Of course, all that depended on what was about to happen.

He frowned in confusion when the guards came up to him next. And then the rest of his team. One by one, they were led to the wooden poles, positioned with their backs to them and then tied in place, their arms around the poles. They were bound so that they could barely move. After that, the guards went away, grinning at each other. Some sovereigns clapped to see the new sight.

The Contest

Bodie stood in place, feeling the wooden pole jammed into his spine, a fresh breeze on his face. All the while, he was sweating and his lips were dry. He swallowed hard, wondering what was about to happen. His fellow teammates were looking around in alarm, their eyes confused, their expressions speculative.

Next, the guards returned to them. In their hands they held blue pieces of round metal. These items were hung above the heads of the team, held in place by a little hook. Bodie guessed the little round plate hung about four inches above his head.

And then a guard started walking towards Jemma. In his hand, he held a bow and several arrows.

Bodie winced. *Shit,* he thought. He now knew exactly what was about to happen.

Because of her plight, her inner turmoil, the position they were in, he saw Jemma still couldn't grasp what was going on. She stared at the proffered bow and arrows in bewilderment, clearly wondering if she'd be allowed to hold a deadly weapon and if she would get shot if she did so.

The guard held it out, told her to take it. Jemma reached out tentatively, then looked around. The man wearing the flowing robe walked up to her. He pointed at the bow and arrow and then at her bound friends, explaining what she had to do. Jemma's face took on a disbelieving expression and her mouth fell open. Where she held the bow, her hands shook.

Bodie swallowed dryly. He could barely believe that he was in this position, tied here, waiting for his friend to take a shot at him. There were guards and guns everywhere, and the nine sovereigns watched with intense interest.

Jemma shook her head, threw the bow to the floor next to the pile of arrows. The robed man shook his head. After a few seconds, the lead guard went up to her and whispered into her ear. Jemma's expression filled with terror and she looked at Bodie.

He felt the dark presence approach him from the rear, and then reach an arm around his throat. The cold touch of a blade wasn't unexpected.

He knew what they'd told her. Do it, or your friend gets his throat cut.

Jemma had tears in her eyes. She stared at the guard as if begging him to change his mind. She couldn't handle it, couldn't handle the decision. Either she watched Bodie get his throat cut, or she fired an arrow at him.

'I've never used a bow and arrow before,' she said in a wavering voice.

'Please don't make her do this,' he heard Lucie say.

'I *won't* do it,' Jemma cried, testing them.

Bodie felt the knife slide into his throat and gasped. Blood flowed. He couldn't move, couldn't resist it as the blade slid through his skin.

'No!' Jemma screamed.

Bodie gasped as the knife was removed. Blood leaked from his throat, but it was just a miniscule amount.

Jemma reached down for the bow.

CHAPTER SEVENTEEN

Jemma was shaking and sweating hard. She had almost got Bodie killed even without using the bow. She could see him now with the red line across his neck, the blood slowly leaking out. It made her shiver despite the heat, made her want to scream out loud.

Jemma did actually have the skill to use a bow and arrow. She wondered if her captors knew that, didn't see how they could. Her career as a cat burglar had made her learn many useful skills, and one of those was how to use a bow. A bow could come in very handy from silently shooting a crossbow bolt into something to rigging a zipline. It wasn't exactly something she'd had to do very often, though.

She hefted the bow, felt its weight. The weapon was well balanced, sturdy. She looked closely at it, saw that it was a good make. It wouldn't let her down. Now, she looked around this new arena, saw the guards with their guns and the sovereigns with their relaxed attitude and nibbles. How easy it would be to put an arrow in them.

And hand her team a death sentence.

They faced overwhelming force. This was how the sovereigns played it. Using threats, and the threat of terrible violence. How long had this been going on?

She realised she was procrastinating. Still, she stood with the bow in their hands. The sovereigns didn't rush her, though. She believed they loved this part: the indecision, the fear, the actual transition from reluctance to action.

And even if she'd wanted to, Jemma couldn't rush it. She now held the lives or deaths of her entire team in her hands. This was her ordeal, and there was nothing she could do to avoid it. The time was now, *right now*.

She wiped the sweat from her face, asked for a towel. They brought it to her quickly, and she wiped her hands, wiped the bow. She picked up an arrow and made her way to the first pole in line.

Yasmine's

Jemma faced the pole. The bright blue target above Yasmine's head stood out clearly. Jemma looked down at the arrow in her hand, the implement of death.

Can I do this? Can I do it to all five of them?

The question terrified her. If she missed the pole, they would die. If she failed, they would die. And, worst of all, what if she hit them?

Her hands shook. Jemma took a deep breath. The sovereigns were all sitting forward now and looked like they were holding their breath. The guards watched, rapt with attention. Not a single weapon was aimed at her.

Deep, profound silence surrounded her.

It was good for concentration. Jemma raised the bow, inserted the arrow. She swallowed, took a deep breath, let it out slowly. She aimed the arrow just a few inches above Yasmine's head.

Time stretched as taut as the bowstring she held between her fingers. The arrow was steady. She breathed again, exhaled again. She was as still as she ever thought she could be.

Jemma loosed the arrow, followed its flight through

THE CONTEST

the air. The audience gasped. Yasmine stayed as still as a rock, her expression revealing nothing. She didn't even close her eyes.

Jemma's breath caught in her throat.

The arrow struck, and there was the loud clang of metal hitting metal. She had struck the target true, at its furthest edge. The arrow flew off to the right, skittering away, but the telltale clang hung in the air.

And suddenly the entire arena erupted in noise. The sovereigns rose to their feet, clapping loudly. The guards roared their approval. The robed man jumped up and down in glee. Jemma tried to keep her concentration.

The applause and shouting went on for a few minutes. Jemma waited patiently, staring at the ground, holding the bow at ease. When the cheering subsided, she looked to the next pole in line.

Heidi.

She cleared her throat and picked up another arrow, walked over to Heidi's pole and positioned herself directly before it. Heidi was looking at her and gave her a brief nod. A smile hovered over her lips. The woman was insanely brave. She was trying to put Jemma at ease even as Jemma held her life in her hands.

Jemma looked around. The sovereigns were settling down; the guards had retaken their original positions and were no longer shouting. They held their guns easily, ready to act if they needed to. The robed man was still grinning from ear to ear, eager for the next shot.

Jemma inserted the arrow and raised the bow. She sighted on Heidi's face and then raised the bow a little, aiming for the round blue target. Again, she took a deep breath and exhaled slowly, trying to calm her mind, to remove any shaking that might remain in her arms, her body. She cleared her mind, concentrated on the target. That was all there was. That was her entire existence. The... little... blue target.

Jemma let the arrow fly. A millisecond later, there was a thud. Her heart sank, and she almost cried out. The arrow had struck the wooden pole, but on the way it had glanced off the target. A mini clang echoed through the air. She staggered as her legs shook and swayed. The bow slipped from her hand.

She had come within millimetres of killing her friend.

But the place erupted in cheering and applause once again. The sovereigns were up out of their seats, the guards almost jumping up and down, high-fiving each other. Jemma had never seen anything so surreal, nor so insane. She took several minutes to collect herself.

The adulation went on and on. The sovereigns saluted her by drinking deeply of their wine, by giving her happy thumbs-up. Guards all around raised their weapons in the air, some actually firing their guns in their eagerness. It all did nothing for Jemma's nerves. She was almost hyperventilating. Had she got lucky so far? How close had she come to missing Heidi's target?

With great reluctance, she looked to see who was next. Lucie. She closed her eyes and bit her bottom lip. The young researcher looked terrified. She couldn't stop shaking and didn't know whether to close her eyes or keep them open.

Jemma walked the few feet to stand in front of Lucie's pole. It felt like a terrible, endless journey, fraught with fear and tension. Her legs dragged. So far, she'd hit the target twice. She still had three to go.

Jemma lined herself up before Lucie. She wanted to concentrate hard, but she couldn't get Lucie's face out of

The Contest

her field of vision. The woman looked so scared. Tears ran from her eyes. She was shaking, her head constantly in motion. It distracted Jemma, took her eyes away from the target.

She lined it up and readied the arrow, felt the bowstring running between her fingers. She focused on the blue target, relaxed her body, tried to put Lucie's heaving frame out of her thoughts.

It was the hardest thing she'd ever done. She delayed, not happy with her concentration. The audience held its breath. Jemma thought about her body standing still, about the ground beneath her feet, the blue skies above, and then she focused, narrowed her eyes, and let the arrow fly.

It struck the target dead centre. Lucie screamed. The arrow fell down across her face, making her start. Once more, the place erupted. The watchers showed their exultation. Several of the guards started making mock bows at her.

But Jemma knew it was far from over. This was the kind of activity that got harder the more you did it. The tension built, the shaking intensified. It became more difficult to hit the target with the perfect shot she so desperately needed.

Next up – Cassidy.

The redhead was standing perfectly still, her face stoic. She nodded when Jemma met her eyes. Her life was in Jemma's hands and she was happy to acknowledge it. Whatever happened would happen. Cassidy showed she trusted Jemma with her life.

Which only increased the tension that Jemma was feeling. And now it ran through her like a physical, snarling thing. It made her hands start to shake, and to sweat.

Jemma walked over to Cassidy, stood before her, head bowed. She couldn't stop the shaking. She looked up, looked down again, and was aware of a current of tension passing through the arena. After a few moments, Phoenix himself rose to his feet.

'You can do this,' he said unexpectedly into the silence. 'This is your moment.'

Jemma looked up at him, wanted to unleash the arrow in his direction. She saw the guards stationed all around, all with their hands on their guns. She couldn't risk it, couldn't risk killing them all at this moment.

She took a deep breath, looked at Cassidy. Slowly, carefully, Jemma raised the bow, feeling it slip slightly through her slick fingers. She wiped them once, twice, and then sighted on Cassidy.

It was now or never.

Holding her breath, sweating, shaking, she let the arrow fly. It winged through the air, shivering along its length. Jemma saw its trajectory through her narrowed eyes, watched it tear ever closer.

Saw it miss the target completely and take a chunk out of the wooden pole.

A terrible silence filled the arena.

CHAPTER EIGHTEEN

What happened next happened very quickly.

Cassidy gasped, flung her head from left to right as if looking for an attack. Jemma almost cried out in despair, but kept her cool, some of the cat burglar level-headedness kicking in. Phoenix surged to his feet. The guards all turned to stare at him. Phoenix was throwing out a hand bunched into a fist. He was turning the hand over, the thumb placed in a downward position.

Even as he did it, Jemma was knocking another arrow. She felt it slide into the bow easily, whipped the bow up, and unleashed a second arrow.

She'd done it without thinking, with consummate skill. The arrow flew toward the target, struck it, and cleaved it in half.

Phoenix froze, his thumb not fully extended. The guards hesitated, seeing what had happened and turning to the sovereign for guidance.

Phoenix bunched his fist, still holding the arm outstretched. He was thinking, deciding Cassidy's fate. Jemma had acted quickly, before he could communicate his decision. Around him, the other sovereigns watched with rapt attention.

Jemma watched him without blinking. Cassidy couldn't see Phoenix from her position, so, instead, she was watching Jemma.

It seemed to take an age but, finally, Phoenix responded with a thumbs up. The whole gathering cheered. Jemma felt relief wash through her like a bucket of ice water. Phoenix went to sit back down, nodding at his fellow sovereigns, taking their praise.

Jemma slumped. The bow almost slipped from her fingers. But she wasn't done yet. She looked up, steeled herself.

The last in line was Bodie.

Jemma didn't feel confident. Yes, she'd just purposely broken a target in half and saved Cassidy's life, but that had all happened in a perfect moment of clarity. She'd just loaded the arrow and let it fly – no thinking, no doubts, no outside influence.

Now she was back to square one. She looked over to Bodie, knowing the crowd was expecting her to walk over, raise her bow, and take a shot. She made them wait, took her time. Again, the tension mounted. Jemma met Cassidy's eyes and received the cool nod in return.

Only when she was ready did she start the walk to Bodie. It felt like the longest trudge; the earth kicking up dirt plumes, the scorching sun blazing down, the eyes of the world upon her. She could feel those eyes burning through her skin, penetrating deep. She kept her head down, looking only at the ground.

Finally, she came to Bodie, stopped, and turned to face him. His eyes were upon her, calm, almost smiling. He had every faith in her, and that somehow made it harder.

Jemma checked her arrows. She had five left. She didn't know why she needed to know that, but it was best to be prepared for what may come. The sweat was beading on her brow, trickling between her shoulder

THE CONTEST

blades. The crowd had grown quiet, the guards staring and grinning and loving every minute.

Jemma wiped her bow. She then wiped an arrow and fitted it to the string. For now, the arrow was pointed at the floor. Her team, in line, watched her, all safe except for Bodie. Jemma now focused on the moment at hand, on Bodie.

She raised the bow, took aim. The arrow quivered in place. She closed one eye, felt the tension in the bow. Waited until everything was perfect.

And then she let loose.

And, as soon as the arrow left the bow, she knew she'd got it all wrong. The shaft wavered, flying off at a slight angle. It missed the pole entirely, shooting past and almost striking a guard. Jemma stared, wide-eyed. The crowd stayed quiet, either in shock or anticipation, or both Jemma didn't know.

Phoenix rose slowly to his feet. His expression told Jemma he didn't really want to do this. He had enjoyed the show, maybe hoped she'd complete her ordeal successfully. Now, he extended his arm, fist bunched.

Jemma couldn't breathe. Bodie still stared at her without expression. Had she just killed him?

Phoenix finally acted. He drew himself straight, gazed out over the gathered crowd, and gave them the thumbs down.

Bodie was dead. Jemma saw it coming. As soon as Phoenix gave the thumbs down, a guard started walking towards Bodie. As he walked, he twirled his knife. He was coming up behind the pole, raising his knife.

There was nothing Jemma could do to save him.

The guard neared Bodie. The knife flashed. Next, she would see Bodie's blood splashing onto the hard-packed earth. She couldn't help him now, couldn't prevent what was about to happen.

Phoenix still stood with his thumb pointed down. Could Jemma appeal to him?

No chance, she thought. These sovereigns lived for moments like this. It had to be the pure anguish of those left behind that they loved.

There was only one way to deal with people like this.

The guard stepped up behind Bodie, raised his knife and aimed for Bodie's neck. Jemma knew she had to throw her own life away. It was the only thing that would work. She nocked another arrow, drew it, and let fly. It flew true, smashing right through the guard's shoulder and knocking him several feet backwards. He cried out, dropped the knife, and tried to stem the flow of blood.

But Jemma wasn't done. She turned and nocked several arrows, shooting each one in turn toward Phoenix and his second-in-charge. The arrows flew in a deadly rain between the two men, making them stiffen and stare.

Jemma immediately started shouting. 'I meant to miss! I could have killed you! Please, *I could have killed you!*'

Phoenix glared at her, surprise and horror on his face. He didn't know what to make of it. The other sovereigns were all silent, frozen. The guards had paused too, and were watching Phoenix. There was a terrible sense of shock in the air. Jemma watched it all, glad she'd done what she'd done, knowing her shots had been accurate and that she'd done all she could to save Bodie's life.

Still, Phoenix stared. He hadn't moved, hadn't even blinked. His outstretched hand trembled. Jemma wished she could tell what was going through his mind.

The Contest

Minutes passed. They stretched interminably. Jemma saw her life in Phoenix's hands. She just hoped she'd saved Bodie's.

Finally, Phoenix started moving. He swallowed. He lowered his arm. To give himself a little more time, he turned away, reached down to the table and picked up a goblet of wine. Slowly, he sipped at it, his eyes now regarding Jemma speculatively. He didn't stop sipping at the wine until he'd drained it.

'I could have killed you,' Jemma said quietly.

Phoenix looked from Jemma to Bodie and then to the crowd. He gave no sign of his inner thoughts. His eyes were blank, his face expressionless. Jemma could barely stand the tension. Around Phoenix, all the other sovereigns stirred, crossing and uncrossing their legs. Shifting to make themselves more comfortable, clearly in a state of apprehension.

This wasn't what they expected.

Jemma tore her eyes away from Phoenix and looked at Bodie. He gave her a nod and a smile, which tore at her heart. She couldn't believe she had missed the target entirely. One slight error, and it had all gone to shit.

Behind Bodie, the guard she'd shot was back on his feet, cradling his arm. Other guards had gone to his aid and were treating the wound. Beyond that activity, all was still and silent and all eyes were on her and Phoenix.

The principal sovereign finally raised both hands.

'Hear me,' he said. 'Hear me. This is an unprecedented moment in our history. Yes, Bodie should die. Jemma missed the target. And that would have happened. I gave the order and the good guard there came forward, knife raised. And then...' he shook his head. 'Then... Jemma did something extraordinary to save her friend's life. She *didn't* kill me.'

Jemma listened, her heart in her mouth. All she wanted was for him to get to the bloody end.

'Jemma loosed four arrows,' he shouted out. 'They all missed, flying between Rahim and me, *purposely*. She chose not to harm either of us, and she did it all to save her friend's life. I think, with that in mind, she deserves our praise.'

And he flung out his arm, fist bunched, and then gave her a thumbs up.

Jemma wilted, the bow falling from her fingers. Guards came up and started untying her team, including Bodie. The crowd was cheering, agreeing with Phoenix. Jemma made sure she gave Phoenix a nod in gratitude. Why not? It couldn't hurt. She was just happy her entire team was alive.

And that she'd completed her contest.

All around her, the raucous noise continued.

CHAPTER NINETEEN

After their ordeal, the relic hunters were taken to their cells and allowed to rest. Bodie spent the rest of the afternoon and evening lying flat out. He couldn't believe how close he had come to dying, and how Jemma had risked everything to save his life. Her quick thinking, her selfless act, it had both humbled and invigorated him. He had hugged her hard without speaking, just let the unsaid sentiments flow.

They spent the rest of the day recovering from their trauma, Bodie especially. He really had thought he'd been about to die. What had flashed through his mind at that point? Surprisingly, very little. Just a touch of regret, love for his friends, sadness at where it had all ended up and what might become of them.

He tried to shrug all that off now as he lay on his bed, staring up at the white ceiling. The fact was, they were all still alive. Contests had been completed. Days had passed. And here they were, still very much in the *game*.

For it was a game, he knew. Phoenix and the others made a game of it. This was what they wanted from their lives – holding life or death over people. Somehow, it made them feel alive, complete.

Bodie gradually drifted off, fell asleep. Normally, on an evening, they were taken to the Core to eat and drink, but nobody came for them that night. Maybe they knew that they just wanted to be left alone.

Bodie woke early the next morning, shifted in his bed and sat up. He drank from the jug of water and just sat there, holding his head in his hands. How had they ended up here, at this time, in this predicament?

There was no genuine answer, no matter how long he thought about it. Eventually, he heard the others stirring and started up a stilted conversation. About an hour after that, the guards arrived, approaching their cells slowly.

Bodie's heart jumped into his mouth. Not another contest? Not yet? He cleared his throat, about to speak up, but one of the guards beat him to it.

'We're taking you to the Core,' he said.

Bodie heaved a sigh of relief. He was hungry too and looked forward to the assortment of foods and drinks on offer. The team lined up at their doors and were then escorted down the corridor, out the exit doors, and across the square to the mess hut. When they entered the mess hut, the guards melted away, leaving them to their own devices. Bodie went straight for the bacon, beans and sausages, and then the coffee.

As he queued, a man jostled his arm. 'Sorry, mate,' the man said.

It was the first interaction Bodie had had with another captive since they arrived. He made the most of it. 'No problem. I'm Bodie.' He held out a hand.

The man took it in a firm grip. He was white-haired with a straggly white beard and blue eyes. His face was lined, but he looked fit and moved capably.

'Bill,' the man said affably. 'How long have you been here?'

It was probably the question on everyone's minds. Three weeks was supposed to be the maximum.

'Just a few days,' Bodie said with a touch of regret. 'You?'

'Two weeks.'

Bodie was unsure what to say next. How do you ask a stranger if his entire team was still alive? How did you ask how things were going in a situation like this?

'We're two down,' the man volunteered the information regretfully. 'Four left. Where'd they grab you from?'

'New York,' Bodie said. 'One night. They were bloody good.'

'That they are, unfortunately,' Bill said. 'You seen a way out yet?'

Bodie looked at him. It was a forward question, considering he'd just met the man. 'Have you?'

'I'm no planner. I was – or am – the tech of my team. Great with the computer shenanigans. All I see are guns and guards.'

To be fair, that was the key problem. 'There are a lot of guards and guns.' Bodie said.

They moved up a little in the queue. Bodie wanted more from the man. 'Any idea where we are? Who these sovereigns really are? If they actually let you go after three weeks?'

Bill leaned in closer. 'I've seen teams vanish. After three weeks, you don't see them ever again. Who knows what happens to them? Hopefully, they will go free. I guess I'll find out in about a week.'

The man looked resigned to his fate. Bodie didn't like to ask what terrible ordeals he and his team had already been forced to endure. He could see, on the man's face, a terrible need for it all to be over.

'Any thoughts at all on the compound?' he asked, a bit

desperately. All he wanted was to get another perspective.

'They're good,' the man sniffed. 'Better than they have any right to be. Yeah, some of them are slack. They drink, they smoke, they even fall asleep on duty. But there are enough of them to cover for each other. You'd need an army to get in here and take them all out.'

'Or a very good strike force,' Bodie said.

'Many of which are already inside,' Bill pointed out.

It was a good point, Bodie thought. Maybe the key here was to rise up from the inside, get all the captives together. Looking around the mess hall, he counted over twenty of them, and not everyone was here. If all these teams were as good as the relic hunters, they might stand a chance.

Or they could risk staying the three weeks.

'The trouble with staying,' Bill said, as if reading his mind. 'Is that you don't know if you're gonna be alive tomorrow.'

Bodie nodded his agreement. The best idea would be to get away as soon as possible. Every day brought a new deadly challenge. Briefly, he wondered what today would bring. Soon, they were at the food, and Bill drifted away with a nod. Bodie decided to keep talking – the more people he engaged, the better. He turned to the person behind him.

A woman. Her name turned out to be Kate. They talked about the compound, the time they'd spent here, the positions of the guards at night. Slowly, Bodie was learning more and more about their new home. He slipped back in the queue, talking to others. Some wouldn't speak, or replied in monosyllabic sentences, but others he got to engage and tried to glean information.

The Contest

Eventually, with his dinner cold, he returned to the table. The others looked up at him.

'Get lost?' Cassidy asked.

'No. I started engaging our fellow prisoners in conversation. We could be in Africa, or Croatia, or even Australia. There are over a hundred guards here. The sovereigns come and go all the time, no pattern. Only Phoenix is a constant. And nobody has any idea what happens after three weeks.'

'Anyone have any ideas about how to get the hell out?' Yasmine asked.

'Everyone is daunted by the amount of guards and their firepower,' Bodie said, munching bacon. 'I get it. It looks overwhelming.' He lowered his voice. 'The only way out I can see is to start a rebellion.'

'You mean from the inside?' Heidi asked.

'Yeah, all the captives together. We could drift between them all, start talking, come up with a plan.'

'We'd have to do it here,' Lucie said. 'We're not free anywhere else.'

'The cells,' Bodie said. 'We'd have to come up with names for each team. Communicate on a night.'

'But we can't be sure the guards aren't listening,' Cassidy pointed out.

Bodie faltered. He had thought the cells idea was a good one. But now he saw Cassidy was right. Maybe they even stationed a guard or two inside at night.

'Then it has to be done here, at the Core,' he said. 'We come twice a day. It's time to mingle and beat out a plan.'

There was no time like the present. On the pretext of grabbing more food, the entire team went up to the buffet and started mingling. They chatted, passed comments, made conversation. They decided who they could talk to, who they couldn't. No teams were less than four strong, and some were as large as eight, which gave them an idea of how many unique challenges there were. They kept the dialogue short, sounding people out and testing their desperation. By the time they'd reconvened around the table and made sure the guards weren't watching them, they knew far more than they had previously.

'Team Bill comprises six people,' Bodie said. 'They've only got a week left and are on the fence. Half of them think they'll be freed, half of them don't.'

'Tricky,' Cassidy said.

'The team I spoke to, let's call them team Blonde,' Heidi said. 'Are up for anything. They lost someone yesterday in what she called the Gauntlet. It was pretty bad.'

This way, they identified those who might help, and those who would. They spoke quietly, sharply, succinctly. They started coming up with a much larger, much more deadly, team. It was a good start, and Bodie was happy with it.

But today was another day, he knew. Whose turn would it be to face death?

CHAPTER TWENTY

The team were returned to their cells. Bodie, conscious of their overall lack of exercise, bent down and did a series of press ups, pull ups and other exercises until his blood pumped. He heard the others doing something similar. Not only did it keep them healthy, but it also passed the time and stopped them from thinking.

About who would be chosen next.

It preyed on all their minds. When would their time come? Bodie completed his exercise routine just as he heard the front door open and then the tread of the guards as they walked towards the cells.

He listened, hoping they would veer off in a different direction, feeling guilty for that. But this time, they didn't. They came right up to the team's cells. The usual guard nodded at them.

'You guys are performing well,' he cast a glance at Jemma. 'You hurt a friend of mine yesterday.'

'Sorry,' Jemma mumbled.

The guard's face brightened. 'Moving on,' he said. 'It's your turn today.'

And his head turned towards Bodie.

'All right,' he said, not knowing what else to say.

'It's a big one. You're going on the Great Hunt.'

Bodie didn't like the sound of that.

'If you refuse, guess what?'

'One of my friends dies,' he knew the drill by now.

'That one,' the guard pointed even though Bodie couldn't see who he was singling out. 'Heidi,' he said.

Bodie closed his eyes briefly. Everyone stepped up to the cell doors, the rest of the team wanting to back up Bodie during his contest. The guard laughed.

'Oh, it's just him today, I'm afraid. You lot don't get to watch.'

'Oh, please,' Lucie said. 'It's just moral support.'

'Too complicated,' the guard shrugged. 'There's a lot of ground to cover. And besides, I don't make the rules.'

He unlocked Bodie's door, beckoned him out, and started walking away. Guards surrounded Bodie and marched him past his colleagues. As he passed them, he caught their eyes, gave them a nod. In the circumstances, it was the best he could do. Soon, they were exiting into the heat, and then the guards took an unusual turn. They went sharply left, leading him in a new direction.

Bodie was taken away from the cell block to a squat building. Draperies hung over the windows, guarding against the direct sun. He went through an oak door and stepped into a lavish hallway, furnished with plush carpeting and gold fittings on the walls. A hat stand stood to the left and on it, strangely, hung an umbrella and a top hat. Bodie had to blink twice. He was then led down the hallway, along a corridor, and shown into a far room.

Phoenix stood at the back of it, behind a wide oak desk. He was staring up at a bookcase, but turned as Bodie came through the door.

'Ah, the man of the moment,' he said. 'Please, sit down.'

Bodie took the only seat, a leather wing chair. The

guards spread out behind him, watching closely in case he tried anything.

'Today you will attempt the Great Hunt,' Phoenix remained on his feet, looking down at Bodie.

'What is that?' He might as well try to glean all the information he could.

'You must get from point A to point B. You will be hunted by three soldiers who have been promised a lot of money if they tag you. It's a long journey. Several hours, in fact. On this property, there are hills, valleys, rivers, streams, plains, caves and a forest. You will be given various items, a ten-minute head start and then allowed to run. What do you think of that?'

Bodie sat back. 'I think it sounds fucking horrendous.'

Phoenix nodded. 'I imagine it would, to you. I understand.'

'And how are you people gonna watch all that?' He wanted all the information, not just some of it.

'Oh, don't worry, we have our ways.' Phoenix pointed at a monitor on his desk. 'There are lots of powerful cameras out there.'

Bodie knew better than to ask any intimate questions. For instance – where the hell are we? It would only get him into trouble and ruin their chances of freedom in what was now less than three weeks. Supposedly. He sat waiting.

'Any questions?' Phoenix asked.

'None that you will answer.'

Phoenix nodded at the guards. Bodie was led out of the room and then the house and marched toward several vehicles, all parked haphazardly. They bundled him into one. Someone started the engine, and they set off, bouncing across the hard earth. They drove through the compound, past the arena and then the Gauntlet, past the wooden poles in the ground, now driving into the distance.

Bodie checked out the landscape as carefully as he could. Soon, he knew, he'd be running through it, hunted. As they drove, the guard sitting next to him spoke up.

'You'll get given a backpack. In it will be a compass, water, food, a knife, a torch, and a rough map of the compound. You must make your way back to the cell building. It's that easy. Understand?'

'How long should it take me?'

'A couple of hours. Maybe three.'

'The soldiers tracking me... are they snipers?'

He knew it was a good question. It would change the way he moved.

The guard shrugged. 'They won't be carrying sniper rifles, if that's what you're asking.'

Bodie nodded.

'Don't forget what happens if you refuse.'

Refuse? How the hell could he refuse? There were three hard-assed soldiers looking for him. He didn't answer the threat, just kept his eyes peeled on the landscape. They drove past a wide gurgling stream that looked heavenly in the blinding heat, past a range of low hills, a forest in the distance. Bodie thought he could see a shimmering lake too, but wasn't sure. A mountain side stood to the right, a vast plain to the left. The truck jounced its way past them all.

The truck drove for a long time, each mile taking him further away from the compound. Bodie turned to the guard.

'Do I get a weapon?'

The Contest

The man grinned. 'I told you... a knife.'

'I mean a proper weapon, considering I'm being chased by soldiers.'

'Just a knife.'

Bodie turned away, unhappy. In reality, he didn't stand a chance. He was in a hostile, strange environment, having to use a compass to navigate which he would find difficult, crossing unknown terrain, and all this whilst being hunted by men with guns. At least, he assumed they had guns.

He asked the question.

'We're not heathens,' the guard laughed. 'They will only carry knives.'

It made Bodie feel a little better. The battles would be up close and personal, and he was good in a scrap like that. He doubted the soldiers would work together, too. They would want the reward for themselves.

Finally, the truck came to a stop. It turned in a semicircle on the banks of a narrow stream before it was turned off. The engine ticked. Doors were flung open and Bodie ushered out.

As he stepped out of the air conditioning, he started sweating.

A guard handed him a backpack. Bodie unstrapped it, checked the contents. The guard was as good as his word. Bodie checked his environs.

'Where are they?' he asked.

'Watching.'

'Any advice?'

'Run like a bastard.'

'Oh, thanks.'

The guards took a quick look around and then started climbing back into their car. The main guard took another look at Bodie.

'Your ten minutes have started,' he said.

Bodie cursed. He couldn't stop to check the compass, the map. He didn't have time. Somehow, he had to get to cover to work all that out and, for now, he could follow the direction they'd come.

The car sped off.

Alone, Bodie shrugged into the backpack and started to run.

CHAPTER TWENTY ONE

Bodie ran in the right direction for a while, until the landscape grew unsure, until his direction become dubious. He ran away from the lake, following a sloping hillside, down and down, until the forest was in front of him. The ground was hard earth, mostly brown with patches of green. There were little shrubs everywhere, perfect for tripping him up. Above, the sun beat down relentlessly and there wasn't a breath of wind in the air.

He jogged steadily, monitoring the time. When ten minutes were up, he felt like panicking, knowing there were now three men hunting him down. But he didn't. He had to maintain his lead, keep moving.

But that would not happen.

Bodie needed to navigate. He ran until he was at the edge of the forest and then slid among the trees. He kept going, staying near the edge but penetrating as far as he dared, keeping the sun in the same position, which he could see clearly through the canopy above. Now, he knelt on a soft bed of loam and shrugged off his backpack, opened it. He took out the map and then the compass, found where he was and the best direction back to the cells. It appeared that he would need to move in a north-easterly direction. Bodie nodded to himself. He would start off and then check his bearing every few minutes, recheck the map every twenty. If he could, he would maintain a watch behind him, looking out for the soldiers.

He swigged water and then started off again, holding the compass out and penetrating deeper into the forest. He stayed on the bearing, rerouting occasionally as he came across a fallen tree or a tangle of underbrush. It was blessedly cooler under the canopy of trees, the sun unable to penetrate fully. Everything was all dappled and green and gold, and then he came across a burbling stream and he splashed water on his face. It was all the time he would allow himself. Without looking around, Bodie leapt across the stream and started on his journey again. He knew he'd left footprints by the stream and silently berated himself. That had been a mistake. He needed to be more careful. But the forest stretched on. He kept his eye on the compass, threading as straight a line as he could. He figured twenty minutes had now passed.

Bodie focused hard, trying not to let his mind wander. He moved as fast as he was able. The soldiers would know which way he went. It was obvious. They would follow him into the forest...

Or would they skirt it, wait for him to come out?

Bodie couldn't let himself think that way. He had to trust his instincts and remain on high alert. The trees were thick before him, and he worked his way through them. He would have been completely lost without the compass.

The minutes marched by. Bodie pushed his way through the greenery relentlessly until, finally, he saw the trees were thinning.

It wasn't a good thing. If he remembered correctly, there was nothing beyond the forest but a wide, flat plain

The Contest

for a while. Bodie slowed as he reached the edges of the forest.

He didn't want to step right out, present an obvious target. He slunk from tree to tree, trying to see where he was going but also aware that he was wasting time. Finally, he reached the very last line of trees, stepped out, and started running along a vast plain.

It was brown and slightly rolling, stretching all around. Bodie could see nothing but the plain and the mountains ahead. He knew he could be seen clearly out here, but hoped the pursuing soldiers were still in the forest.

He ran as fast as he could for as long as he could, happy to find that the landscape had dips. They weren't deep enough to completely hide him unless he lay down, but they at least offered a modicum of cover.

Bodie stopped when he reached a deep fold, knelt down and swigged some more water. He ate a couple of power bars too, keeping his strength up. The water was half gone already, and he wondered if he might after ration it. He figured he'd been running for about fifty minutes now. If the guard had been telling the truth, he guessed he was about two hours away from the compound.

A big *if*.

Bodie packed the water away, and then slowly rose to his feet. He looked back towards the forest. There was no sign of anyone. The soldiers could be anywhere, even ahead of him. He withdrew the knife now, wondered why he hadn't done so earlier, and knew he was in a panicked state of mind. He couldn't relax, couldn't focus exactly right. Bodie put the backpack on and kept hold of the knife.

And back at the edge of the forest there was movement. Or was there? Was it a shadow? Bodie flung himself to the floor, keeping out of sight. After a moment, he rose slightly, peeking his head over the fold to look at the forest's edge. Now he could see nothing. No shadow. No movement. Had it even been there?

Now what? He couldn't stay there, had to risk moving. He crawled out of the dip, reached higher ground, and kept crawling. The progress was slow, and he couldn't keep moving like this. He had to get a damn move on. Bracing himself, Bodie rose to his feet once more and started running.

He looked back over his shoulder towards the forest.

Nothing lurked there. He was aching, sweating so badly it flew off him in rivers. The sun beat down, and by now, it was early afternoon. There were birds in the air, circling. Bodie hoped to hell they weren't bloody vultures.

He kept running up and down the folding landscape. The plain still stretched widely on all sides. He took another compass bearing, switched his course marginally. One thing he was doing right — he was following the compass and the map to the letter. If he kept the mountains ahead, he even knew which direction to run without constantly staring at the compass. It helped and, right now, he needed all the help he could get.

He kept looking back, even though he knew he shouldn't. All the way back to the forest was still clear, and he looked around its perimeter, scanned the plain. He saw no sign of movement.

Ahead, darkness rose.

He only saw it out of the corner of his eye. One

The Contest

moment, the way ahead was clear, the next something dark blocked it.

Bodie almost ran point blank into a knife. He just couldn't believe his eyes. A figure had popped up, a figure dressed in desert fatigues and wearing sunglasses and a baseball cap. It was broad, solid. Its face was grim, as if set in stone. Bodie saw all this in a split instant as he still ran towards the knife.

Slowing, digging his boots into the earth, he flung himself to the right. He staggered, caught himself. The soldier had been waiting in a fold of land, just laying there ready to pounce as Bodie approached. He must have been lying in wait for a long time.

Bodie gripped his own knife between sweating fingers. He panted hard, wiped sweat quickly away before it trickled into his eyes. The soldier looked calm and collected as he approached warily.

'Can't we talk about this?' Bodie said. 'Join the same team.'

The soldier didn't even reply. He advanced steadily, closing the gap. Bodie circled him, wanting to shrug out of his backpack but knowing there wasn't time.

The soldier lunged. Too soon. Bodie evaded the thrust easily, saw the knife pass harmlessly by. His right foot hit a stone that wouldn't budge, made him stumble. The soldier's eyes narrowed, perhaps thinking Bodie had stumbled on purpose to draw him in. It was a cat-and-mouse situation. The soldier wasn't about to take any chances, though.

Bodie swallowed. His mouth was dry. Perversely, he was very much aware that tangling with this soldier right now would allow the other two to catch up. Or find better positions. It was an all round critical situation.

The soldier shot forward fast. He swung underhand with the knife. It sliced through the air right in front of Bodie who backed away and then it slashed towards his face. Bodie ducked, losing his footing. He hit the earth with a crash, rolled out of range. He came up again, now facing the soldier on his knees.

The man pressed his advantage, still coming but not rushing into anything. Bodie flung his knife up to ward off the other man's attack and the blades clashed, ringing across the plains. Bodie felt a heavy vibration run through his wrist. He forced himself up, faced the other man once again.

They were close now.

The soldier lunged once, twice, then backed away. Bodie evaded the thrusts. The two circled each other under the blazing sun, droplets of sweat running off their faces and down their backs. They moved with purpose, dangerously, and their very lives depended on where they put their next step.

Bodie hadn't made the first move yet. Now, consigned to a fight to the death, he did. He swiped the knife from left to right, making it seem like a clumsy movement. When the soldier evaded and then lunged in, Bodie was ready, slashing towards his oncoming frame. The blade nicked the soldier's ribcage before he could stop his forward momentum, ripping clothes and flesh. Soon, the material was soaked with blood. Bodie felt no satisfaction at drawing it first.

'We can work together,' he said.

'Shut the hell up,' the soldier murmured.

Bodie struck as the man spoke, this time slashing across the forehead. This was a much deeper cut. Blood flowed down into the man's eyes and he backed away,

THE CONTEST

wiping at it with his sleeve. Bodie didn't press his advantage at first.

'Last chance,' he said.

The man wiped furiously. The blood flowed. Frantically, he tried to keep his eyes on Bodie and waved the knife around, skills forgotten. Bodie kept him close, ready to attack.

'I'm sorry then,' Bodie said.

He lunged, made a feint, and then waited until a fresh wash of blood invaded the soldier's eyes before striking. The knife plunged into the soldier's heart and then withdrew. The man stiffened, grunted and fell backwards in the dirt, hitting the ground with a heavy thump. Bodie stood over him, his head downcast.

'Sorry again, mate,' he said.

With a heavy heart, he knelt at the soldier's side, put fingers over his eyes and closed them. Then he looked up, searching the landscape for enemies. He was glad to see no figures out there, no approaching soldiers. But the panorama was vast; they could be on their stomachs watching from anywhere.

Bodie rose to his feet, put the knife away and took a long swig of the water. He deserved it. Maybe he'd come across another stream soon, get a top up. But it wasn't the end of the world – he figured he was about ninety minutes from the compound. He looked in the general direction, but saw nothing except a hazy kind of mirage. He broke out the compass, freshened his heading, and then took off as fast as his aching body could carry him.

CHAPTER TWENTY TWO

Bodie hurried through the arid landscape, highly aware there were still two killers on his tail.

The landscape started to get hilly as the mountains grew closer. He followed the hills, rushing up and then down and then up again. The mountains grew clearer and clearer until he could make out most of the details. After a while, he realised he had climbed to a decent elevated level and paused atop one rise to look back the way he'd come.

And saw them instantly. Two distant figures coming through the scenery. They were close together, moving efficiently, following his trail. Bodie cursed on seeing them, wondering why they were working together. Maybe they would share the prize. He knew without a doubt he couldn't take two on at the same time. He put his head down and started moving faster, harder, trying to make the compound before they caught up.

At the bottom of a dip he found a stream, knelt on the banks and filled up his water bottle. The water tasted refreshing and reinvigorated him. He wiped his brow, saw the filth on the back of his hand and the fresh sweat. He thought about his team, his friends, back at the compound and wondered if he would ever see them again. And then, for the first time, he remembered Phoenix's revelation that there were numerous cameras

The Contest

placed around the panorama. He hadn't seen one yet, though he hadn't really been looking. He looked now, saw nothing obvious. Maybe they were high in the trees, powerful and small. Maybe Phoenix had been lying.

He doubted it. The man was nothing but a terrible, warped watcher. A viewer of the macabre. His power came from forcing others to do his bidding. He was a parasite and had to be taken out.

Bodie wasted little time. He waded through the river, feeling its gentle pull carry him upstream a few yards. On the other side, he felt a little cooler and started off again, head down, climbing the next hill. Soon, as the hills grew steeper and craggier, he spied a shallow cave ahead and entered it. The inside was cool and felt misleadingly safe. He stopped for a few minutes, tried to catch his breath.

He looked out of the cave. Again, he was in an elevated position and could look back across the landscape. Again, he spied them, closer now, definitely closing. He figured they were about twenty minutes behind him. Maybe they had lost time in the forest, maybe somewhere else. Maybe they hadn't tracked him as well as they should have, but they were definitely tracking him now. Even as he watched, Bodie saw one of them stop and pull out a set of field glasses from his backpack.

He hit the dirt, but kept watching. Saw the soldier focus immediately on his position. They knew where he was then. At least, roughly. The soldier stared for a few seconds, then shouted to his colleague, pointed. The other man nodded. Bodie doubted they could see him prone on the ground. It was hard enough knowing they had a good idea where he was.

He waited for the men to pack away the binocs and

start to move again. When they did, he followed suit, exiting the cave and choosing the easiest way across the craggy hillsides. Truth be told, there was no easy way, and he found himself skirting the mountains. But at least the heat up here was more subdued, and there was a light breeze in the air.

He kept going, leaving a trail but unable to do anything about it. He found the ground on the hillsides softer now and came up with an idea.

Knowing he was wasting time, but risking it anyway, he dug several ankle-breaker holes amid his track and covered them over with loose material. It was worth a try. The holes were right where he was walking, which would attract the soldiers, and maybe they wouldn't think he was wily enough to think about laying a trap. Bodie knelt in the sandy earth for a while, digging the traps, and then continued on, filthy, flagging.

He was really feeling it now. In relative terms, he hadn't been on the go for that long, but the entire situation was desperate. It sapped all the energy from him.

He pushed hard, figuring they were still closing the gap. What were they now? Fifteen minutes behind? Less? He couldn't just keep rushing blindly onwards. He was too far from the compound to make it before they caught him. This realisation was the one he'd been refuting all along. Now... it hit him hard.

He would not escape them.

Bodie's flagging mind wrestled with the problem. Almost an impossible conundrum. He couldn't keep running, couldn't wait for them, couldn't...

Wait.

A thought occurred to him as he stumbled on. He'd

The Contest

already seen them following his trail to the nth degree. They were relying on that trail. They had their heads down and were moving unerringly along it. Maybe, just maybe, that presented him with an opportunity.

Bodie kept moving, but kept a closer eye on the surrounding landscape. He slowed slightly, fully aware of the risks. His mind was now focused; he knew there was only one way out of this. And that way was to fight. It was everything that bastard Phoenix had been hoping for.

Bodie soon found the perfect spot to hatch his plan. There was a fold in the surrounding landscape, a place where he could hide. He had to hope the following soldiers weren't at the very top of their game. He didn't think so – otherwise they wouldn't have been relying on following his spoor so closely.

Bodie went past the delve for a while, and then, carefully, doubled back. He walked backwards, treading in his own footprints all the way back to the fold in the landscape. When he was there, he hid, flattened himself, and controlled his breathing. It wasn't easy. His heart was pounding, his chest heaving. He found it hard to focus, because his mind was racing. Slowly, Bodie took out the knife and held it ready. He set himself, ready for a swift attack, ready for an ambush.

It was his last roll of the dice.

CHAPTER TWENTY THREE

Minutes passed like hours, slogging by. Bodie was able to control his breathing, steady his nerves. He wiped his face, his brow, got a firm grip on the knife. He was as ready as he was ever going to be.

His eyes were focused on rock, and making sure he stayed well hidden. His ears were attuned for the slightest noise. The worst thing that could happen here was that the soldiers passed him by and he didn't notice.

Nothing happened for a while. Five minutes passed, then seven and eight. He counted in his head, body taut and ready. The tautness made his muscles shake, and he had to make an enormous effort to steady them. This wasn't natural to Bodie. None of this was. He didn't fight for a living, didn't make his way through treacherous landscapes whilst being hunted. Even as he stood there, waiting, it felt bizarre, otherworldly. It felt as if someone else was in his body standing there.

What the hell was he doing?

His thoughts turned to Heidi and Cassidy and the others. Were they being allowed to watch this? And then something else occurred to him. How trustworthy was Phoenix in this situation? If he was watching, would he somehow reveal Bodie's position to the soldiers?

The sudden realisation unsettled him tremendously. Phoenix couldn't be trusted an inch. He listened intently,

The Contest

ready for any sound of boots crunching on grit.

And then it came.

Bodie knew his life was in his own hands. Everything would decide on the next few seconds, the next few minutes.

A boot came down just a few metres beyond the fold, and then another. The men were walking at a steady pace. Bodie couldn't hear them breathing, but he could imagine them focused on his trail. The boots came down in double time, meaning there were two men walking by. Bodie let them go, and then eased himself out of his hiding place.

He came around the fold, looked down the trail he'd engineered. The lead soldier was following it blindly, not even looking ahead. The second soldier walked behind. Both wore fatigues and baseball caps and wraparound sunglasses. Both carried exposed knives in their hands. Bodie was glad about that. He didn't want to kill an unarmed man.

Guilt flashed through him. This would not be easy to do.

But it was kill or be killed. He was the prey in a very twisted game of cat-and-mouse. And, as he vacillated, the two soldiers walked further away.

Bodie leapt forward. He struck the back of the second soldier, pushing him forwards. At the same time, he thrust in with the knife, wincing but determined. The sharp blade penetrated through clothing and then flesh and buried itself in the soldier's ribcage. The man stiffened and then let out a scream, falling to his knees. Bodie whipped the knife back out and stood above the fallen man, the blade dripping.

The lead soldier whirled and stared in disbelief. He

looked from the downed man to Bodie, his eyes wide. And then he tightened the grip on his weapon and narrowed his eyes. Bodie didn't move. The man he'd stabbed fell onto his face, bleeding out. He was breathing shallowly, ever more slowly. Bodie felt sorry for him even as he eyed up his new adversary.

The soldier reached down, grabbed a handful of dirt, and launched it at Bodie. The dirt filled his eyes, and he backed away, giving himself some space. He sensed rather than heard his opponent move.

The man came in swiftly, but the body of his colleague hampered his attack. He had to leap over the prone man, and that upset his flow. He landed and twisted awkwardly, ending up throwing a wild slash at Bodie.

Staggering back, wiping at his eyes, Bodie felt the blade slash through his sleeve. It didn't penetrate flesh, but the feeling of the knife so close sent a bolt of adrenaline through him. He blinked rapidly. His vision cleared.

The soldier was pressing his advantage, coming forward fast, now more stable. He didn't spare a glance for his dying colleague. He attacked Bodie with a flurry of strikes, unrelenting, unstoppable.

Bodie just backed up. He couldn't match the man's fury and decided just to stay out of the way of it. He backed around the fold, went up the hill, hoped to God his foot wouldn't get stuck in some hole or trip over some underbrush. The attack was relentless, dizzying. All Bodie saw was the flashing blade and occasional glimpses of the crazed face behind it, the wide, dead eyes.

He moved steadily, holding his own blade slightly in front of him. Once the other blade struck it, almost

The Contest

knocking it from his hands. After that, Bodie held it more carefully, more tightly. If he lost his blade now, he was dead.

Gradually, he realised he was above his attacker. That gave him the higher ground. But there was no sign of the other man's assault wilting. It was strong and unbeatable. If Bodie fought back now, he would die.

He kept going. The guy couldn't keep it up forever. He moved from bright sunlight to shadow to a dappled light, all the time in the lee of the higher mountain and backing up the slope.

The soldier finally relented, pausing his attack. Bodie chanced a look back, saw that he was on the very edge of a precipice. The soldier didn't know that. Bodie felt his heart climb into his mouth.

There were several ways to handle this. One of them was to simply launch himself on the other guy since he had the height advantage, but that was all down to chance. Another was to fight back, to force the man back down the trail. Bodie decided that was the way to go. He struck out, aiming for the ribs, forced the man back a step, struck again and again, slicing towards the chest and face. The man backed up, a tiny step at a time. It appeared they were evenly matched, but surely the soldier was more experienced?

Bodie wasn't so sure. In his life, he'd had more than his fair share of experience. He backed the man up now, heading down the slope. His opponent was panting hard, feeling the effects of the crazed attack he'd launched. Now was Bodie's best chance of taking advantage.

He kept going, carefully, steadily. He could feel his muscles growing tired as he searched for an opening. Striking high and low, he sought to penetrate the other man's defence. It was a hard, silent battle, neither man speaking, both knowing the struggle would end up with one of them lying dead among the rocks.

Bodie went for it. He slashed hard across the other man's throat, missing by an inch, and then followed it up with a heavy punch to the ribs. The other guy slipped, grunted. Bodie threw another punch, this one to the face, and went low with the knife. The punch connected with a jaw; the knife went through skin, but only about a millimetre.

The soldier jumped back, massaging his jaw with one hand. He stared at Bodie as if Bodie were his next meal, his lips working soundlessly.

It was now or never. Bodie had gained a slight advantage. He thrust outward with the knife and launched an attack, leaping up and down, smashing into the soldier and driving him backward. The man backpedalled uncontrollably, hit a rock with his foot and fell to the ground, momentum sending him rolling head over heels. Bodie followed as fast as he could, but the man was rolling violently, unable to control himself. Bodie scrambled after him.

The soldier rolled down the slope and hit level ground, still going. He flew across the trail and then hit a rock hard with his shoulder. He cried out, looked dazed. Bodie raced after him, careful not to trip. He didn't want to end up rolling after the soldier. That would not only look ridiculous, it would be suicide.

Bodie hit level ground. He saw the soldier was injured. The man was holding his shoulder, the knife between his legs. He looked up at Bodie with a pained expression.

'Do it,' he said.

The Contest

Bodie would never kill an unarmed man in cold blood. He shook his head. 'I can't do that,' he said.

'If you don't kill me, I'll kill you,'

Bodie almost smiled. 'And how are you gonna do that?'

'Like this,' the man suddenly uncurled, let go of his shoulder, grabbed the knife between his legs and flung it end over end at Bodie. The blade whickered through the air fast, catching the light. Bodie ducked to the side at the last moment, felt it fly by his temple and flung his own knife in retaliation. The blade slammed to the hilt in the man's neck, pinning him back. He slumped instantly, and blood flowed.

Bodie was left staring at the dead body.

He almost collapsed on the spot. His legs were weak, his blood pumping hard, but the adrenaline seemed to surge out of his body.

And then he did collapse.

Minutes passed. Bodie lay on the floor, unmoving. The two dead soldiers lay close, their eyes staring at the sky. After a while, Bodie forced himself to his feet, broke out the map and the compass and started making his way back to the compound. It was about a sixty-minute slog away.

Bodie tried to close his mind to everything that had happened. He didn't want to think how he'd been forced to kill three men, how he'd stepped up and won the day. He was glad to be alive, but it didn't feel right.

Their ordeal continued.

CHAPTER TWENTY FOUR

Reilly geared up for his meet with the man called Sten from Blackoak One. It was a tentative thread he was pulling, and a dangerous one, but it was the only thread he had.

He exited the hotel, flagged down a cab, and reeled off the address he'd been given. The driver eyed him in the rearview.

'Are you sure?'

Reilly's anxiety rose a notch. 'Is it that bad?'

'Not bad, so long as you know what you're doing.'

Reilly thought about that. He liked to think he knew what he was doing, that he was au fait with *this* world. Not that that was a good thing. It wasn't, and he wished it was otherwise. But tonight... he needed to be part of that world.

He told the cabbie to drive, settled back for the journey. He had no weapons with him and felt vulnerable. The night was utterly dark outside, not even a star in the sky. The only illumination came from the lighted facades they passed.

Roughly a half hour later, they came to a darker side of town. The buildings weren't as well lit; the cars parked in hulking shadow at the side of the street. Reilly paid the man and got out, walked three blocks as he'd been told. He stayed on high alert, watching every door, every

The Contest

alleyway. From some of them, the darker ones, he heard conversation and once a shout, but he ignored it all and continued on.

Reilly eventually came to a small parking area. He'd been told to look for a white SUV and there it was, parked at the far end. Reilly scanned the area, saw no signs of trouble, no one lying in wait, and entered the lot, started walking. The place was half full. Nobody sat in their cars.

Reilly reached the white SUV and rapped a knuckle on the front passenger window. It slid down almost immediately. The driver leaned across and looked up at him.

'You Reilly?' he asked.

Reilly nodded, then saw the gun in the man's pocket. He backed away, walked around to the driver's window and rapped again. When it opened, the man looking nonplussed, Reilly leaned in.

'Yeah, I'm Reilly,' he said. 'Who are you?'

The guy, up close, stank of body odour. He wore a denim jacket and had gold earrings. Reilly didn't want to get this close, but he leaned in some more. He readied himself. The guy glared up at him.

'You've got some nerve,' he said. 'Name's-'

Reilly snaked his arm into the car faster than a striking viper. He plucked the gun out of the man's side holster and held it pointed to the side, non threatening. 'Now, why do you need a gun to meet me?'

The man blustered, threw himself around a little, but there wasn't a lot he could do sitting in the car's front seat. Reilly held out a placating hand. 'I'm not here to fight anyone.'

'Then give me my goddamn gun back.'

'I don't trust guns. You'll get it back when we've concluded our business, I promise.'

From the back seat of the car, there came a low chuckle. Reilly didn't move. He'd known someone had been sitting there, watching everything, but had chosen to ignore the figure. He guessed this man was the man in charge.

'I want to see Sten,' Reilly said. 'The man I spoke to on the... internet.'

The back door opened, and a man stepped out. He was short and fat and wore tight-fitting clothes that only accentuated his bulk. When he faced Reilly, his cheeks wobbled.

'Give him back the gun. We are here to take you to Sten.'

'Are you kidding? I thought he was meeting me here.'

'Sten doesn't do meetings that way. We will take you to him.'

Reilly didn't like it. He didn't like it one bit. But did he even have a choice? He stared at the large man and then at the car, then at the driver, who was staring at him with expectant eyes.

'Sten didn't mention I'd have to go on a drive.'

'Sten's a man of few words. Loves to type an essay on his computer, but doesn't talk for shit. Look, we can help you. If you don't come, you've wasted our time and yours. Make your mind up.'

Reilly knew the man was right. Standing here, he was no further forward. He sighed, reached in and handed the driver his gun back, then approached the guy at the back. 'Lead the way,' he said.

They set off at a steady pace, the driver not wanting to attract any unwanted attention. He stayed within the

The Contest

rules of the road, driving steadily. The overlarge man didn't say a word to Reilly as they sped through the night. Inside, the car was pungent. Reilly had to take shallow breaths. He sat in the leather, made sure his seat belt was tight, and stared out the window at the passing dark establishments, wondering where he was being taken. He stayed alert without appearing so, kept his attention on both men in case they tried something.

He needn't have bothered. They were docile the whole way, just collection boys. They accompanied Reilly until the driver turned off the main road into an industrial area.

They passed a few dark warehouses. It was almost eleven p.m. now, and the traffic around here was light. Reilly still felt anxious inside – he couldn't stop thinking about what was going to happen – but he hid it well, exuded a cool outer demeanour. Soon, the car pulled up outside a dark warehouse and the driver turned it off.

He turned to the back seat. 'Out,' he said. 'And just so you know, there's gonna be a lot of guys with guns inside. I'd advise you to stay cool.'

Reilly nodded. He did not know where he was. He stepped out of the car and waited for the other two to lead the way. They took him right up to the front door and knocked. Almost instantly, it opened. A bearded man stood inside. He took one look at the driver and then beckoned everyone in. He too was armed, his gun close at hand in his waistband. Reilly followed silently. Soon, the large man led the way and took Reilly from the open warehouse space to a set of back offices, following a series of narrow corridors. Reilly felt like he was being led further and further into an inescapable maze.

Finally, the big guy stopped and knocked at a white

door. There was no name plaque on it, just the number 9. A voice shouted 'enter' and they walked in. Reilly now faced a thin, short man with thinning hair and enormous glasses. He didn't look imposing, just appeared to be pissed off.

'What?' he asked.

'Sten, this is the guy who wanted to see you.'

'Guy? What guy?'

'The guy from the internet. Jon Reilly, you called him.'

'Oh, yeah, that guy. Well, give us a little space then.'

Reilly stepped forward as the large man and the driver stepped back. He now stood before the guy's plastic desk.

'This is Blackoak's HQ?'

'Are you fucking kidding?' the man said irritably. 'That's a proper building in Midtown. This is a rat infested shithole.'

'You wanted a face to face. Here I am.'

'Yeah, yeah, just sit the fuck down, all right? I don't enjoy talking and I don't like meetings.'

'I didn't ask for this,' Reilly said, sitting. 'You did.' The guy's attitude was annoying him.

Sten waved his words away. 'You want an actual face to face with one of our employees. You're willing to pay for the privilege. Am I right?'

'Yes. The man's name, as you know, is Jacko White.'

Sten nodded. 'Why do you want to meet Mr White?'

This was the whole crux of the matter, Reilly knew. He needed a perfectly plausible reason.

'The guy owes me money. I'm not proud of it. I shouldn't have lent him it. But he's dropped out of sight and I need it. You are my only recourse.'

Sten stared as if weighing up the explanation. He

The Contest

licked thin lips, took a drink of water from a tumbler. At least, Reilly thought it was water. It could have been vodka for all he knew.

'He owes you money?'

Reilly nodded. 'Enough to be worrying.'

Sten turned to his computer and started tapping. Reilly wondered if he was digging into White's history, checking some on screen data. Sten was clearly a computer guy.

'Hmm, I can understand you,' Sten said after a while, staring at the screen. 'Knowing his history, I don't understand why you let him borrow money in the first place. He's well known for his gambling problems.'

Reilly shrugged at that, thinking the less he said, the better. As the silence stretched, he said, 'I thought the guy was a friend.'

'And how did you two become friends?'

Reilly winced inside. This was something he had to get right. 'The Amazon,' he said shortly. 'Jacko came through with a gang of drug dealers who were being guarded by Blackoak One.'

At that, Sten glared at him. 'We would never do that,' he said. Still, he tapped some more on his screen and then seemed satisfied. He nodded.

'If you're paying for our time, for Mr White's time, I see no reason you can't have a face to face. You're essentially a paying customer.'

Reilly nodded. It was all about the money. 'When?' he asked. 'It's urgent.'

'Let me work on that.'

The way he said it, the laid-back manner, twisted in Reilly's gut. He needed this meeting yesterday, was desperate for it. Outwardly, though, he remained calm.

'Urgent,' he said eventually. 'Please.'

CHAPTER TWENTY FIVE

Bodie got back to the compound, had a shower and a change of clothes and then laid down on his bed for a short while. The others were happy to see him; he didn't return their greetings with anything more than a quick smile and a wave. What he'd done out there haunted him, and the cuts and bruises on his body would only heal into scars, forever reminders of what he'd done.

He'd washed the dirt and the blood off, head down. He was alive, but at what cost? The good thing was that the soldiers had willingly been paid to kill him. At least he hadn't been forced to fight a civilian. Bodie couldn't deal with that.

He was still lying flat out when the guards came again. His heart fell immediately on hearing their footsteps, wondering what they wanted this time, but it was just to escort them to the Core for their evening meal. The team respected his silence as they traipsed toward the building, giving him brief smiles.

Inside, Bodie saw another chance to mingle. He found a table first, laid a napkin out, and turned to the others.

'You have your friends,' he said. 'Let's start talking to them about getting the hell out of here.'

The team all inclined their heads silently, then melted away. Bodie sought his contact, Bill, and the rest of the man's team, and sidled up to them, plate in hand.

THE CONTEST

'You all okay today?' Bodie asked.

'Day off,' the man shrugged. 'Must have been another big event happening.'

Bodie said nothing about that. He pretended to laugh at something Bill had told him. 'Any news?'

'Yeah, I spoke to my team. We're all pretty damn observant, as I'm guessing you guys are. The sovereigns didn't pick us as contestants for our pretty faces. They picked us for our experience and what we can bring to the table.'

Bodie nodded. 'Yeah, I get that too.'

'So... the guards who attend the cell blocks are always the same. They work between the cells and the Core. They're here now. We count nine in total, all armed with Glocks and HKs. They also carry military equipment like KA-Bar knives, smoke grenades and stun grenades. They're fully prepared for an assault. And you have to assume they're well trained. Out in the arenas, it's different...'

Bill paused and looked away for a while. Bodie pretended to be grazing for extra food. After a minute or so, they came back together.

'We count at least thirty, similarly armed. We can't be one hundred per cent certain the thirty aren't part of the cell crew too, but we don't believe they are. So chalk up another thirty of the enemy. Some also wear body armour, by the way. Now, besides these guards, you have the ones stationed in the posh house and the other office buildings, the maintenance shed, the guard towers. We think these rarely change their stations either. We believe each man sticks to his post. You can add at least another twenty there, probably more.' He shrugged almost imperceptibly. 'That's a lot of firepower.'

Bodie, happy with the information, felt a sinking feeling. That was a hell of a lot of firepower to deal with. It was the main reason the sovereigns held the sway of power here.

'Are they mercenaries?' he asked.

'Good question. I see your thinking. Mercenaries can be bought and paid for. They can be reasoned with. But no, I think these men and women are paid employees, stationed here permanently.'

'Where's the fun in that?'

'I know what you mean. Maybe they work for a set period and then take time off, working under a non-disclosure agreement. They, more than anyone, would know the consequences of blabbing.'

'Anything else?' Bodie asked.

'Isn't that enough?'

Bodie laughed, keeping up appearances. Around the perimeter of the mess hall, the guards looked at ease, some of them swiping on their phones.

'It's plenty,' he said. 'But we need all the information we can get.'

'The sovereigns,' Bill said, picking a small chunk of cheese off a plate. 'There are ten of them, including Phoenix. I've seen them all. Don't recognise a single one of them, though I have their faces committed to memory. Believe me, when I get out, I'll always be on the lookout.'

And that was the problem, Bodie thought. *That* was the problem with getting out. The sovereigns knew that Bill, and others, would search for them. Consequently, why would they let them live?

'Any clues?' he asked.

Bill shrugged. 'I'm no expert on human behaviour. None of us are. I couldn't tell you what one man does, where he lives, just by looking at him. Some people can, but that's not me.'

'Worth asking,' Bodie said.

'Sure. Let me know if you need anything else.'

Bodie nodded. Bill had only confirmed what he and the others had already suspected. They were dealing with a tight setup, a well-controlled and able crew. They couldn't launch a full-on frontal assault. The only way out of here was by stealth.

And with over a hundred guards, was that even possible?

Bodie broke it down. They had the perfect cat burglar – Jemma. She could pick any lock. They had the covert muscle if they needed it — Cassidy. They had a researcher and map reader in Lucie. Yasmine was fast and sleek and deadly. Heidi had planning ability, and could always be relied upon. She always came through. Their team was equipped to escape this hellhole.

He meandered back to his table, attracting no attention. The others joined him at random intervals, and then leaned forward as they ate, imparting their information.

Bodie heard several versions of the information Bill had already given him, but at least it confirmed the man's observations. So far, they had four teams on board. Team Bill, team Blonde, team Bison, and team Six. All appeared capable and looked like they could keep their mouths shut. In fact, Bodie thought, every operative in the mess hall looked talented and qualified for anything.

He ate, savouring the bacon and the coffee, the hash browns. He wasn't a picky eater, usually went for the staples. Of course, he was desperately hungry after his ordeal of the day, but sought not to rush his food. The team took their time, and so did the others, in case they needed to chat any further.

Bodie rose to his feet, signalled Bill and another team leader with his eyes. When they met him in the queue, he asked, 'Any clues about how the sovereigns arrive, and when?'

'I've heard helicopters,' the other man who called himself Terry answered. 'Mostly landing in the morning. When they leave, they take off late at night. Before midnight.'

'The early hours are quiet?'

'Silent as the grave.'

Bodie had thought so. He'd been hoping the others might have glimpsed the choppers. He said as much.

'Once,' Terry said. 'I saw it during the day, when I was being dragged to the box for insubordination. It was a big, black Sikorsky with no markings. The pilots were just standing around smoking.'

'The box?' Bodie couldn't help asking. This was a new one to him.

'Yeah, a wooden box so narrow that you have to stand up all day. They leave you in it to cook in the heat, teach you a lesson. It's a pretty ordinary torture.'

Bodie nodded, getting the idea. 'So no clues who these sovereigns are?' he prodded, pushed as hard as he could. 'Nothing at all?'

The men shook their heads, went back to their tables. Bodie noticed a guard watching him and piled his plate before wandering back to his own. He sat there for a while, eating, ignoring his team.

Ten minutes later, he leaned forward. 'It's going to have to be a stealth escape,' he said. 'Nothing else for it. And we're gonna need provisions.'

'Because we don't know if we're thirty miles from civilisation or three hundred,' Jemma said.

'Exactly. And we'll be hunted. We have to escape in the early hours, well before they usually come for us. At least that's routine. I reckon we could get a good six or seven hours head start if we do it right.'

'So the planning starts,' Cassidy said.

'We've planned harder heists,' Bodie said. 'Harder jobs. We're good at this. We all have our individual jobs and then can combine them into a perfect whole. Are you all ready?'

'Since the day I arrived here,' Yasmine said.

'Then let's get started.'

CHAPTER TWENTY SIX

The guards came for them the next morning at the usual time and took them to the Core for breakfast. After they'd finished, they were returned to their cells and left to rest for a while. The morning passed sluggishly by, but they couldn't relax. They all knew, uncategorically, that there would be a new contest today.

And just before 11 a.m., the guards returned.

By now, the entire team recognised and hated the approach of the booted footsteps. At this time of the day, it meant one of them was about to face death.

The guards stopped outside their cells, facing them with smug smiles on their faces as if they knew what their presence did to their captives' minds. And, of course they did. They revelled in it.

This time, they opened Yasmine's cell. Bodie heard her sigh. He waited for his own cell to be unlocked, but it didn't happen. As the guards turned away, he grabbed hold of the bars.

'Wait,' he said. 'Please tell us where you are taking her. What's going to happen?'

The lead guard turned to him, licked his lips, and smiled. 'You really wanna know? Okay then. We will lead your friend here, on her own, out of the cellblock. Then she's going to the Killing Pit, which is a one-on-one fight to the death. Opponents are chosen at random, so there's

The Contest

no knowing who she will fight. If she's still in one piece at the end of it all, we'll bring her back here.'

Bodie gripped the bars until his knuckles hurt. No doubt the sovereigns would look forward to it, squirming in their seats, believing they would see a fine spectacle. And all the while, Yasmine would be fighting for her life.

'We can't attend?' Heidi asked. 'To give moral support.'

'It's a tight spot,' the guard said. 'But the fight will be streamed locally. We might let you watch.'

And with that, he grinned and turned away, taking Yasmine with him. The black-haired woman gave them one last look, a brief, confident smile, and then she was gone.

Yasmine followed the guards out into the bright afternoon sunshine. There was no point arguing with them; it would just sap her energy. Outside, she was already sweating, and squinted her eyes. They led her across the square, past the mess hall and on, soon heading past the bleachers. There was nobody around – it was actually as quiet as the grave and she could see for quite a distance. She wondered where everyone was.

The eight guards didn't speak to her, and their hands never strayed far from their weapons. She went past the bleachers, giving their wooden heights a long look. The arena itself was dry and dusty, covered in splotches that could only be dried blood. She wondered if there'd already been a contest held there today and if somebody had been carried away.

They led her past the wooden poles to a nondescript building that she'd never really noticed. It was wooden, without windows, and had a flat roof. It looked like a utility building of sorts, but one of the guards led her straight to the front door and then opened it.

A wash of noise came out.

Clearly, there were a few people inside. Yasmine steeled herself as she walked in through the front door. She had no idea what to expect. What she actually saw surprised her.

Inside, the building was empty apart from a wide circular staircase set into the ground. The staircase was almost as wide as the building. Its metal risers went deep underground, Yasmine saw, as she came up to them. The guards motioned for her to start her descent. Yasmine stepped onto the first riser.

The circular steps went on and on. The good thing was, it was cooler down here – they clearly had the air con working, which probably meant the sovereigns were going to be present. She descended riser after riser, seeing nothing below, and then she leaned over the banister rail.

Directly below, illuminated in a yellowish light, she could see a sandy floor. That was all, but it filled her with a sense of dread. She already had a very good idea of what this killing pit would entail.

She went down twenty steps and then thirty and then lost count. Eventually, the steps ended, and she walked out into a wide, sandy pit. The walls were jagged, hewn rock, the lighting coming from spotlights. She could see a couple of air conditioning units. The pit itself was circular, a basic, sandy floor ringed by blocks. Around the perimeter were gathered an assortment of people, some of whom she recognised. There were a couple of guards she knew by sight. There was Phoenix and six of

The Contest

his sovereigns. As she studied them, she saw, behind them, a CCTV camera fixed to the wall. She saw others too, fixed all around at high angles.

Yasmine let out a long, deep breath. She rolled her shoulders. This was going to be sheer hell.

She waited in place, not moving. A swell of conversation drifted all around her. It was as if these people were here to watch a friendly sporting a challenge, a fun match. They were all happy, eager, charged with enthusiasm. Yasmine had never seen anything like it.

Long minutes passed. Yasmine kept her head down, not wanting to be noticed. Her heart was hammering. She wondered who her opponent might be.

That question was answered a few minutes later as she heard the heavy clanging of descending boots on the metal staircase.

The guards showed Yasmine to the other side of the pit. She moved over and then turned to look at who might be coming down. The person took their time, stepping heavily riser by riser. Finally, a head appeared and then a bare chest and soon she was looking at a broad chested man wearing nothing but the customary grey trousers. He had a thick head of hair and a beard and well-defined arms. If Yasmine guessed, she imagined he might be a wrestler. The man entered the arena, looking around, and then his eyes rested on her.

He smiled with confidence.

Yasmine gave him a blank expression. She would reveal nothing of her character. The problem was – this other man wasn't a soldier; he wasn't a guard. He was just the same as her – an unfortunate who had been kidnapped. He was here to fight until either he died or he earned his release. How was she supposed to kill someone like that?

The crowd quietened briefly as the two opponents stared at each other. People wanted to assess the contestants' reactions. When nothing happened, they returned to their conversations, at least until Phoenix surged to his feet.

'My friends!' he cried. 'My friends! Welcome to the Killing Pit. It is here, in this small place, that our contestants will find out who they really are. How much they revere their lives. It is here that they will live or die. My friends, we gather here today to watch a very special fight. We will pit Yasmine against Zano, two formidable opponents, and we shall see who survives. Who else wants to see that?'

The crowd roared. The other sovereigns surged to their feet, clapping. Yasmine saw they had goblets of wine and finger food in their hands. They were certainly here to enjoy themselves.

'The Killing Pit always delivers a hard-fought battle,' Phoenix went on. 'And today will be no different. Our two titans know the consequences of not fighting...'

At that moment, a guard leaned into Yasmine and whispered into her ear. 'Lucie will get her throat cut.'

At the same time, she saw a guard whisper to Zano. The man's face blanched. They had no choice but to fight.

Phoenix went on, 'And I am sure they will fight hard. Only one can remain standing. But let us be clear. Only one can remain *alive.*' A cheer interrupted him. Phoenix let it ring out for a while and then waved for silence.

'So let us move forward and get the fun started,' he shouted. 'Isn't it a great day to be alive?'

The Contest

Yasmine tuned out the cheering, the yells of acknowledgement. She rolled her shoulders slowly, flexed her fingers, warmed her muscles up. This was the last thing she wanted to do, but there was no way out of it.

Zano, being more obvious, started swinging his arms and stomping his feet. His face was set into a scowl, his throat muscles bulging. His eyes were set into flinty stones, and he looked like he wanted to kill her. Yasmine, not at all in the same space, felt a little intimidated. But she knew she had to step up.

As Phoenix said, this was kill or be killed. There would be no second chances.

Minutes passed. Phoenix let the crowd roar. Yasmine saw betting slips passing between hands. She saw food and alcohol being consumed. She noticed men and women kissing, holding hands. The situation was entirely surreal.

And still, Zano bobbed up and down before her.

Phoenix clapped his hands. 'Let battle commence,' he cried.

CHAPTER TWENTY SEVEN

Yasmine felt her muscles tense as Phoenix shouted for the fight to begin. Zano dropped into a crouch. The man looked ready for it, ready to fight. Yasmine felt exactly the opposite. Every sense screamed that this was wrong, that it would end up tragically. Zano's eyes were wide, assessing her; he kept a low centre of gravity.

The crowd chattered and conversed. Some of the assembled throng weren't even watching the fight. It meant little to them. They used the time to catch up with friends and acquaintances, maybe make plans. Meanwhile, Yasmine was locked in a life or death struggle.

The two opponents slowly circled each other. They both stayed low, ready for any aggressive movement. They wore their issue clothing, the grey outfit, and Yasmine was glad for the first time that it was loose and airy. The temperature down here wasn't too bad due to air conditioning for the sovereigns, but she was already sweating.

Zano closed the gap. They were just a few feet away from each other now. She watched him carefully, looking for any telltale signs she might use. At first she saw nothing, but then she saw both his hands flex before he lunged, telegraphing the move.

She skipped to the right, evaded his outstretched

The Contest

arms. She didn't want to strike back, but knew she had to. The man's side was exposed. She delivered a hard kick to the ribs, made the air whistle between his teeth.

Zano staggered. He came around fast. Once more, his hands flexed and then he attacked. Yasmine leapt away to the edge of the pit, upsetting the direction of his attack. She span and delivered another kick. This one caught him across the face, sent him to his knees.

Now the crowd shouted, baying for blood. They saw a man down and a chance to earn money on their bets. The sovereigns were also on their feet, angling to get a better view, still with their wine goblets clasped in their hands.

Yasmine couldn't press her advantage. Deep down, she knew she should. The crowd urged her on. But she just couldn't do it. Attack a downed, innocent man, beat him to death. She backed off and let him regain his feet. The crowd roared its disapproval. Zano was panting hard as he faced her.

'That won't happen again,' he said.

Yasmine didn't speak. She felt sick, couldn't bring herself to do anything but survive. This whole scenario was beyond her experience, and she didn't know how to handle it.

Zano now appeared to be waiting for her to attack. She couldn't do it. The crowd started getting restless. She saw the sovereigns looking at each other and wondered what they would do. One of them shouted at a guard. This man held up a knife, waved it at Yasmine, and mimed slitting a throat.

It was obvious what he was telling her.

All this time, Phoenix was smiling quietly. He knew that, eventually, he would get what he wanted and all this was merely build up. It made the whole spectacle better. In effect, the crowd was forcing Yasmine to act, playing with her emotions, stretching them every which way.

She lunged now with little effort. Her lax attack worked against her though as Zano easily deflected it and came back with a strike of his own. He smashed her on the cheek and in the stomach. Yasmine now understood that she had to fight well or that he would beat her. The realisation made her feel even worse.

Zano's hands flexed. He struck again. Yasmine saw it coming and, this time, stepped into it. She threw a rising elbow into Zano's face. Zano ran full on into it. The impact sent his head snapping up and then back and a gout of blood to fly from his nose and mouth across the dry sand.

Now there was another roar, this one spicier. Zano staggered away, taking his eyes off Yasmine, something a fighter should never do. She could have broken his leg right then, maybe struck his ears and debilitated him, but still couldn't bring herself to go that far. A part of her still held back from the final viciousness. Instead, she walked up to him and threw a few hard punches into his ribs, breaking at least one. Zano wheezed and then threw his arms about, catching her a glancing blow on the side of the head.

Yasmine felt the pain explode in her brain. She lunged away, creating some space between them. Zano must have sensed an opportunity because, still bleeding freely and clutching his ribcage, he stumbled towards her, balling his fists.

Yasmine sensed him coming. Again, she could have targeted his legs, his knees, but she held back. That

The Contest

failure enabled Zano to close in, to rain tremendous blows down on her. She felt impacts on her side, her ribs, her neck. She staggered to her knees. He was grunting, breathing hard, coming at her with full force. Yasmine felt the blows in her bones. Her head was down. If she didn't fight back soon, she knew this man would kill her.

Gritting her teeth, she kicked out. Her right boot caught him on the shin. She kicked again, higher, bending his knee back. Zano howled. He reached down to rub his knee. She delivered an uppercut to his chin that made his eyes roll.

She kicked the other knee, made him fall to the ground. Zano struck out blindly, hoping to catch her in the chaos. His blows did land, but Yasmine ignored them. Instead, she positioned herself at the top of his head, put her thighs about his neck and squeezed. She held his arms in a tight grip as she did so, turned her face away from his and locked on hard.

Yasmine sobbed and bled as she choked the life from the man.

When it was over, she sat back. The crowd cheered. She couldn't bring herself to look up, to see their eyes, to witness the spectacle of their glee. She could only stare into the dirt, disgusted with herself.

But it was over. She had done everything they had asked. It was strange then, when the guard with the knife walked up to her and cleared his throat.

'Hey.'

She looked up. The guard held a spear in his left hand. She looked confused.

'Did you think it was just one fight?' he grinned. 'Get ready for round two.'

Yasmine closed her eyes, tried to take it in. She rose to

her knees. The guard handed her the spear and, almost unconsciously, her hand closed around the shaft. She was bleeding, battered, and bruised. Deep down, she was reeling, having just killed another human being to save her own life. Yes, the guy had also been trying to kill her, but was that the point?

Yasmine dragged herself up to her feet. The spear was about two metres long with a pointed metal head. She looked at it for a moment, then looked to where the sovereigns were sitting. The thought going through her head was pretty obvious.

'Do it and you all die horribly,' the guard said, though he made no move to stop her. Yasmine didn't doubt something like that had happened in the past.

She stood, feeling alone in the noisy chaos. The spear felt alien in her grip. She quickly checked herself, probed her ribs. Nothing seemed broken, and she was no longer bleeding. Her jaw was bruised, but was okay.

Yasmine waited.

She didn't have to wait long. There were footsteps on the stairs. She looked up to see a tall woman with blonde hair making her way down. The woman looked fit and strong. Her face was set hard, the eyes like flint, and Yasmine saw no emotion there. The woman entered the fighting pit and then turned to stare at Yasmine.

Her face remained hard.

Yasmine stepped back, hating the confrontation. At that moment, Phoenix spoke up.

'Yasmine, meet Maria. Maria, this is Yasmine.' The leader of the sovereigns sounded pleased with himself. 'You don't know each other, but you're about to.'

Maria was handed a spear.

There was some laughter among the crowd, most of it

The Contest

forced. Yasmine didn't take her eyes off Maria. It would only take one thrust with that deadly weapon, and the fight would be quickly over.

The guard backed away. The crowd went silent. Phoenix was still on his feet, arms in the air. And then, abruptly, he lowered them, signalling the start of the fight.

Yasmine didn't move at first. Maria balanced her spear in her right hand and rolled her shoulders. She looked confident, weighed the spear expertly. Yasmine wondered if it was her weapon of choice.

The two women faced each other, heads lowered, eyes locked. The crowd started murmuring, passing bets and letting out a few catcalls. Maria then moved in and thrust with her spear. Yasmine darted to the side, and the bladed head passed inches from her flesh. She balanced her own spear so that the head pointed towards Maria.

It didn't get any easier. This would be a bloodier fight, something to entertain the watchers. She watched her opponent once more, trying to work out that tell that told her when Maria was about to strike.

She saw it quickly. Maria's eyes widened, and then she attacked. Yasmine got a millisecond of warning, which was enough to give her an advantage. The spear again flashed harmlessly by.

The sovereigns were again out of their seats; most of the crowd screaming and shouting. The pit rang with the noise, a terrible ululation of bloodlust. It seemed to spur Maria on. She thrust her spear hard and fast at Yasmine, time and time again, trying to close in as she did so. Yasmine retreated to the farthest edge of the pit, staying out of the way. But Maria was edging ever closer.

Now she attacked with a thrust Yasmine could not

evade. Instead, she caught the spear head with her own, the metal clashing like swords. She deflected the blow and then performed the same feat again. The sound of the spear heads clashing spurred the crowd on to greater volumes.

Yasmine then met the next attack. She avoided the spear, came up close to her opponent, and punched her in the throat. Maria hadn't been expecting it. She instantly dropped her spear and folded. Yasmine had all the advantage in the world.

She held back. The crowd sensed it, saw it. They screamed at her. Maria staggered away, holding her throat. Yasmine kicked her spear to the edge of the pit. Maria looked up then, looked straight at her.

'No,' she said.

Yasmine couldn't do it. She had her own spear poised to strike, to run her opponent through. But she just couldn't force herself to act.

'*Kill!*' Phoenix yelled.

Yasmine had frozen in place. Right then, Maria clearly understood Yasmine's hesitation for what it was and lunged. Instead of going for her own spear, she grabbed Yasmine's and yanked it out of her hands. Yasmine fell forward. Now, Maria had the only spear, and she was trying to point it at Yasmine.

With a lunge, Yasmine targeted Maria's eyes and then, once more, instinct took over and she made a grab for the spear. Just as she did, so the head was pointing at Maria's stomach. Yasmine's lunge forced it through the flesh, forced it into the other woman's abdomen. Maria's eyes went wide. She fell to her knees. The shaft of the spear slapped the floor.

Yasmine stood back as the other woman's eyes closed.

THE CONTEST

The crowd erupted. Yasmine was shaking with emotion. She bowed under the weight of what they had forced her to do. She couldn't take any more of the cheering, couldn't go on.

And then Phoenix's voice cut through the din. 'And now you have a choice,' he said. 'You can choose to fight a third and final fighter now, or you can finish and fight another three tomorrow.'

Yasmine couldn't believe she wasn't done yet. Her head was spinning, her heart and soul heavy with guilt. How did you ever recover from something like this? Phoenix's words seemed to wash right over her.

She turned to him, and the crowd hushed. 'I have to fight again?'

'Yes, a third battle in the fighting pit is required.'

'Why?'

'Because we are the sovereigns and the sovereigns make their own rules.'

'Are two deaths not enough for you?'

Phoenix laughed. 'Two? On a good day, we see dozens.'

Yasmine shuddered. 'You are all... depraved.'

'Of course. That is why life is so good.'

Phoenix's harsh laugher brayed across the room.

'Why do you do all this? Why do you make strangers fight to the death?' It was a question that she imagined was on everyone's mind, even the guards who worked here, even the soldiers who were paid by the sovereigns.

And to be fair, Phoenix did look at her, and took his time to answer. 'Because,' he said. 'By doing this we have proven that *we the sovereigns* can make anyone do our bidding, even the basest of labours like killing. And in that, we have proven that we are the kings of the world. Nobody and nothing rates higher than us.'

In his face, Yasmine saw pride, arrogance, and madness. She felt nauseous, felt her bile rise. At that moment, she knew she couldn't face another day in the pit.

'I'll fight the third opponent now,' she said.

CHAPTER TWENTY EIGHT

One final warrior came into the fighting pit.

Yasmine couldn't believe her eyes. They'd pitted her against a brutal figure for her third fight. She was already bruised, beaten, bleeding. She hurt like hell. And yet the man they brought forward was wide and rippled with muscle and had a head that looked like a rock – all hard and misshapen. His eyes were flinty pits, his forehead like a shovel. His hands were twice the size of hers and flexed constantly. The guy was bald and had blood-red lines for lips and breathed loudly. When he spoke, his voice came out in a low growl.

'Get ready to die,' he said.

Yasmine had to get a hold of herself. This guy wasn't like the other two. He really wanted to kill her, to fight and maim and break bones. She could see it in his face, in the set of his body, in his every movement. For this man, she had to step up her game and think firmly about survival.

They faced each other at the centre of the pit, just a few metres apart. Neither opponent moved, but Yasmine could feel the slow trickle of blood from a scalp wound, the throb of bruises. She waited for Phoenix to start the fight and wondered how the hell she was going to survive this one.

Nothing happened. Then, slowly, two guards pushed

their way out of the crowd and approached the fighters. In their hands, they held two weapons.

Machetes

Yasmine winced outwardly.

'And just so you know,' Phoenix said, reinforcing his earlier point. 'Your sovereigns have provided the machetes so that we can watch you hack each other apart.'

Yasmine swallowed. She gripped the handle of her machete and licked her lips. Her mouth was dry, and she still felt like throwing up. The crowd was stoked by now, more voluble than any football crowd she'd ever seen, every man and woman shouting for their favoured opponent and, in the same moment, for blood and death.

The noise swelled around the room, completely filled it. Yasmine could barely think straight. Her opponent, all muscle and bone and brawn, held his machete so tightly his muscles had turned white.

'Fight!' Phoenix yelled.

Yasmine waited, but her opponent didn't. He exploded into sudden action, startling her. He'd covered half the distance between them before she even started reacting. Yasmine blinked. He was fast for a big man. She was forced to go down into a crouch and crab walk to the side, evading his grasp. Sand flew from under her boots as she performed the unorthodox move. She stayed low, knowing he would find it hard to run after her and crouch. Seconds later, she was on the other side of the pit, eyes narrowed, watching his every movement.

That had been close.

He came on, still breathing loudly, gripped his machete hard. He didn't slow, just moved purposefully towards her in a straight line. Of course, where could she

The Contest

go? He closed in, raised his machete, swung it at her.

Yasmine darted to the side. He blocked her path. He was close now. She kicked out, caught him in the groin, made him stagger back.

But he did not go down.

He grunted, coughed, didn't look phased one bit. Yasmine had stopped him in his tracks, though, made him think again. She needed to sow doubt in his mind. With a yell, she lunged forward, machete held high in the air. The man staggered away. She brought it down at his head, barely missed, almost took the top of his ear off.

The guy, clearly rattled, staggered backwards. He must have felt the blade fly past his head, known how close he'd come. Now he held his weapon up as Yasmine attacked again.

Their blades clashed. Yasmine sliced sideways and forwards time after time, not giving him any respite. Her third attack took a chunk off his left knuckle. The flesh went flying, followed by a spurt of blood. The man gasped. He backed up more and more, his feet dragging through the sand. Yasmine knew this was the only chance she'd get to press her advantage.

She came on, swinging back and forth. Her opponent was too big and heavy to move easily, though he was fast. He managed to get a hand under one of her blows and gripped her around the wrist. Then he tried to snap it.

Yasmine yanked her wrist back, but couldn't break his grip. He had hold of the hand in which she gripped the machete. Thinking quickly, she let it drop, caught it close to the floor with her other hand.

Now she had a free swipe as the man still concentrated on breaking her bones.

With little room to manoeuvre, she swung the

machete down at the man's boots. The blade pierced the leather, cutting straight through and embedded itself into flesh. A scream issued from the man's mouth. Instantly, his grip flew away from her wrist and he staggered backwards. She let him go. He looked down at his feet, saw her machete fixed in his foot.

Looked back up at her and grinned.

'That worked out well,' he said.

Yasmine couldn't believe what she was hearing. She backed up. The guy, walking with her machete planted in his foot, shambled after her, leaving bloody footprints on the ground. As he came on, the crowd backed him raucously.

Yasmine spread her arms and crouched. She was far from done yet. Balanced properly, she waited, her eyes fixed on her opponent.

The big man approached, waving his machete warily. Yasmine stood her ground. When he lifted the machete to strike, she dived in and targeted the weak spots. She hit him in the solar plexus, then the throat, and then jabbed at the eyes. Her attacks staggered him, made him pull up short and gasp. She didn't let up. She targeted the arm that held the machete next, punching the bicep and then striking at the elbow. The man grunted, tried to swing the weapon, but there was no room. Yasmine was right in his face.

With his free hand, he grabbed hold of her top, tried to yank her out of the way and create more space. She stood her ground, feeling the top rip but giving no quarter. She hit the elbow again, caused him to hiss between his teeth in pain. He tried to back off, but she wouldn't let him, just stayed right up close.

The man abandoned his grip on her, then balled his

The Contest

fist up and punched her in the stomach. Yasmine flexed her muscles, but it wasn't enough. The blow was devastating. She doubled over, lost her grip on him, and her head went down.

She felt the machete being swung at the side of her skull.

She tried to whip her head up, but wasn't quite fast enough. The blade sliced into her head and then passed her by, carrying on through its arc. It left a narrow, long wound in her head which started gushing blood. Yasmine fell to her knees, crying out.

The big man rushed in, machete raised.

And fell right into her trap.

With a surge, Yasmine rose and came up with her machete, burying it in his gut as he towered above her. The blade sank in deeply. The man's eyes flew open, and he uttered a piercing shriek, dropped his own machete to the floor. He stared at her in disbelief, unable to process defeat.

Yasmine didn't push the issue, she stepped away quickly and let him fall to the ground. He actually fell on the machete, which drove it deeper. He uttered a groan, his hands and legs still moving. Yasmine stared down at him, wondering what to do.

'You must kill him,' Phoenix said.

'He's practically dead,' Yasmine had won. It was clear. She wanted nothing else to do with the dying man.

'Your opponent must be dead,' Phoenix said. 'Or you will forfeit the contest.'

Yasmine stared at him, at the faces of the other sovereigns. This was what they loved. The torture, the pain, the soul-searching. The warped sense of right and wrong. Yasmine looked from them to the guards scattered around, who now appeared to be placing new bets.

Would she or wouldn't she?

Yasmine looked down at the twitching man. 'He's dying anyway,' she said. 'What do you want me to do?'

Phoenix shrugged. 'Rules are rules,' he said with glee written across his face.

Yasmine reached down and hauled the man onto his back. His face was covered in sand, plastered there by sweat, and a wide patch of red surrounded the machete's handle. It was spreading rapidly and, even as she watched, Yasmine saw a new puddle of red leak out and spill to the floor. The man's eyes were no longer open, and what she could see of his face was ashen.

'He's dead,' she said with relief in her voice.

Phoenix said nothing but, when she looked over at him, she saw a flush of disappointment on his face.

'Fuck. You,' she said.

CHAPTER TWENTY NINE

Reilly settled back in his plane seat, en route to Spain. He was now a client of Blackoak One, having paid them a chunk of money for a face to face with their employee, Jacko White.

The plane took off, and a meal was served. Reilly found he was too wired to sleep. Apparently, Spain was about halfway between Reilly and Jacko, so had been determined the best meeting place. Still, it was a weary journey for Reilly.

He thought about what he'd learned so far. For the money he'd spent, it wasn't a great deal. All he knew was that Jacko had been involved in his friends' kidnapping and that he worked for Blackoak One. The company, being run entirely as a money-making machine, responded to the offer of more money, especially for something as simple as a face to face. For them, it was easy cash.

But Reilly felt as though he were making headway. All he needed now was a successful meeting with Jacko. The man was a mercenary. He was loyal only to himself. Surely he'd be amenable to a few searching questions about his current job.

On the quiet.

Reilly put his head back, seeking rest. The plane flew with a gentle roar, the din of the passengers drowning out the engines. He distracted himself by reading the in-flight brochure and then watching a movie but, all the time, he was as on edge as he'd ever been.

The plane landed safely, and he cleared airport control, thinking of nothing but his meeting with Jacko. Not knowing how long he needed in this city in Spain, he'd booked a hotel and went directly there now. He was three hours early for his meet.

Reilly killed time eating and drinking at a local bar and, fifteen minutes before his scheduled meet time, exited the place and went directly to the café. He stopped outside, took a good look around, used his time-honoured skills of observation to scan the area for watchers, and saw nothing untoward. He wandered inside, checked the place out, and wandered back out again. It was a fair size, and it looked completely innocent to him.

He looked from another angle, walked the perimeter. Still, nothing shady stood out. When the appointed time came, he entered the café and found a table and assumed Jacko would do exactly the same as he'd just done.

Ten minutes passed. Reilly, already on edge and weary from the travel, started to get antsy. He bit his bottom lip, felt nerves in his chest. It was an unusual feeling for him, and he understood right then how much he cared for this new team he'd adopted. Their welfare was important to him.

The café door opened. A broad, tall man stood there whom Reilly instantly recognised. The two men locked eyes and then the newcomer made his way over.

'Jacko,' he said as the other man took a seat.

'Reilly.'

'It's been a while.'

Jacko was part-shaven, sporting a facial stubble. His eyes were black and his face was lined with weariness. Reilly sensed a pall over the man, as if he was into something he couldn't handle. He waited whilst he ordered coffee and a croissant, and then took a sip of his own.

'Thanks for coming.'

'Don't thank me. Apparently, it will be worth my while.'

Reilly thought about that. He'd already paid Blackoak and wondered what they had told Jacko.

'Did they tell you anything?'

'Just that you needed my help, and that you were a good customer. Someone I should put myself out for. Hence, the reason I flew all this way to damned Spain.'

Reilly remained quiet as Jacko's food and drink came. He let the man eat for a minute as he took a long sip of the hot coffee.

'I need your help,' he finally began. 'Some of my friends were recently abducted from New York city,' he reeled off the date and names. 'Your face was on the security footage.'

Jacko winced at that statement. 'It was? Shit.' He didn't deny anything.

'I'm trying to find my friends,' Reilly pushed on. 'And you're gonna be a significant source of information. At least, that's what Blackoak tells me.'

Jacko stared at him, the croissant halfway to his mouth. 'They said that? My super secretive, under-the-radar covert employer told you that?'

Reilly knew he couldn't back down now. He had to keep moving forward. 'Like you said, I'm a good client. They want you to help me.'

'You paid them for my time,' Jacko said. 'Now you have to pay me for more.'

Reilly sat back, sighing. He didn't have a great deal of money left, but was willing to use it for information. Of course, it had to be the *right* information.

'First,' he said. 'I need to know if the money is worth the information.'

Jacko leaned forward. 'I know the people you're looking for. I was hand-picked for that abduction team. We all were. The targets were considered highly dangerous but worth the risk, but only if the team abducting them was the best.' He kept his voice pitched low beneath the general murmur of conversation that pervaded the place.

'So they knew exactly who they were taking?' Reilly said.

Jacko nodded. 'Why the hell do you want these guys? I thought you were happy down in the Amazon.'

Reilly shrugged, not wanting to give too much away. Surprisingly, he didn't want to get into his feelings with Jacko. 'They saved my life,' he said. 'In more ways than one.'

'What the hell does that mean?'

'It doesn't matter, mate. Now, what can you do for me?'

To buy himself time, Jacko went up to the counter and ordered another croissant and a coffee. Whilst he waited, Reilly finished his drink off. He met Jacko's eyes when the man sat down again.

'You got ten thousand?' he asked hopefully.

Reilly choked. 'I don't even have half that.'

'How much did you pay Blackoak?'

'Two.' It had actually been double that.

The Contest

'Two then. I'll take two.'

'And for that...' Reilly let it hang.

'I give you everything. I don't care about them. Why should I care about their secret operation? I'm here for the money.'

'I knew you'd be the right man to speak to. As soon as I saw your face on that tape, I had high hopes that you were the Jacko I remembered.'

Jacko grinned, maybe seeing that as a compliment. He blinked and opened his mouth to speak, thought better of it. 'That's me,' he said finally.

Reilly put his wallet on the table, showed Jacko the two thousand. 'Over to you,' he said.

'You want to know *now?*'

Reilly frowned. 'Sure,' he said. 'Time is imperative.'

Jacko licked his lips nervously. 'All right,' he said. 'But listen. This never came from me. These people, they're hardcore. You must never mention my name.'

Reilly saw the fear in Jacko's eyes and didn't like it. 'They're that bad?'

'Worse. These people are the worse kind of animals. They care little for human life, except where they can use it to amuse themselves. They're what I would call *evil*, and I've seen some of the worst evil out there. These people... they're beyond anything you can imagine.'

'I've lived with some pretty bad people,' Reilly said, recalling the Bratva and his days in the Amazon.

'Not like this. I'll try to explain. They kidnap capable people and force them to do things on pain of death. If they refuse, their companions are killed, not them.'

'What things?' Reilly was already shuddering.

'Contests,' Jacko said. 'Challenges. Fights and events and races. Things that even you or I would find formidable. They force the contestants into these deadly challenges where some win and some lose. Those who lose invariably die.'

Reilly had heard nothing like it. He gawped at Jacko. 'Who are these people?'

'I don't rightly know. They go by nicknames like Phoenix and Reaper. They're rich beyond belief. You know the sort. Depraved and loaded. Phoenix is the big boss.'

'Tell me more.'

'I don't know a lot. They call themselves the sovereigns. It's a vast compound in Sierra Leone. Well guarded, well armed, well funded. The action never stops. Every day, they're at it. They must kidnap new people every week to keep it all going. I see all sorts, from bounty hunters to cops to military types and so many others. Your team is doing well.'

Reilly felt his heartbeat triple. 'Are they all... okay?'

'When I left, yes. I can't remember the when's or the who's, but they're all still alive.'

'I need to know exactly where this compound is.'

'And I need my two grand.'

Reilly placed it on the table in front of Jacko, saw his eyes grow hungry. Yes, he'd got lucky to see Jacko in the first place, but he'd also had the foresight to know a greedy, money grabbing bastard when he saw one.

'Yours,' he said. 'As soon as I get my location.'

Jacko grinned.

THE CONTEST

CHAPTER THIRTY

Lucie hadn't slept all night. By process of elimination, it was clear that it would soon be her turn to take part in a contest. There was only herself and Heidi who hadn't been called yet, and a fresh day was dawning. She was no fighter, no capable warrior. Yet the people who were doing this to them appeared to have knowledge of their skill sets. What on earth would her challenge be?

She lay in her bed, worrying. Hours later, she heard the approach of the guards and felt her heartbeat quicken, the butterflies start in her stomach. This steady approach was both tense and maddening. It signified the start of a terrible endurance.

The guards stopped outside their cells. Of course, they knew exactly what fears their approach wrought within their captives. Now, though, one of them stepped forward and announced that it was breakfast time. Lucie sighed with relief, caught a guard watching her, and tried to mask her feelings. He smiled knowingly and mouthed the word, 'Later.'

She tried to ignore it. The guy was playing with her, trying to set her on edge. The trouble was, his attempt was working. She almost tripped up as she exited her cell, tripped over nothing but her own feet. Her time was coming, and she could think of little else.

They went to the mess hall, grabbed their food and

started up conversation with the other teams. Team Bill was reticent today – they were approaching the end of their stay and, Bodie reported, being a little cagey with him. Bodie had told them he didn't think anyone was ever properly released, but he didn't think Bill believed him. Or didn't *want* to believe him.

Cassidy approached team Blonde and reported that there'd been a guard change. Several fresh faces were in evidence, but there had been no weakening of their numbers. They guessed Phoenix couldn't keep the same guards here all year round and assumed they were well paid for their silence.

Team Bison and team Six had little to say. Both had lost people the previous day and weren't in the best of head spaces. Lucie respected that. She wondered if the relic hunters had got lucky so far, or if they were just that good and experienced. She ate slowly, taking her time, and caught Bodie's eye.

'Try not to worry too much,' he said. 'You've got this.'

It was that obvious; she knew. It was written all over her face. She attempted a smile, looked away. She finished her food and sipped a mouthful of hot coffee.

All too soon, they were led back to their cell block. Lucie wanted to take a hot shower – anything to take her mind off what she thought was to come – but they could only do that in the early evenings. She couldn't think of any other way to fill the time.

She sat on her bunk, head in her hands.

There was little conversation on the cell block. Most of the prisoners, she guessed, were resigned to their lot by now, and constantly worried about their position. Would they be next? Would their best friend? And would they feel guilty if it wasn't them?

The Contest

The sound of approaching boots interrupted her thoughts. The guards were coming for them. For one of them. A minute passed. She looked askance, saw boots pass her cell and then stop. A face was right outside her bars.

'Your turn,' the man said.

Lucie rose on shaking legs. She heard the words of encouragement from her team. The man facing her was the same one who mouthed 'Later' to her earlier. He looked pleased with himself.

'Hurry.'

She was ushered out of the cell and led away from the block. The guards surrounded her and the sun beat down. She guessed it was just before midday. They took her into a fancy house and she knew, from the others' descriptions, that this was where Phoenix lived.

Lucie was shown into a study with a brown desk and bookcases lining the walls. Phoenix hung up a phone and turned to look at her.

'Ah, the researcher,' he said. 'Are you fit?'

She blinked, unable to comprehend his meaning at first. 'Am I fit? Yes, I think so.'

'That will be required for your contest.'

She held on to the back of a chair to steady herself. 'Which is?'

Phoenix now looked pleased with himself. 'No fighting,' he said. 'You will be part of a race from the river to a cave in the mountains. It will be a desperate race,' he grinned. 'For the two who finish last will die.'

The last two will die? Lucie shuddered, unable to take it in. Was she really going to be part of such a barbaric contest? 'Please,' she couldn't help herself saying. 'Please don't do this.'

'Oh, but I am doing it. W*e* are doing it. You see, we love your anguish, your torment, your anxiety. That this is the last thing on earth that you want to do. It is what makes this whole thing worthwhile.'

'It is quite a setup,' Lucie said. She didn't know if she was playing for time, or offering a jot of admiration.

'Once you have the infrastructure, it's not too bad.' Phoenix shrugged. 'And the payoffs are worth all the hassle.'

They led Lucie out of the room and across a square to the nearest car. She was bundled in the back. At first, it was stifling, but then the air con kicked in and made the ride much more pleasant. They bounced their way across a tarmacked and then down a dirt road, taking her far away from the compound. She lost track of time. All she could do was to survey the surrounding, passing landscape and try to still her shaking legs.

Some time later, the car stopped. She was pushed out and stood on the dirt road, surrounded by tyre tracks and clumps of brush. A flat plain stretched out before her, running all the way to the mountains. Behind her, a river flowed.

She waited. Soon enough, other cars started arriving. They deposited people out into the dirt and left them to stand there, to eye each other, to sweat under the scorching sun. Lucie counted nine other competitors.

A guard with a megaphone stepped forward and spoke into it. 'You will race,' he said. 'Simple as that. You will race in any way possible to a cave in those distant mountains. The cave is directly in front of you as the crow flies, but will also be signposted. *There are no rules,*' he added with a knowing smile. 'But know this. The last two people to reach the cave will be put to death.'

The Contest

With that, some of the assembled competitors gasped and Lucie realised not everyone got to see Phoenix. She wondered why she had. Maybe it was because her team was doing so well in the contest. It didn't really matter. The guard with the megaphone was looking over the assembled competitors as if gauging their readiness.

Lucie squinted into the distance. She thought she might be able to see the cave complex they were heading for. Some others were limbering up, stretching muscles. Lucie straightened her back, but her legs were still shaky and she didn't even know if she could run on them.

The guard yelled at them. 'Ready? *Go!*'

Lucie breathed deeply and put one foot in front of the other. The race was on. The plain stretched ahead of her, full of pitfalls. How could she possibly hope to survive?

Lucie did not know.

CHAPTER THIRTY ONE

Not a single competitor looked up for the race, but they all set off together. They were spaced apart, at least for now, and running with their eyes fixed on the horizon. Lucie wasn't a particularly fast runner. Truth be told, she'd never run for any length of time in her life. Should she pace herself? Or just try to get in the lead?

She figured there'd be less hassle at the front of the pack. But she just couldn't make it. There were others faster, fitter, than her. Luckily, there were stragglers too – people who just weren't made to run. Lucie fell somewhere in the middle.

She ran, feet pounding the ground. The race was hot and well contested as people pulled out ahead and others struggled to keep up. Lucie ran with her head down mostly, pounding up and down the slopes that stood between her and the cliffs. As she ran, the cliffs didn't appear to be coming any closer.

She topped another rise, saw folded hills ahead of her, and went down the next slope. To her left, a man laboured, his face bright red. To the right were two fleet women, both with long, flowing blonde hair. As she glanced their way, one woman got her feet tangled and fell head first, tumbling down another slope. Lucie lost track of her as she ran, trying not to feel anything. *This is where your feelings really betrayed you.* Two people were going to die, the *last* two. But did you rejoice in someone else's downfall, or did it pierce your heart with guilt?

She tried to focus on the running, just keeping one foot in front of the other. The slopes kept coming, up and down, up and down. Lucie's calves ached, her legs throbbed, her chest was heaving. She had to slow and, as she did so, a young man struggled past her.

Worried, she looked back. There were three people behind her, which meant she was fourth last. The two blonde women – who looked her equal, a stout man and an older woman. They were all struggling to keep up.

Ahead, the rest of the competitors streamed at a different pace. One man, a broad individual, was running hard and with confidence, clearly a seasoned runner. Someone else was just behind, looking over their shoulder. Still more were running at pace, keeping their attention on their own performances.

Lucie kept going, struggling, chest heaving, but determined to save her own life. Ahead, a new obstacle appeared.

It was a wide, slow-running stream. The competitors plunged through it, lifting their legs and trying to stay at pace. The stream was probably along their route to slow them down, to tire them, and it instantly slowed the front runners. Lucie came to it at a steady pace, jumped in, and started slogging through the current. The waters, at first, were nice, offering some solace from the beating sun, but then the heavy flow started to drag at her lower legs and hold her back. Lucie struggled hard, but she took a second to dip her head into the cold flow.

The stream took just seconds to negotiate, but it added an additional element to the race. One of the guys ahead started slowing, panting hard. Clearly, he'd lost his wind. Lucie started catching him up ever so slowly. At first, she left wet footprints in the sand, but then her wet clothing dried out and she ran on, trying to keep an even breath.

The cliffs grew marginally closer.

Lucie hadn't been able to gauge the distance at first. Now she saw the cliffs were farther away than she'd initially thought, and she was glad she hadn't set off at pace. This would be a marathon more than a sprint, and she slowed marginally when she realised it.

She was breathing steadily now, used to the pace. She kept it up, took another glance back. Her fellow competitors were closer than she'd like. None of them were lagging too far behind. Lucie started along a low, flat plain for a while, the monotony of the run making her lose focus. She lost track of where she was in the race.

The cave system grew closer. Now it was clearly discernible, and she could even make out the crude signposts. She felt her anxiety rise another notch. They were zeroing in on their goal.

She wondered how much she had left in the tank. Not being a runner, she did not know how to gauge it. All she knew was that her chest was on fire, her legs were throbbing and shaky, her feet were hurting. But she kept going, fired by adrenalin and the knowledge that this was life or death. She thought of her friends – of Bodie and Cassidy and the others – and knew they'd be rooting for her, cheering her on.

She assumed there were cameras along this route which enabled the sovereigns to watch the progress. She could imagine them in their ivory tower, stretched out,

The Contest

nibbling cheese and grapes and drinking wine and spirits, watching avidly and placing their bets. They would be on the edge of their seats, immersed in the tension and the promise of violence.

She ran on, dripping sweat. Her face felt like it was on fire. A man was to her right, having caught her up, and now slipped past her. She tried to run harder, faster, but there was nothing more in the tank. She couldn't speed up, just couldn't. The ground flew beneath her feet, all hard and earthy. She ran up and down slopes and tried not to stumble, kept an eye on the terrain. Now, though, the hills that led to the caves were approaching. They grew rockier, more craggy. There were more sharp edges. Lucie suddenly found herself jumping from rock to rock.

She looked ahead, saw that she was now sixth of eight. The caves were in sight up ahead, and a sign pointed to the correct one. Already, the leader of the pack was approaching it and looked to be barely breathing hard. Clearly, this was his forte, and he'd had an advantage. But that wouldn't matter when it came to the killing.

She ran on, leaping between rocks, taking advantage of the flat slopes. The man in front of her pulled away slightly, and she wondered if there was anything she could do to catch him up. Right now, she was so close to the rear runners it terrified her.

They ran on. The day grew hotter. The slopes steepened. Ahead, a woman cried out as she fell and twisted her ankle. She screamed in anger and kept going, dragging herself along on one leg until she reached the caves second. Then she collapsed, rubbing her injured ankle. Lucie saw her, rejoiced with her even though she knew her own plight was highly dangerous.

She could hear someone directly behind her, someone putting on a spurt of speed. Maybe they'd saved themselves for the end. That was what some people did, wasn't it? They saved a load of energy for the end of the race. It was risky, but it might work. It was going to work. The person was in Lucie's vision now, pulling alongside her, then edging ahead. It was a middle-aged man with a balding head and narrow shoulders. He looked built for running.

Lucie couldn't let it happen. This put her in seventh place out of eight. She sped up, pushing her body beyond its limits. She leapt between rocks, sometimes landing nimbly, sometimes coming down hard. Her balance was fraught. The caves loomed ahead, maybe a hundred yards away.

She hated the fact that she was trying to send another person to their deaths. This was the dilemma the sovereigns loved. It was why they did what they did. Lucie detested it, and tried to quash the feeling, concentrated on the balding man's back.

And then she fell. With minutes to go in the race, she went sprawling. Her ribs hit a rock and then the side of her head. She rolled, seeing stars before coming to rest, staring at the sky and the white-hot sun. She breathed.

It was over. The back marker was approaching.

Lucie screamed in anger. The adrenaline seared her nerve endings. It made her move, made her roll over and force herself to her feet. Without pause, she started shambling forward, every synapse on fire.

The balding guy was three metres ahead. She made herself leap over enormous gaps, land and then keep leaping and running. She dug deeper than she'd ever done in her life and kept running despite all the blinding pain. And all the time, she knew this was exactly what the sovereigns wanted to see.

But she couldn't finish in the last two. She just couldn't. The cave entrance was just up ahead. The balding man was finally slowing, his last reserves spent. Lucie was gaining on him.

She made a last desperate effort, summoned up every dreg of will she could muster. She practically threw her legs forward, making them sprint, ignoring the tearing pains in her chest and her stomach. Lucie was just seconds behind the balding guy.

There are no rules, she thought.

And then he crossed the finish line, running into the cave.

Except he didn't. At the least possible instant, Lucie reached out and grabbed hold of his top. She yanked on it, yanked him sideways with brute force, and sent him crashing into the rock at the side of the cave. He hit hard and bounced off, fell down.

Lucie ran into the cave, finishing sixth.

The man was on his knees, head in hand, bleeding. Just then, the woman in last place ran up, eyes betraying her terror. The balding man finally dragged himself over the line.

Lucie couldn't meet his eyes. She had snapped, fought like a wild animal in a desperate situation. She hadn't known she had it in her. She still didn't. Could hardly believe what she'd done.

Had that really happened?

It was incredible what a trapped, cornered human could do. She'd literally been fighting for her life and had sacrificed another person in her stead. The man was now staring at her and she couldn't meet his eyes, couldn't get up off her knees. She was sobbing, her entire body wracked with agony.

Minutes passed before a shadow fell across the entrance to the cave. Several guards walked inside, holding their weapons low. They looked around, staring at everyone, gauging their awareness. The only person standing and breathing easily was the guy who'd won the race.

Lucie looked up, aware now of a small CCTV camera mounted inside the cave. Even here, they were being watched.

'You did well,' one guard said, stepping forward. 'Most of you. But where there are winners, there are also losers. When you started this race, you knew the rules.'

The guards all came forward now, grabbing hold of the woman who had finished last and the balding guy. They dragged them out of the cave and back into the direct sunshine. The remaining guards urged the rest of the runners out of the cave.

Lucie rose last of all and only when she was forced to. Her chest was still heaving, and it felt like her ribs were on fire. She felt sick, unwell. Her head was spinning. She didn't know which way to turn, which way to look. All she knew was that she'd somehow managed to get a man killed.

Soon, she was out in the sunlight again. The two who'd finished last were shoved and pushed until their backs were to the edge of the closest slope and there were about three metres between them and the guards.

Two guards raised their guns and took aim.

Lucie gasped. A firing squad? Surely not. She opened her mouth to protest, felt it glued shut with a terrible dryness, and then heard two shots. Her eyes flew wide

THE CONTEST

open, and she gawped. The guards had fired on the two people, who instantly flew back off the ledge amid two gouts of blood. Lucie couldn't believe her eyes and, judging by their gasps, neither could her fellow competitors.

All that was left was blood in the sand.

Lucie felt the tears spring from her eyes. The guards came around, offering water, and even though she desperately craved it, she ignored it. Never in her life had she felt so unutterably evil, so vile.

How can I live with what I've done?

A practical part of her insisted that there'd been no choice. It had been life or death, and in the end, she'd chosen life. She hadn't made up the rules nor carried out the sentence. It could have been worse, too. They could have made the competitors shoot each other.

On the other hand, she'd been actively involved in instigating another person's death. She'd caused it to happen. But she wasn't the architect... and yet...

The questions fired through her brain like machine-gun bullets. She couldn't focus, could barely stand upright. When a guard came up to her, she couldn't look him in the eyes.

'Don't blame yourself,' he said kindly. 'It was life or death out there.'

It was the first nice thing any guard had ever said to her.

Lucie nodded, bit her bottom lip. The tears still leaked from her eyes. A part of her knew the sovereigns would be lapping this up. They, at least, had had a successful day.

The guards let them all rest for a while, handed out more water and energy bars. Lucie finally swigged a little water, but couldn't stomach the food. She sat on a rock, gazing into the distance.

She'd survived, but at what cost?

Lucie waited for the guards to round them up, to escort them off the rock and to a bunch of waiting cars, to drive them back to the compound.

Soon, she would be reunited with her team, and they would be ecstatic.

Lucie would never speak about what happened. She couldn't, couldn't bring herself to explain. She had found out the basest, worst, and vilest thing about herself. It had to stay hidden.

Forever.

CHAPTER THIRTY TWO

Bodie woke early the next day and lay staring at the ceiling. The trouble with their captivity was that there was nothing to do except wonder what vile contest was coming next, and who might take part in it. Of course, they all knew who was next. Only Heidi remained. Only Heidi hadn't been forced to perform yet.

Bodie shifted, rolling his shoulders. At this time of the morning, the cell block and the compound were cast in utter silence. It was the best part of the day. All the other hours were fraught with worry, with terrible anticipation. He actually looked forward to waking early to lie in a little peace and quiet, to chill.

Lucie had returned yesterday and, though he hadn't seen her, he sensed by her silence that it had been an awful experience. All she'd told them was that she was okay and didn't want to discuss anything. She needed rest. Having been there himself, Bodie respected her wishes.

An hour passed. Bodie heard his surroundings start springing to life. Car engines started up. People walked by outside the walls. Conversation struck up through the cell block. Cassidy started talking to Yasmine about something inconsequential, about what they were going to do when they returned to civilisation. It kept their spirits up.

They had embraced the habit of speaking their names every morning at 8 a.m. just to let the others know they were okay. They did it now, Lucie included. Bodie wondered what kind of night she'd had and if she'd got even a moment's sleep.

The guards came shortly after, leading them to breakfast. It was a brief affair; they were ushered through their queues by the guards who stayed among them, giving them no chance to chat. Bodie ate his fill and drank coffee and watched it all unfold, curious. Why was today different?

They didn't find out for a while.

Heidi was clearly nervous. Today it would be her turn. She was the last of the six to go. She finished her breakfast in silence and cast a lot of glances at the guards. When they were led back to their cells, she kept her head down and remained uncommunicative. Bodie tried to lift her spirits, to no avail. He didn't really blame her.

They were left alone for an hour. Then, the front doors opened, and they heard, with dread, the approach of the guards. The shuffling feet stopped outside their cells, all their cells, and the man who they'd become accustomed to as their leader spoke up.

'A delightful surprise for you today,' he said.

Bodie looked at him suspiciously.

'Don't be like that. The sovereigns like to keep you on your toes.'

With that, *all* their cell doors were opened, and they were ushered out into the corridor. The guards led them out and across the square in a silent line, their weapons slightly raised. As usual, it was hot as hell out here and Bodie found himself instantly sweating. He kept his eyes

The Contest

peeled to all sides, absorbing everything in case he needed to use it in the future. By now, he'd got a pretty good idea of the compound's layout, of its comings and goings, and he knew his companions would have the same knowledge. He hoped the information would soon become pertinent.

Surprisingly, they were led back into the arena. Bodie didn't like it. What the hell was going on? The bleachers all around were occupied by lounging guards. The sovereigns were just filing towards their seats, nine of them. Bodie watched them laugh and smile amongst themselves, wondering who they were and exactly what would happen next.

The sovereigns took their seats and were served with great golden goblets of wine. They sat back, reaching for their nibbles, still chatting. They deigned to look over the arena, observing the new competitors. Bodie narrowed his eyes when he realised it was just the relic hunters inside there, and he had a terrible feeling.

But then everything changed.

There was a commotion behind him. Bodie turned to see a crowd approaching. He saw what he assumed was one of the other teams, surrounded by guards. The team numbered six, the same as his, and Bodie began to get a feeling of foreboding. He didn't like the look of this.

The new team was led into the arena and left standing. The guards walked away. Bodie and the others eyed the newcomers, wondering what to make of them. They all stood in silence, unsure of what to do. Bodie saw three men and three women on the other team, all looking fit and capable. He wondered where they hailed from, what they did, and how they had ended up in this godforsaken place.

Time passed, and silence reigned, at least in the arena. The sovereigns on the bleachers looked to be having a whale of a time. The guards fanned out warily. Those on duty, at least. Others sat in their seats and watched proceedings with an interested air.

Bodie and the others were made to wait. Finally, the sovereigns turned their attention to the arena and seemed to notice those who stood waiting below. They started taking an interest. Phoenix, clad in his usual white suit, rose to his feet.

'We decided to do things differently today,' he said. 'So here you are, waiting on our pleasure. There's no rush. Take sustenance, relax. We will be with you when we are ready.'

Bodie swallowed hard. The tension was building. He knew that was the real point of all this, to let their anxieties run riot. He watched as Phoenix retook his seat and started up another conversation with a fellow sovereign.

They were given bottles of water, and oddly, paper plates loaded with pastries. Bodie ate what he could and drank all the water. He saw Lucie refuse it all, saw the drawn look on her face, and wondered whether he should try to draw her out a little. They had all been put through the wringer though, and were dealing with it in their own ways.

As the sun blazed and a weak wind blew, stirring up mini dust devils, Phoenix finally turned his attention back to the arena. He made a gesture. Several guards left the area and then returned. All carried armfuls of baseball bats and handed them out. Soon, Bodie, his team, and the new team, all held a baseball bat in their hands. The guards backed away, leaving them alone.

The Contest

Bodie faced Phoenix. This was what he'd been dreading.

'You may think you know what's about to happen, but you don't,' Phoenix said. 'we're nothing if not innovative. Now, keep watching.'

Bodie heard more noise and turned. From the other side of the arena, he saw a group of guards approaching. They also carried baseball bats. They entered the arena and fanned out, facing the relic hunters and the other team.

'Guards versus contestants,' Phoenix said with glee. 'A fine battle, to be sure. A real battle. A melee. This will be a mass fight and I want to see everyone involved. You don't have to kill each other, but you do have to fight. Those who refuse will be shot. Now... are you ready?'

Bodie took the time to wander over to the other group. They would fight better together. He nodded at a few of them, blinked his eyes at the others. Everyone appeared on edge, holding their weapons in sweating hands.

He watched the guards, who twirled their bats and looked supremely confident. They were looking forward to this.

'Fight!' Phoenix yelled.

CHAPTER THIRTY THREE

Bodie lifted his baseball bat as the guards advanced. The guards themselves were dressed in their usual uniform of black and now fanned out. They all looked supremely confident. The relic hunters and the other civilian team were bunched up together. They weren't ready for this.

The guards came on. They would give no quarter, Bodie knew. The gap was closing. There was a moment of stasis when the guards breathed deeply and stared their opponents in their eyes, a moment when the opponents wished to be anywhere else than here. It was loaded with tension and fear and danger and it sent the sovereigns to their feet.

And then the guards rushed in.

Bodie half crouched, making ready. He was at the front of his team, and would take the brunt of the first attack at least. A guard came at him, swinging down towards his head. Bodie flung his bat in the air, smashed the other one away. There was a loud clunk as the weapons struck each other. Bodie was unbalanced by his own swing and staggered to the side.

Guards came in among his team, swinging hard. Cassidy yelled in anger as she combated one of them, swinging her own bat and wincing as the weapons struck and vibrated against each other. The vibration ran through the length of the wood and up her arm, making

The Contest

her bones rattle. Cassidy almost dropped her own bat, but managed to hold on. The guard fell to the side, his bat now lying on the floor.

Cassidy smashed him across the face. Not hard enough to do much damage, but hard enough to take him out of the fight.

The guard sprawled to the left, lying flat out. His place was immediately taken by another who came up against Cassidy with a yell of bloodlust. The two exchanged blows.

All around Bodie, his team fought the guards. The guards ran among them, swinging their makeshift clubs. Yasmine and Heidi met the challenges head on, deflecting blows and then fighting back. Lucie backed off as much as she could, intermingling with the other group as she sought not to get too involved. Of course, Phoenix's threat meant that she had to fight. He and all the other sovereigns were watching closely.

Bodie ducked aside as a bat whistled through the air next to his head. The blow glanced off his shoulder, making him wince. It felt like his bones were throbbing. He rolled the shoulder. Nothing broken, but there was pain. The guard was still coming, swinging again. Bodie stepped into the swing so that he was right in the guard's face and head butted him. The guard fell away, his bat falling to the floor.

Jemma was moving like a shadow, flitting between attackers and delivering swift, hard blows. None of them were meant to be debilitating, but every strike hurt and sapped strength and drew the enemy's attention. She was a thorn in their side, always slinking and sliding through their ranks.

The other group was rallying too, standing up to their

own attackers. As Bodie fought, he saw one slight man at the back, shying away from the combat. The man had already dropped his bat and looked like he didn't want to be a part of the battle. He turned away as a guard came up to him, offering his exposed back to the descending bat. The bat came down, but was caught by one of the man's colleagues, who then received a punch to the face for his good will. Even as he fell back, the man yelled at his colleague to fight.

Bodie heard the sound of battle all around him. He was right in the thick of it. Baseball bats struck each other left and right, the sound ringing through his head. There was also the sound of bats striking flesh, which was sickening, and the yells of those hit. Bodie saw Yasmine take a blow to the stomach. He saw Cassidy double over as a bat pounded her midriff. Both women recovered quickly, but then backed up as attacks overwhelmed them.

Some civilians were still not totally involved.

Bodie saw it wasn't the people on his team. It was two on the other team. The slight man he'd seen earlier and another, a big man wearing large glasses. They were shying away from the action and, even as he watched, Bodie saw guards stalking towards them.

The guards all held guns.

'Hey!' He yelled. 'Fight!'

His words were either lost under the din, or the two men just ignored him. They didn't respond. Bodie had to turn away then to deal with another attack and, by the time he turned back, half a minute later, the two men still weren't engaged.

Bodie cast a quick glance at Phoenix. The white-clad man was on his feet, standing tall. He held out a bunched up fist and then stuck his thumb out so that it faced down. Bodie flinched. The guards raised their weapons. One of them fired, hitting the large man in the chest. Blood exploded everywhere, and the man flew backwards, staggering into his own colleagues. There was a brief lull in the fighting as the shot man landed hard on the ground.

Bodie was aghast. He hadn't expected the suddenness of the assault. Phoenix was brandishing a fist at them. 'You will fight!' he almost screamed.

The slight man saw that he was about to die. He somehow found the courage to launch himself at a guard and received a slap in the face with a bat for his trouble. He went down, bloodied, but the attack saved his life.

The guards with the guns backed off.

Bodie came up with another ploy. He took it from Jemma's example. There were no rules here. He forced himself out of the melee and started darting around the outskirts of the crowd. He attacked the fighting guards from behind, targeting their skulls, rushing from one to the other and knocking them to the ground. Bodie managed three before a guard met him head on with an assault.

To left and right, they all struggled. The guards were no pushovers. Yasmine was on one knee, trying to protect herself from a downward swing. Cassidy was staggering to the side, holding her shoulder. Jemma was still flitting around the battle, but had just been tripped up by a sharp-eyed guard.

Bodie saw Lucie take a blow to the face, saw her waver. Blood streamed from her nose. The guard who'd felled her now stood over her with a triumphant grin on his face. He raised his bat, ready to bring it crashing down on her head.

Bodie couldn't let it happen. He flung his own bat, watched it fly through the air and then strike the guard full in the face. The man looked surprised and then shook his shaggy head violently as he staggered back. Lucie stayed down for a few seconds and then forced herself to her feet. Showing her resilience, she immediately hooked a foot behind her opponent's boot and send him crashing backwards to the floor. Then *she* towered over *him*. She brought her bat down hard.

Bodie had saved her, but was now without a weapon. A guard had noticed. He broke away from his attack on Heidi just to target Bodie. He came in swinging. Bodie used the width of the arena to his advantage, backing away and moving from side to side. The two opponents were soon separated from the group.

Bodie waited, watched for the right time to act. The guard wasn't exactly subtle. He followed Bodie around with his bat raised, but didn't stray too close. Bodie wouldn't have time to make a surprise attack. He had to wait for the guard to strike.

The two paced back and forth, waiting for the other to act. Bodie wouldn't be drawn into it. He waited and then pretended to lose focus and let his eyes drift to the scene of the battle. This galvanised his opponent to attack.

The man leapt forward, swinging down with his bat. Bodie tried nothing fancy. The man's swing was short, so short that all Bodie had to do was reach up a hand and close it on the descending bat.

He gripped it hard, stopped the attack. The guard looked shocked. With a wrench, Bodie yanked it out of the other man's hand and then, trying the element of surprise, threw it at him. The bat smacked the man full in the face, sent him stumbling. Bodie reached down to

The Contest

pick it up. Now he was the one with the weapon. The guard's eyes flitted every which way, looking for a chance to escape.

Bodie pressed his advantage. He stepped in hard and fast with quick swings. As the man focused on the bat, Bodie kicked him in the gut. The man folded, Bodie brought the bat down on the top of his head, staggering him.

The man went down, barely moving. Bodie looked up. His own team was dealing with their guards quite successfully. Cassidy had felled two, as had Yasmine, taking the pressure off Lucie. Heidi and Jemma were engaging still more, helping out the other team. The sound of chaos still reigned, and the sovereigns were all on their feet, cheering and eating and spilling their wine.

Bodie ran back across to the fight. He took out another guard and then traded blows with another. Cassidy fell to the floor, hit from behind. Bodie darted in to slow down her opponent, ignoring his own. It was a frenzied mess of battle, men and women trying to best the other with baseball bats and kicks and punches.

The sovereigns looked to be loving the spectacle. The guards lounging around the bleachers cheered and scoffed. Some of their own friends were probably out there fighting, and they commented loudly on their successes or defeats.

Bodie kicked his opponent in the chest, and then whirled to face his own guard. The man was already swinging his bat. Bodie managed to duck the attack and felt a certain satisfaction when it connected with another guard's shoulder. He drove the point of his bat into the man's groin, sending him down to the floor.

By now, most of the guards were down. Bodie noticed

the slight man lying on the floor, seemingly unconscious, along with a load of guards. He counted four opponents now standing and knew the fighting wouldn't last too much longer. He looked around, saw Cassidy staggering and holding her shoulder, saw Yasmine cupping her chin and rubbing it. Heidi looked okay, but Lucie was limping. They looked a sorry bunch.

And then Phoenix's voice rang out over everything. 'Let it stop!' he yelled. 'We sovereigns have seen enough, and it has been a mighty and tumultuous skirmish. We don't want you to exhaust yourselves, for there are many more contests to come! This has been...' he smiled. 'A bit of fun, mostly for the guards' entertainment. I hope you enjoyed!'

Bodie hated his blasé off-the-cuff comments, his view that their fighting hell had been nothing more than a bit of fun. They were all drained and bruised and at least Cassidy had taken a blow to the head. He hoped it hadn't disorientated her too much. And Heidi – she had to be incredibly uncertain – she had been due to fight her own contest today.

As if on cue, Phoenix waved beyond the arena to the ominous looking wooden contraption called the gauntlet.

'And some of you have that to look forward to tomorrow,' he said. 'I suggest you all get a good night's sleep.'

Bodie staggered out of the arena.

CHAPTER THIRTY FOUR

Reilly had a lot of work to do. He'd paid for the location of the compound, using Jacko's greed and unprofessionalism. But he was one man alone and knew he was up against a shitload of opposition.

Reilly spent some time wondering what happened next. What did you do in this situation? He had the last of his money and a faint idea of what to do. But he also needed to act quickly. Where did he go from here?

Reilly didn't rush into his decision like a fool. He considered it, considered every part. It was a difficult few hours, but there was only one solution. At least, only one solution he could think of.

He was going to need help.

As soon as he'd made the decision, Reilly didn't dither. He started making phone calls. Colleagues were currently in short supply, so he called the only people he knew – old friends, old acquaintances – but only the people he trusted. Reilly was aware he still didn't really know where he stood with the Bratva, so he tried to use the people he'd met during his Amazon days.

And there were more than he cared to admit. Thank God for phones, he thought, as he dialled up their numbers and made the calls.

He offered them money and asked for a meeting. Most of the people he knew were motivated by money.

Reilly had about a dozen people to choose from. He ended up with six who were willing to make the journey.

'Wylde. Mira. Carter. Flores. Chase. And Rytter.' He murmured to himself, mulling over their names. They were all on their way to Spain.

Reilly made the best of it. He wanted to talk to them all at once. He knew they were all capable, and that they would watch his back, knew they would walk through fire if they agreed to help. The important thing would be *not* to play down what they were up against. Reilly tried not to chafe about the lost time.

Eventually they all turned up, four men and the women – Mira and Rytter. They were a scarred, capable bunch, and Reilly sat them all down in a quiet corner of his hotel lobby, the surface strewn with bottles of alcohol.

'A grand reunion,' Wylde said with a huge grin.

'I'm asking you to risk your lives,' Reilly said.

'It's all about the money,' Rytter said.

'Are you sure? This is a big ask.' Reilly was determined not to play it down.

'Yet you said we have friends on the inside,' Carter said. 'Lots of them. That should help a great deal.'

'And that's the whole crux of the plan,' Reilly said. 'That's our way of overwhelming the compound's guards. If we can free the prisoners, we're on to a winner.'

'And a big payday,' Rytter reiterated. Rytter would do anything for a sizeable chunk of cash. Reilly had known right away that she'd agree to come to Spain the moment he mentioned the greenbacks.

'You say we're headed for Sierra Leone?' Flores asked. Reilly nodded.

'Where are we getting our weapons from?'

The Contest

It was a good question. They would have to fly to Sierra Leone first as they couldn't exactly take any guns in with them. They'd have to equip in country.

'I've thought about that,' Reilly said. 'I have a friend who moved from the Amazon to West Africa a few years ago. He dabbled in weapons.'

'Have you contacted him before we go?' Flores asked, always the stickler for detail.

'Yeah. He's still in the trade. We can count on him.'

'And the money?' Rytter shifted in her seat, her tight blue jeans reminding Reilly they had once done more than just talk. 'When do we see the cash?'

'As soon as we're done,' Reilly said. He knew these people were all loners and there'd be no point in paying them until the job was finished. It wasn't as if they could leave the money to anyone. And, of course, they knew the realities of what might happen too.

'How long we in country for?' Chase asked.

Reilly hadn't thought about that. He took a sip of beer to give himself time to compute. 'I'm guessing two or three days. If we can't do it in that time...' he spread his arms.

'You're not painting a fantastic picture,' Mira said.

'I'm not trying to. Listen...' And Reilly leaned forward. 'These people are capable, trained, and always ready for an assault. I don't know how many they number, but it could be over fifty. We stand no chance if we can't reach the prisoners, so that's our most important recce. If we fail, they die and we die. This is a ride or die mission.'

The team he'd assembled looked up for it, which impressed Reilly. Clearly, he'd picked the right people. He sat back now and considered them.

'One last good night before we dive in to hell?' Wylde said, holding up a glass.

'I'd say that's a given.' Carter said.

'How about it?' Rytter was looking at him and raising her eyes. 'One last good night?'

Reilly knew what she meant and ignored it. His feelings for Yasmine these days meant he had to consider every angle. And if Rytter and Yasmine ever met – which they *should* – then he didn't want things to get too messy.

'Drink up,' he said. 'I'll organise the flights.'

The next day, they left Spain and took a quick hop on a plane. The flight time was roughly five hours, so not too bad all in all. Reilly organised everything, from the flights themselves to the landing in Freetown and the onward journey to his friend who lived close – a man named Sharpe. They landed in good time, breezed through customs, and then found a taxi to take them to a car rental place. They hadn't wanted to use the airport ones to help keep a low profile.

Soon enough, they were in a small truck with canvas sides. Two upfront and four in the back. The team had argued about who went where, causing Reilly to shake his head and wonder about the risks of the mission. It all turned out amicable in the end, though. He drove and, being the leader, told them that Wylde was going to be his passenger. No one argued, and he hadn't chosen Wylde for any reason.

They left the capital, Freetown, behind and drove a few miles until they came to an industrial area populated by large buildings and warehouses. The place was overgrown with shrubbery and vegetation, and huge weeds forced their way up through cracks in the road. People were everywhere, sitting and staring, working on

THE CONTEST

cars and trucks, drinking out of bottles, repairing machines, and

There was an affirmation, and then the door opened. Reilly found himself staring at a familiar face.

'Sharpe,' he said, holding out a hand. 'Good to see you again.'

'And you, my friend.'

They all entered the room. Sharpe went behind a desk and then turned a shrewd eye on them. There was nowhere to sit, so everyone remained on their feet. Reilly found there wasn't a lot of space in the room, and started to think he should have left a few of them behind. He felt a bit like a schoolkid standing in his headteacher's office.

'What do you have for us?' he asked quickly.

'First, why are you here, my friend? Are you going to step on anyone's toes?'

Reilly thought it a fair question. 'Have you heard of a compound run by a man named Phoenix that forces people to become contestants in some brutal game?' He told Sharpe all he knew.

'No. Where?'

'It's right on the outskirts of your country. Run by a bunch of mega-wealthy dudes. I'm not surprised you haven't heard of it.'

'I'm poorly travelled,' Sharpe said with a touch of irony. 'Don't get out much. It's too friggin' hot out there.' He laughed.

Reilly looked around the room. It wasn't exactly appealing in here. 'The weapons?' he asked.

Sharpe nodded and sat forward. 'Got the usual and ubiquitous AK's, a few Glocks, a Sig Sauer and a few cheapo Taurus'. A shitload of ammo and six Kevlar vests along with military knives and a night vision goggle set up. Will that do for you?'

Reilly nodded with pursed lips. That all sounded just fine. 'I have the money.'

Sharpe held out a hand. 'Are you guys gonna start a war in my backyard?'

Reilly sensed this was an important answer. He met the other man's eyes. 'Not for long,' he said. 'It's a quick in and out, just a few hours. We're trying to rescue people, not start anything prolonged.'

'On that note,' Wylde said. 'How about you join us?'

Reilly winced. He didn't have the money for that, didn't have the right connections to get any more money. He barely had enough to pay the six people right here and procure weapons.

'I live here,' Sharpe said. 'I don't get involved in any kind of shit in my backyard. I'm sure you know what I mean.'

Reilly nodded. 'Sure,' he said. 'As mentioned, it's a quick in and out.'

'All right then. Let me show you the stash.'

It all went smoothly from there. Reilly was soon the owner of several sets of guns and ammo and was loading them all into two small four-wheel-drive vehicles they'd rented locally for the duration, along with provisions. When they were ready, Reilly programmed their journey into the sat nav and then they gauged the timings.

'Gonna be too late by the time we get there,' Mira pointed out. 'It'll be almost dawn.'

'Then we take it easy, park up, and hit the place tomorrow night,' Reilly said. 'Agreed?'

There were nods all round. The new team jumped into their trucks.

Reilly took a deep breath and followed them. This was one hell of a risky venture. He just hoped he wasn't leading them all into captivity… or worse.

CHAPTER THIRTY FIVE

Heidi woke with fear in her heart. Truth be told, she'd barely slept.

Today would be her day. She was the only member of the team who hadn't taken part in one of the horrendous contests yet, the only one unscathed. Today, all that would change. Today... she would face death.

Hesitantly, she swung a leg out of bed, then another, and sat up. She bowed her head. This was a far cry from being part of a relic hunting team that swept the globe for lost and ancient artefacts and from her old job in the CIA. It was ironic too, because it had happened right when she and Bodie were finally getting together. Effectively, it had driven them apart once more.

In the silence, she took a deep breath, then another. She knew it was early morning, knew she had about an hour before the guards came to take them to breakfast. She had to make the most of that hour.

Sat in a cell, in grey fatigues, surrounded by guards... yes, she had to make the most of it.

Heidi focused on her good times, which, she found, centred mostly around the relic hunters. They had been on some incredible missions from Greece to New York to the Amazon and even to Atlantis and, despite the danger, she had loved every one of them. The memories brought a smile to her lips. Further back was the memory of a daughter who wanted nothing to do with her and an ex-husband who blamed her job for her absence and punished her with divorce. Heidi chose not to dwell on all that.

She lost herself in splendid memories for an hour and remained quiet, chilling. Eventually, the guards came. They looked on edge today, almost excited when they looked at her, and she wondered why. What could they possibly have in store? Now, however, they wanted nothing except to escort her to breakfast.

Heidi followed the usual routine, filled her plate from the buffet and sat down to eat. Today, she wasn't in the mood to converse with her fellow inmates. Bodie and the others did, though, gathering valuable information. When Bodie came back to the table, he told them he they'd garnered enough information to possibly make a move. He figured Jemma could engineer something that could break them out of their cells, that they could gather all the prisoners together, to break out en masse. Once outside, they could commandeer trucks and vans and cars, enough to take them anywhere. If the vehicles had sat nav, they could figure out where they were and where was best to go.

Which left the problem of the guards and their guns.

They could overwhelm some of them, but not all. There was no sign of them guarding the perimeter on watch towers or anything like that, no sign of gatekeepers. Bodie had a vague sense of where they were housed, but nothing concrete. It was the massive flaw in their plan, and the one thing that could get them all killed.

Still, they had six teams on board now. Two had abstained, and team Bill was sitting on the fence. They were close to their end date now, but they had also recently lost a member of their team to the Killing Pit. They were devastated, and they were uncertain.

Heidi sat in edgy silence. The others made conversation, but didn't push her too hard. They knew what she was going through. Heidi finished her meal and thought about going up for seconds, but didn't want to overeat. Not today. Not when...

She didn't like the tail end of that thought. Instead, she finished her coffee and set about going up for a refill instead.

Soon, they headed back to their cells. Heidi thought about when she'd woke this morning with hours to go and the inexorable passage of time. You couldn't stop it and the more you fought against it, the faster the world seemed to turn. It ticked, and it ticked, irresistible, inescapable, pitching you towards whatever uncertain and unwanted future awaited. Every second felt like a death knell.

And soon... they came.

Heidi looked up as she heard the dreaded sound of approaching boots. The main guard stood outside her cell, a smug smile on his face.

'Today is good,' he said. 'I hope you are ready.'

'For what?' Heidi ventured, rising to her feet.

'Ah, my favourite. You will see.'

Heidi walked to the bars, stood waiting. As the guards unlocked her cells, the one who'd spoken leaned over and said, 'If you don't do as we ask, Bodie dies. That is who you will sacrifice today if you say no.'

Heidi had expected something similar, but wondered

why they'd chosen Bodie. Did they know of their potential relationship, or was it just a random guess? Soon, it didn't matter. She wasn't about to refuse to do as they asked. She was resigned to it all by now. A dangerous place to be. But she couldn't help how she felt. They'd been here for a week, and despite Bodie's big plan taking shape, she felt they were no nearer to getting out of here in one piece than they had been when they arrived.

She soon found herself outside in the heat, walking across the square, shielding her eyes. At first, she saw no activity around her whatsoever. The arena was empty; the Killing Pit building was still. And then she heard something. The sound of chatter and laughter in the wind. The sound of hilarity, of content conversation, of a crowd. She looked ahead and knew exactly what she was heading for.

The gauntlet.

It had been standing there like a dire warning all the time they'd been at the compound. Always in their visions, in their thoughts. It had looked like the worse kind of obstacle – a Devil hovering at the edge of vision – and now it was real. Now she was really going up against it.

But on the bright side, she thought, she didn't have to face a human opponent.

The guards manoeuvred Heidi towards the gigantic contraption. It became more daunting the closer it grew, a vast hellish feature of sharpened wood, beaten metal, and infernal angles. There was a pathway across it, but that pathway was pitted with snares and hazards.

Heidi saw the crowd now, gathered in seats arranged in front of the gauntlet. There were dozens of rows of

The Contest

seats, and the sovereigns were all arrayed in the first row. Heidi counted ten. A full compliment. The biggest turnout yet. She could already see Phoenix, the white-clad man, turning his head to see her approach. He looked excited.

Heidi stopped in front of the gauntlet. It towered above her. She could see the wooden steps she'd have to climb to reach its heights. She turned now, stared into the crowd.

A set of evil bastards who didn't deserve to live.

Phoenix surged to his feet. 'And now we have it,' he said. 'The return of the gauntlet. It's been a while!'

The crowd roared and clapped, some rising to their feet. The guards held their weapons tighter and smiled.

'The gauntlet is the greatest of our contests,' Phoenix went on. 'It pits machine against mind in the most perfect way. Who will win, and where will she die? Ladies and gentlemen, start placing your bets!'

Heidi cringed a little at the aloofness of it all, the disdain in which they held her. Did these people infect each other with callousness, one to the next to the next? She watched helplessly as people rose and turned to their neighbours, pulling out cash and betting slips and shouting in their excitement. She heard words like snakes and swords and the executioner. Her mouth was bone dry.

The guards gave her water and then urged her towards the bottom rung of the ladder. They stood below her as she started climbing, looking up. Heidi felt the thick, sharp wood under her hands, the grainy surface. She climbed step by step until she reached the top and then stepped up onto a wooden platform.

The gauntlet spread before her, all terrible wooden

angles. There was a single path through, broken intermittently, which she knew she'd have to follow.

'Start up the machine!' Phoenix yelled.

Heidi watched in horrific anticipation. A shudder ran through the gauntlet, and then it started to shake gently. Soon, many contraptions ahead were whirring and turning, their sound drowning out even the shouts from the crowd. Heidi turned to them, saw the gestures, the jeers, the eagerness. They were all anxious for her to get started.

Heidi felt the sun beating down, the sweat beaded on her brow. She closed her eyes for a moment, sought concentration. Suddenly, Phoenix yelled, 'Begin!' and she snapped her eyes open.

She was ready.

Ahead, the wooden structure shook gently. There was the hum and roar of machinery. Things turned and spun and rotated at various speeds. She put one step in front of the other, heard the urging of the crowd, wondered what she'd come up against first.

Ahead, the ropes slashed and whirled.

CHAPTER THIRTY SIX

Heidi approached the whipping ropes slowly and with trepidation. They blocked the way in front of her and were arranged in straight rows. She would have to avoid one before walking towards the next. She stopped before the first, balanced on the soles of her feet.

The thick rope sliced the air in front of her, winding back and forth, slashing like a blade. If one of those cords hit her, it would cause serious damage, hurt her chances of finishing the entire contraption. She stood in front of it, waiting, as the crowd bayed.

She tried to tune the crowd and its noise out. She was aware of the first line of sovereigns looking up at her from the right, of their relaxed attitudes and the way they sat back and ate and drank their fill, watching the entertainment. She couldn't get their icy heartlessness out of her head.

Heidi watched the snapping rope, gauging its frequency. It curled and then snapped and she reckoned she had a three second window where it curled before striking. The sound of the rope was like a blade cutting the air. She crouched slightly, knew she only had a few feet in which to jump because, beyond this rope, lay the next one.

She hesitated, counted the seconds down. When the first rope had snapped and then curled, she leapt past it, stopped abruptly in the space beyond it. Now she was in a no-man's-land, a small space between ropes, and she had to concentrate on the next.

This one was slightly different, curling and twining for just a second or two longer. But it then let go with an even harder snap, something that might break a bone or snap a finger. She watched its movement and counted the seconds and then leapt past it.

Once past, she drew up abruptly, now in front of the third rope. This one coiled and coiled, but then, as she was about to set off, it snapped abruptly, arresting her forward momentum. Heidi froze in place and watched it carefully. One time it coiled for three seconds, the next five; the next, it snapped three quick times in succession.

It was random.

The crowd cheered as it sensed her working this out. She glanced at them, concentration broken. The sovereigns all leaned forward as if sensing blood.

Heidi tried to figure it out. The crowd was yelling at her to get a move on. It seemed the rope might not be random after all, but after the three sudden snaps reverted to type. Heidi waited for the next three snaps against the wishes of the crowd and then jumped past. She sensed the curling of the rope and let out a deep breath of relief. She had guessed correctly.

Now she faced the fourth and final rope. It hung in front of her, curling upward and striking straight down. If she jumped past it, she might just touch it. Perhaps that was the idea.

She watched, counted, and waited. This rope seemed to be on some kind of timer, unleashing every five seconds. Heidi didn't rush. She knew only too well it could be some kind of trap.

The Contest

Finally, she made her move, leaping through the rope. Her hair touched it and that set it off, but the snapping of the rough cord just missed her back, though it brushed her clothing still, propelling her forward. Heidi landed on her hands and knees, breathing hard but unharmed.

The crowd shouted its appreciation. Some betting slips were thrown away, others amended with more money changing hands. The sovereigns were clapping gently in appreciation.

It was far from over. Heidi rose to her feet. Up ahead, the gauntlet seemed to end. The pathway disappeared and there was the top of a ladder standing up. Heidi approached it and looked down the ladder.

It was a pit suspended in the air. The ladder led to the bottom of the pit, in which lay coils and coils of hissing snakes. As Heidi watched, they rolled and slid over each other, their forked tongues flicking, their scales shining. There was a raised ledge that passed above them, the only way across to a ladder on the other side of the pit. Heidi guessed she would have to walk across it.

Snakes. The last thing she needed. Though, as she looked once more at the sovereigns, she thought it kind of fitted.

Heidi grasped hold of the ladder, climbed on, and started down. She went slowly and, as they sensed her presence, the snakes started writhing harder; they reared up and spat at her, their forked tongues flicking. The closer she got, the more agitated they became.

Heidi reached the bottom of the ladder. The ledge she would have to cross was right in front of her. She stepped off the ladder onto the ledge and now she was standing about two feet above the snake pit on a five inch wide plank of wood. She faced forward, looked to the other ladder, the one that led upwards.

It stood about twelve feet in front of her, twelve feet of hell.

Heidi could only walk by placing one foot tentatively in front of the other. She held her arms out for balance, breathed out slowly, and inched her way forward. To her right, gaps in the wooden structure enabled the audience to watch with rapt attention.

One step, then two. The snakes slithered toward her and started to raise up. They coiled and uncoiled, rearing their vicious looking heads. The sound of their combined hissing filled her ears.

Heidi fought to keep her balance as she walked across the plank. Snakes heaved to both sides, sliding across each other, approaching the plank and striking. Heidi saw several of them strike the plank itself, saw fangs hit the wood and pull away. The wood was just inches below her boots.

She soldiered on, one foot in front of the other. It felt like a mile across, and she wasn't even halfway. She could rush it, but that would only increase the risk. But was that true? Going slow was only allowing more snakes time to strike at her.

Their incessant hissing filled her ears. They lunged up from the bottom of the pit, their fangs inches from her boots. One snake got higher, grazing the leather on her soles. Heidi let out a strange noise and held her breath, frozen in place.

She couldn't just stop here.

The snakes were gathering, bulging over each other. The pile was growing, bringing them closer to her. They moved with a steady malevolence, each one as deadly as

The Contest

the next and with only one thought in mind. *Attack*.

Heidi stepped forward, waving her arms for balance. She felt petrified and unhinged. She had done nothing like this before in her life. It surely couldn't be happening, being forced to do this. Finally, she thought she was halfway across the plank. Her feet were aching because of the pressure, her eyes were stinging because the sweat was dripping into them.

Heidi blinked. Right then, a snake slithered up and over her boot, falling down the other side. They were that close. She felt an impact against her boot, saw a fang sticking into the leather. It hadn't penetrated her foot though – there was no pain. The snake fell away, disappearing among its brethren. Heidi lunged forward, feeling claustrophobic with fear. She came down on the plank, flapped her arms for balance, fell to the left.

And somehow managed to wrench herself straight. She wavered in place for a while as the crowd cheered.

One foot in front of the other. That was all she needed to do. Block out the snakes, block out the thin plank of wood beneath her. Just walk. Walk to the end of the plank and reach the ladder.

Finally, she did it. She started to climb out of the pit, using the ladder. There was a commotion behind her, the snakes shifting fast. Two then reared up, striking quickly, their fangs hitting the wood beneath her right boot. Heidi shuddered and climbed faster, making sure of her handholds every time before hauling herself up. The last thing she needed was to fall backwards now.

Up into the open air, she came again. Those who had bet on her to succeed laughed and whooped. Those who hadn't cursed. Heidi took several moments to steady herself before looking towards what came next.

She saw an open stretch of wide planking, no obstacle. It looked too good to be true. Heidi knew it was. What awaited her here? She approached the section tentatively, one foot in front of the other. The crowd urged her on, screaming with a whole lot of schadenfreude in their voices. Heidi ignored them, unsure what was coming next.

Entering the clear section, she swallowed drily. There was a sudden rush of air, a pop, and then a white-hot streak lit her arm up with pain. She froze on the spot, lifted her arm. The grey material had split and something had sliced her flesh just barely. She looked to where the implement currently sat quivering in a plank of wood. An arrow. Was someone shooting at her?

Heidi looked around, saw no one in evidence. She took another step forward and then, just barely, felt the floor give a little.

She flung herself forward.

Two more arrows split the air above her, barely missing. She understood now. There were pressure points all along the wide planking. Stepping on a pressure point released an arrow.

Heidi climbed to her knees, the sound of the crowd falling over her like a surge of water. They knew she had just understood her peril. She looked ahead. At least another twenty steps to go. The massive wooden contraption shuddered and shook all around her. A terrible, living beast that just wanted to maim and kill.

The crowd urged her on.

Heidi started crawling forward. There was another pop and an arrow split the air above her. Maybe she could just stay down here. But it wouldn't be that easy, she knew. They would have thought of that. Eventually,

The Contest

she would come across an arrow positioned low. Heidi rose to her feet and looked carefully at the wooden planking.

She saw it immediately. The pressure points were delineated by small silver bolts that stood slightly proud of the wood. She tested the theory now, sticking her leg out to tap the bolt and then quickly withdrawing it. Sure enough, an arrow shot through the air. This one would have jammed itself into her neck. Heidi now felt a rush of elation. She was beating the machine.

She kept her eyes on the planking and avoided the pressure points for the next fifteen steps. She heard a definite gloomy note enter the crowd's voice as it realised she had figured it out. Heidi got all the way to the end of the planking without another mishap.

But she still had a long way to go. She rested for a few minutes as she tried to figure out what came next.

Her heart rate went up.

You've got to be fucking kidding me.

CHAPTER THIRTY SEVEN

Dead ahead of Heidi, blocking her path, were several rows of swinging swords. The swords were full size and heavy looking. They whooshed through the air as they sliced it apart. Heidi stopped before the first one, gauging its swing.

Simple enough. Just left to right, swinging relatively wide. It wouldn't be too tricky to step beyond it. The trouble was, Heidi saw, the swords were set pretty close. There wasn't an awful lot of room between them. She would have to be extremely careful.

The crowd was regaining its voice again, sensing blood. Heidi took a quick glance at the sovereigns. They were sitting on the edges of their seats, sloshing their wine goblets and eating heavily, entranced by the spectacle. They were laughing and gesticulating, berating and praising her. Some of them looked annoyed, as if they'd already lost their bets. Heidi heard the shouting and tried to block it out. She could taste nothing except dry sand in her mouth. As she waited, she laid her hands on the wooden supports, feeling the rough wood beneath her fingers.

The first sword swung by heavily. She stepped forward briskly, made sure she was past its swing, and then stopped instantly. The second sword roared past, the deadly blade inches from the edge of her nose. So

The Contest

close, in fact, she could feel the wind it generated as it passed.

Heidi held her position, not daring to move, arms by her side. The sword swung by again, its momentum shaking her. The instant when it passed was terrible, curdling her insides. It was as if horrific death had come within inches of taking her life. Heidi counted and saw she had four more sets of swords to negotiate.

Taking a deep breath, she waited for the sword to pass and stepped forward. She held her breath. One enormous blade swung behind her and one in front. The sound of their passing was indescribably terrifying. It made Heidi cringe. She waited again and stepped forward once more...

... realised she'd stepped forward too far.

Heidi had split seconds in which to act. She sensed she was too far forward, had to inch herself back, but only a little. Her entire body shook. The sword was coming; she could see it out of the corner of her eye. The blade shone in the sunlight, reflecting brightly as it started on its arc towards her. She inched herself back a short way, but how far was too far?

Heidi had lost all sense of where she should stand. The swords were coming. All she could do was hold her position and hope. She flinched as the two swords approached at speed.

They passed within an inch of her, slicing the air, rushing by. Heidi felt the breeze as they passed. She now faced the last sword in line and took a deep breath, waited for it to pass her by, and then lunged.

She landed on the other side, clear, on her knees.

There was a roar from the crowd, a respectful cheer. They loved her. She loved the fact that she was still alive.

Her arm smarted where the arrow had struck, and her throat felt like extra dry sandpaper, but apart from that, she was okay.

Heidi stayed prone for a little while, catching her breath. She could hear footsteps in front of her. She could see some movement out of the corner of her eye, but hadn't had a chance to focus.

Now she looked up.

She was almost at the end of the gauntlet. That was the good news. The bad news was that a muscle-bound hulk of a man now stood between her and her goal. He wore a black leather mask, leather trousers and a leather vest and that was all. In his big, meaty hands, he held a thick noose. Next to him stood a gallows. Heidi had been wondering how that might be used. Now she knew.

Was she supposed to defeat him? Get round him? The voice of the crowd was suddenly raised. She heard them shout, *'Evade, evade!'* and figured that was what she would do. The trouble was, the guy took up most of the pathway.

But there was the gallows beside him. She would have to...

Heidi didn't like it. She gathered herself, rose to her feet. The big guy just stood there, rippling his muscles, noose in hand. His black eyes glittered through the holes in his mask. Heidi assessed him, figured his bulk would slow him down. This was all about speed.

She walked forward, got as close as she dared. She could smell him now, a thick smell like bad meat. His forehead dripped sweat and his mouth was drawn tight, his teeth bared. He thrust the noose towards her.

'For you,' he growled.

Heidi knew it was now or never. As the man spoke,

she darted towards him, making him start. His free hand shot out, grabbing for her. Heidi then stopped and kicked, hoping to surprise him. She succeeded. Her kick struck the centre of his stomach and pushed in, the fat bulging out to both sides. Still, he staggered a little. Heidi used the distraction to dart to her left. She went under the gallows, its terrible shadow hanging over her, and through to the other side.

The big guy grasped for her, unbalanced, and unable to walk, but Heidi went beyond him, moving as quickly as she could. She sprinted for the end of the gauntlet, reached the stairs that led down and stopped for a moment, looked back at her opponent.

He hadn't moved.

And judging by the cheers of the crowd, by the way they were standing on their feet and clapping, Heidi had to assume that she'd won the contest.

CHAPTER THIRTY EIGHT

Heidi waited for the guards to surround her. The adrenaline started to fade. Her legs shook, her arm smarted. She found she was hyperventilating and tried to get a hold of herself. The tension, the closeness to death – it all hit her now. She had come incredibly close to losing her life.

She stood in the shade of the gauntlet, sweating profusely, glad for a moment to be out of the glare of the red-hot sun. The guards said nothing to her, just stood warily around as Phoenix walked over.

'Bravo,' he said. 'What a performance. I have rarely seen anything like it.'

Heidi wasn't sure how to respond to a sick madman with seemingly endless resources, so said nothing.

'You people are the best of the best,' he went on. 'Your team, I mean. I can see we're going to have to switch things up a gear next week.' He smiled benevolently at her, then waved at the guards to take her away.

Heidi fell in with them, happy to leave the site of the gauntlet. They led her back to the cell block, which, oddly, she found a little comforting. It was far better than what waited for her outside, and it was cool. She entered her cell and sat down on the edge of the bed. She was dirty, sweating, and bleeding. The guards told her someone would take care of her wound soon and then

The Contest

she'd be allowed to shower and change. Heidi nodded without looking up.

She sat for a while, numb. The intensity of the contest was overwhelming, and it all surged through her mind in waves of disbelief and terror and shock. This was how everyone else had felt. They had all gone before her, and now she knew all about the trauma they had experienced.

As she sat there, she heard Bodie's voice. 'Heidi? You okay?'

'I think so,' she breathed. 'I survived.'

They didn't need to ask if her ordeal had been tough. Bodie said, 'Do you want to talk about it?'

'Not really. They took me to the gauntlet.'

There was a respectful silence. Heidi felt as if her team didn't quite know how to respond. She said, 'I survived. I'm okay.'

'That's seven contests we've completed,' Lucie said. 'Which means seven days. That's our first week done.'

Bodie whistled softly. 'You're right. I think we've been here long enough, don't you?'

'Are you kidding?' Yasmine said. 'One day was long enough.'

They chatted on. Heidi found she couldn't take part in the conversation. She remained too traumatised to think properly. After a while, someone came to take care of her wound and then she could shower and change. Soon, she was back in her cell and counting down the last hour or two before dinner.

Bodie broke a new silence. 'We are close to making our move.'

They had determined long ago that no guards remained in the cell blocks between appearances.

Jemma answered quickly. 'I am almost ready.'

Heidi knew she had been making a tool to pick their locks from implements they had stolen from the mess hall.

'The teams are up for it,' Yasmine said. 'Most of them.'

'You think we stand a chance?' Lucie said.

'More of a chance than staying here for another two weeks,' Cassidy spoke up. 'Do you seriously believe they're gonna let us go?'

'Team Bill is due to finish next week,' Bodie said. 'They've elected to stay. I can't seem to get through to them.'

'The truth is,' Heidi finally spoke up. 'We don't know what happens when we leave. Nobody does. They might take you into the desert and shoot you and then bury you. They might set you free on some desert island to starve to death. And of course... they might set you down in the middle of New York, free. I mean, what can we prove if we don't even know where we are?'

They chatted a little while longer. Soon, the guards appeared and led them to the mess hall, where they started in on their evening meal. Bodie and the others soon drifted away to start up their conversations with the other teams. Tonight, Heidi couldn't seem to bring herself to talk to anyone.

Her stomach turned and rolled wildly, spoiling her appetite. Her arm hurt. She could feel the tight bandage and it only reminded her of the gauntlet. The trauma of her experience stood at the forefront of her mind. She sat there, staring, unable to focus both physically and mentally. What the hell would happen to them next?

Heidi didn't know what to think. Bodie was hell bent

The Contest

on getting them out of here, and his focus was admirable. But was that the right way to go? There were dozens of guards, all armed, and other dangers beyond that. They had no idea what landscape lay all around them except for dry, deadly plains and hostile mountains. Of course, if they could commandeer the compound's vehicles, that might make a world of difference. One look at a sat nav, and they'd know instantly where they were.

Heidi watched Bodie and the other relic hunters work the room as the guards stood on the perimeter with indifference. They were getting close to a major decision. It would soon be now or never.

Could this be all part of the contest?

CHAPTER THIRTY NINE

Reilly and his team drove as close as they dared to the coordinates they'd been given and then decided to hide the vehicles. They found a thick stand of trees and parked them under the overhanging branches, drove them in deep. And then they all got out and met up under the concealment of yet more trees.

Reilly checked his AK, his Glock, and readjusted his Kevlar vest around his chest. The night was dark; it was just before midnight. There were surprisingly few stars in the sky and a bit of cloud cover. The moon was nowhere to be seen. In short, it was the perfect night for a covert infiltration.

Reilly scanned the team. They were ready. They had talked this through, and each person knew their job. It was all about getting in and out as quietly as possible, though the consensus was that would not happen when they released forty or so prisoners. Still, all plans were fluid, and Reilly knew they'd have to adapt this one before it was finished.

They left the tree cover, broke out the GPS and set off across country towards the coordinates. They walked for a few miles in silence, each man and woman looking out for themselves and monitoring the perimeter. Reilly watched everything as they traversed hills and a plain and then a wide river.

The Contest

Their destination then became obvious. Ahead, a long, high chain-link fence stretched across the landscape. The fence shone weirdly in the apparent wilderness, an incongruous obstacle. It appeared to go on for miles.

They traversed it until, ahead, stood a high gate, bordered by a wooden H-frame. Two wide gates stood in the middle, both currently closed. Reilly and the team sank to their stomachs and watched for a while. They saw no sign of guards.

'Too easy,' Reilly said eventually.

'Or they're incredibly complacent,' Wylde answered. 'Which is understandable if they've been here a while.'

Reilly led them away from the gate, still observing the compound beyond. From here, all they could see was a winding dirt trail and, in the distance, a huddle of shadow-strewn buildings. It was too dark to make out anything else. Reilly approached the fence.

He waited for Mira, who had the bolt cutters. She made quick work of the chain-link fence and soon they were through, crouching on the other side. Reilly saw there was quite a distance to the buildings, stayed low and signalled that they should start forward.

They took their time and kept to the shadows. Reilly tried to stay as quiet as possible, but found it difficult with all their gear. Still, there wasn't a guard in sight. He had to assume that was soon going to change.

The buildings loomed larger. There was no noise, not a sound stirred the compound. Reilly found it unnerving. He could now make out several buildings to left and right, all couched in shadow. The team paused for a few minutes and took stock.

'Where do we start?' Rytter asked.

'Look at the buildings,' Reilly said. 'To the left, that's clearly a house, an upmarket one. Next to it is an upscale hotel, both probably used to house the sovereigns we were told about. Then there are...' he squinted. 'At least three long, low buildings. They have to be cell blocks or guard barracks.'

'Well, we'd better be sure which is which,' Wylde said, half jokingly. 'Because choosing the wrong one could end messily.'

'I see a few other huts around,' Flores said. 'Maybe storage sheds.'

A brief noise shut the team up and made them hunker down. To their right, a guard finally appeared, drifting across their field of vision. He wore all black and a bullet-proof vest and carried an assault rifle. The guard looked bored, unhappy, and whistled tunelessly to himself. He was headed their way.

'Are we a go?' Wylde whispered to Reilly.

It was a damn good question. They'd come all this way. They were all tooled up and ready to go and yet still did not know exactly where his friends were being kept. In truth, they weren't even positive this was the right compound.

But Reilly had to believe they were right, that they were just in what they were doing, that they were here to do the right thing and free his friends, along with countless other prisoners. And it would not work without the help of those other prisoners.

'We are a go,' he said and tried to quell all the misgivings he felt about being right here at this time, about to commit murder.

The guard sauntered nearer. He really wasn't paying attention. Wylde was the closest to him and took the responsibility. The powerful man rose from the shadows just as the guard strolled by, grabbed him around the neck and got him in a choke hold. The guard struggled, but only briefly. His gun clattered to the floor. Soon, he was dangling limply in Wylde's arms, and then being dragged further into shadow.

'Let's move,' Reilly said, noting that Chase picked up the guy's gun for one of the prisoners.

They penetrated further into the compound. Now to the far right, they could see what appeared to be a large arena surrounded by wooden stands. It was faintly floodlit and looked old, barbaric. Reilly wondered if these were part of the trials his friends had been facing. Were there other spectacles like this scattered about?

He focused. They ran to the nearest building, breaking cover for just a few seconds. Then they were in the lee of the building and Rytter was looking through the front door.

'I see bunks,' she breathed. 'Must be the guards' quarters.'

Reilly cursed. That was the one thing they didn't need. He turned to the right. Saw a larger building standing in a square of hard-packed earth, motioned at it.

'We'll try that one.'

Before he could move, Rytter jumped sharply back. She motioned frantically, and the group melted away, disappearing into the deeper shadow at the side of the building. Seconds later, the door opened and two guards came out. Reilly was crouched low, looking up at them. This time, the team drew their knives.

They waited. The guards came right past them, holding weapons in one hand and radios in the other.

Since Reilly had already sanctioned the mission, the team didn't hold back. Two of them leapt out at the ideal moment and drew the edges of their knives across the guards' throats. Then, as they bled out, they were dragged into deeper shadow, their radios turned off and their guns taken.

'No going back now,' Reilly said tensely.

They ran to the next building, staying low and unseen. Their equipment jangled a little in the silent night, but it wasn't loud enough to cause concern. This time, Reilly found himself at the head of the crew and slowly approached the front doors of the building. Flores was at his side.

Together, they looked through the long narrow vision panel.

The first thing Reilly saw was cell doors. Dozens of them marching away down a corridor. He smiled grimly and turned to the others.

'Jackpot,' he said.

They tried the front doors, found them locked. Mira stepped forward, lock picks in hand. It took her nine seconds to pick the lock, and then she pushed the doors open. Without a sound, they went inside.

Went to the first cell and looked inside. Saw a man sleeping in a grey outfit, covers bunched around his ankles.

Reilly took a look down the length of the cell block. There were two passageways to traverse, both with cell blocks on either side. This was going to take a while. Of course, his entire team was versed in lock picking, as was he, so they could all work separately. Sooner or later, he thought, they would get to Bodie and the others.

Seconds ticked past. He gave the go. The team split up

The Contest

and started towards the cell doors, drawing out their lock picking tools. They didn't speak, just went into the cells first and then roused the occupant, figuring that was the quietest way to do it. Six of them, working together, ought to get this done in no time.

Reilly worked on his first cell. He was inside quickly, then bent over the sleeping figure and shook his shoulder gently.

The eyes opened. Reilly whispered, 'We're here to rescue you. Remain calm and quiet. Do you want to be rescued?'

The figure nodded, eyes quickly comprehending. Reilly went on with the second part of his rehearsed speech. 'This will not be easy. We're gonna come under fire. Are you ready?'

Again, the nod. Reilly motioned for the man to get up and then left the cell. Quickly, he walked past his team to the next cell and repeated the routine. Soon, he had freed three men and was moving to the next available cell.

Through the bars, he recognised Cassidy.

His heart leapt. He rejoiced. She recognised him immediately and sat up with a start. Her face crumpled into a grin.

'Reilly?'

'Yes, it's me. I've come to get you out.'

'Oh, well done, bud. Well done. Do we get to fight these assholes?'

'Yes, you most certainly do.'

Cassidy looked pleased. She waited for Reilly to pick the lock. As he did so, he was aware of the other relic hunters being released down the line of cells. Soon, he was staring into the face of Guy Bodie.

'You are a sight for sore eyes,' Bodie said. 'Literally. I don't know how you found us, but thank you.'

'We're far from out of this yet, but you're welcome.' Reilly shook his hand.

Bodie gathered around with his friends. 'What's the plan?'

Reilly balked a little at that. 'There isn't much of one,' he admitted. 'We release the prisoners, who become our army, and then we go incapacitate or kill all the guards. We take over the compound. Then, we escape.'

Bodie nodded. 'Sounds good.'

Reilly looked briefly at his friends because time was at a premium. They looked worn, bowed by their ordeal. But there was a new light in their eyes now – the light of hope.

He looked around, up and down the cell block. The prisoners were all released on this side and being apprised of the plan. Seconds later, Rytter appeared, saying all the prisoners on the other side were free.

They stood in silence for a moment. So far, the plan was going well. He looked Bodie in the eye.

'Shall we?' he said.

'You're the boss.'

Reilly first connected with his own team, made sure they'd explained the plan to all the prisoners and that they were on board. Surprisingly, he was told there'd been three abstentions – people who wanted no part of it. He shook his head. Each to their own. But all the rest were ready.

He looked towards the doors.

'Let's do this,' he said.

CHAPTER FORTY

Reilly led the way back out into the night.

The prisoners trailed him in a long line. They were too many to hide properly but still tried to merge with the surrounding shadow. It would now all be about surprise. If they could despatch a few guards in silence, it would make their jobs far easier.

The whole new forty strong team knew this.

Reilly waved them away. Not everyone had a weapon, of course, but they were all capable operatives. They had to be – being here. Reilly knew that. Now, in the dark, various people explained that they knew several guard positions and hurried off to take care of them. Reilly looked from the cell block to the other buildings.

'Any idea which one of these is guarded?' he asked.

Bodie pointed ahead. 'That's the mess hall, so unlikely. That's the hotel they put the sovereigns up in, and that right there – that's Phoenix's house.'

'Phoenix?' Reilly said. 'Is he the boss?'

'Head asshole,' Cassidy said. 'We gotta take him down.'

All around, figures were dashing off into the darkness, some kind of vengeance on their minds. The night writhed with malevolent shadows. Reilly heard nothing, but he knew exactly what was happening out there.

'The guard's barracks would be an obvious target,' Jemma said.

'Too many of them, and then it'd get noisy,' Reilly mimed the use of a gun. 'We need to start by taking as many as we can, as quietly as we can. That's the 'Reilly' way.'

'I must confess,' Cassidy said. 'I like the 'Reilly' way.'

Reilly now realised there were twelve people in his immediate team. Quite a large number. Where could they go? He nodded at Phoenix's house. 'Let's do it.'

They arrowed off, keeping to the shadows of the buildings but heading for the house in question. It reared up ahead of them, ostentatious, completely out of place with its surroundings. Purposely so, Reilly thought. Phoenix was clearly that kind of man.

They reached the front and flattened themselves against the building. Now Mira stepped forward and again used her lock picking tools. The door opened inwards, and they were filing inside. Bodie and his team insisted on going first.

They came to a reception room where a guard lounged over a semi-circular desk. He didn't even look up as they approached.

'Yeah?'

These people were incredibly complacent, Reilly thought. They had been stationed here for far too long. He saw Cassidy run and vault over the desk, kick the guy in the throat and then follow him down to the ground. There were a few death gurgles, but nothing too loud. The team continued past the reception room. Cassidy pocketed the guard's handgun.

A circular room lay beyond, populated by desks and computers. Reilly guessed this was a kind of information hub during the day where techs worked. They didn't slow, went to the next room.

The Contest

Found three guards lounging around on sofas watching a game on a 60 inch TV.

The twelve strong team exploded into action, lunging at the guards. For their part, the guards had left their weapons propped in a corner and had no chance of reaching them. Bodie took one man, Heidi and Jemma another. Some of Reilly's team became spectators, but others barged in on the action.

The guards fell beneath a barrage of blows. Knives were used. Soon, there was the sound of blood leaking and pooling on the floor. Reilly didn't know what had been done to the relic hunters, and in what way, but he guessed it was pretty bad.

Bodie looked up from the floor, his knife dripping with blood. 'Next,' he said.

They advanced through the house, eventually reaching the first floor staircase. Here, they would be exposed. Reilly led the way up, now holding his gun in front of him. They were approaching the point where they may have to go loud, but he would keep it quiet for as long as he could.

They reached the landing without incident, started along a wide corridor papered with plush wallpaper and lined with gilt-edged paintings. As they walked, a guard appeared ahead, saw them, and gawped in surprise. His mouth fell open. Reilly was too far away to rush the man before he brought his gun up, so, reluctantly, aimed his own gun.

Cassidy's well-aimed blade slammed through the air, missing Reilly's left ear by less than an inch. The point entered the guard's throat and made him choke, brought him to his knees. Seconds later, he was dead. Reilly turned to Cassidy and raised an eyebrow.

'Great throw. Didn't know you had a knife.'

'Pulled it off the guard back there,' she showed him another. 'Want one?'

He smiled and shook his head. They continued on, traversing the top floor corridor. When they came to a window, Reilly stopped and peered through. He could see shapes out there, shapes dealing death and destruction. They flitted through the darkness with their deadly weapons, their movements quick and shocking, their intentions merciless. They had been abused for too long and were now extracting their revenge. He saw guards fall, shadows rise, blades flash. And, scarily, it was all soundless.

They checked one room and then another. They found a white-robed man in the third room they checked – not Phoenix. Bodie said he vaguely recognised him as a frequent sovereign. The man didn't put up a struggle as they bound and gagged him and then left him tied to the bed.

They moved on. It was the fifth bedroom before they found Phoenix. Cassidy entered the room first and found the man sleeping alone atop the bedsheets, his face turned towards them. At that moment, he looked serene, harmless.

In reality, he was one of the most evil bastards alive.

Bodie stared at the sleeping figure. He could barely believe they had him, and it was all down to Reilly. Their new friend had really come through. Bodie couldn't begin to describe the relief he'd felt when he first saw the man and, even now, when everything was still uncertain, he was still on a high. They were free for the first time in a week, free to do as they pleased.

The Contest

And they were here – right in the madman's room.

Cassidy strode over to the bed, put a gun against Phoenix's left temple and ground it in until he woke. The man's eyes first filled with fear, and then went calm. He sat up in bed.

'Aren't you having a really bad dream?' Cassidy breathed in his ear.

'An interesting development,' Phoenix said. 'I wonder how many escaped.'

'All of us,' Bodie said, walking forward. 'Which means you are fucked.'

'I have contingencies for that,' Phoenix said.

'You do? What are they?'

'They're called *guards*.'

'Well, at the moment, pal,' Bodie went on. 'Your guards are all meeting the business ends of some mighty sharp blades. We're taking over.'

Phoenix looked unsure for the first time. 'You have organised into a fighting force?'

'You thought we would just try to flee with our tails between our legs?' Cassidy asked. 'You thought you could hunt us down? That it'd be a new sport for you? I bet you did. But it ain't gonna happen that way. *We're* hunting *you* down.'

'And we're killing you all,' Heidi said.

Phoenix inched backwards on the bed, looking from face to face. 'I own you,' he said. 'You're mine.'

Bodie borrowed a knife and brought it close to Phoenix's face. 'Out of interest,' he said. 'What *does* happen to the teams that survive their three weeks?'

Phoenix looked on with tightly drawn lips. 'The burning question,' he said. 'I understand why you ask it now. The truth is... we set them free.'

'Bollocks,' Jemma said and smashed her fist across Phoenix's smug face. His lips mashed against his teeth, drawing blood.

'It is true! They are-'

Jemma punched him again, getting blood on her knuckles.

'Try again,' Cassidy said.

Phoenix stared wildly from grim face to grim face. 'It's a big fucking territory,' he said finally. 'You figure it out.'

Bodie wasn't surprised, but he was horrified. All the teams who had fought here, all the people who reached the end of their term, all the hopeful souls. They were all just taken into the landscape, shot, and buried.

He felt an urge to thrust his blade right through Phoenix's face, fought it. He couldn't bring himself down to the man's level. Instead, he turned to his team, the people who'd stood by his side throughout this ordeal.

'Tie the bastard up,' he said. 'Justice will deal with him.'

Cassidy didn't look happy about it. 'Isn't the system built to allow rich pricks like this to slip through? Doesn't it happen all the time?'

Bodie agreed, but what was the alternative? 'If they fight us, we hurt them back,' he said. 'If they sit there looking sorry for themselves,' he indicated Phoenix. 'We tie them up and hand them over to the authorities. They're murderers ten or a hundred times over.'

Phoenix swiped out as Jemma and Cassidy bent to tie him. They laughed, caught his ineffectual swings and almost broke fingers and arms. Phoenix squealed. It was good to see him on the receiving end. Bodie watched, a half smile on his lips.

'Phoenix is neutralised,' he said. 'Who's got the other sovereigns?'

The Contest

Reilly reeled off a list of names. Bodie didn't know them, but knew, if they'd come with Reilly, they'd be decent operatives. He had to assume the other sovereigns were taken care of. Once Phoenix was secure, he turned away.

'I think we're gonna have to take care of the rest of the guards,' he said.

This was going to be the hard part, he knew. They checked the rest of the house and then went back outside. In the dark night he could hear the sound of guards being taken down, see the slinking of nightmare shadows carrying knives and rocks and anything else that came to hand. The darkness was a seething mass of horrors, of dozens of men and women reaping vengeance on scattered guards for what had been done to them. He heard the sound of metal and stone on flesh, the death throes of the dying, saw blades flashing, gleaming in the half light.

At the horizon, a false dawn was coming.

Bodie turned towards the guard's barracks.

'Let's end this,' he said.

CHAPTER FORTY ONE

Silently, the entire team crept towards the guardhouse, keeping to the shadows for now. Around them, the sounds of death remained muted and soon they were being joined by several others. As they approached the barracks, Bodie guessed their number had swelled to over twenty.

They possessed about eight guns between them and numerous knives. Reilly's team, of course, was fully equipped.

Bodie slowed as they approached the front doors of the barracks. The entire team crowded around, listening. It was Reilly who spoke up first, the unofficial leader of their incredible coup.

'No killing for killing's sake,' he said. 'We do this the right way.'

There were nods from some, steely silence from others. Bodie readied himself. It came as no surprise to find the front door of the barracks unlocked. They waited for a moment, braced themselves, and then walked straight in.

It was cool inside, the regulated temperature soothing. They stood in a wide reception room lined with armchairs. There was a counter ahead, unmanned, and several vending machines and sofas. The guards had it good.

Bodie led the way to the back, gun in hand. There was

The Contest

a narrow corridor with doors to either side. People barged through the doors, finding nobody on duty. Of course, it was coming up to dawn, probably the quietest time of the night for the guards.

Beyond the corridor they came to a wide open space. It was surprising. The place just opened out to left and right, and there were bunks running down it in several rows. Quite a few of the bunks were occupied. Bodie thought it would be a dream to visit every bunk before they woke, neutralise every guard.

But that would never happen.

There was a guard sitting up in bed, thumbing through a magazine. When he heard an inrush of noise, he looked over, eyebrows raising in surprise.

'Hey!' he yelled.

The team rushed forward. When the guard reached for a gun and turned it on them, they shot him. Other guards were swinging themselves out of bed, some faster than others. More guards were waking. Gunshots rang out.

Bodie raced down the nearest row of bunks, came across a guard at ground level and smashed him across the head. He fell back, unconscious. Bodie grabbed the weapon that was lying next to him and threw it to a teammate. He moved on, reaching a swinging set of legs as a man tried to jump out of bed. Bodie caught him halfway, smashed his gun across the man's face. The guy fell back, bleeding, but reaching for his weapon.

Bodie leapt on him, on the bunk, and brought his gun down again. The guards didn't deserve to die unnecessarily; he thought. Yes, some of them enjoyed their job – maybe even took pleasure in it – but not all of them. He clonked his opponent on the temple twice and watched him slide into oblivion.

Bodie climbed off the bunk. There was chaos all around. He saw Cassidy and Heidi meeting guards in the centre of the row, jabbing and punching at them. There was the sound of gunshots coming from other rows, either the retaliation of the guards or the onslaught of the now ex-prisoners.

Bodie saw another guard leaping into the fray. This one already had his gun up and was aiming. Bodie was forced to drop to one knee to present less of a target and then open fire. His bullets stitched a line across the man's stomach, dropping him. Almost instantly, another guard replaced him, this man with his gun up. Bodie fired again, taking off the top of his head.

To left and right guards were waking and jumping down. Bodie found he was in the thick of it. He lashed out constantly, watching for weapons. He grabbed a gun, yanked it away from a guard, and shot him in the leg. A man swung at him as he leapt from the top bunk, grazing Bodie's head. He caught the swinging arm and yanked on it, brought the man tumbling down. Ahead, he saw a guard using the top bunk to his advantage, firing down on the prisoners and tagging a man. Yasmine shot him through the mattress and he fell back, bleeding through the grey sheets.

They worked their way down the aisle. Some guards wanted none of it and sat or stood with their arms in the air. They were herded to the back of the room. Some leapt into the battle with gusto, not even firing but swinging their arms left and right, up for a fight, even as guns pointed at them. Bodie saw it all in the eyes of his enemies: anger, frustration, fear, outright terror. He saw suspicion and pure rage and utter disbelief. Some of these men thought they were supposed to fight to the death.

The Contest

Bodie pressed on. He saw bedlam on both sides, men and women in a turmoil of battle. He heard shots and shouts and gasps, the death rattle of many. Prisoners fell and guards twisted and collapsed off their bunks. The smell of sweat and fear tainted the air, and all he had was the feel of the hard steel weapon in his hands.

It coughed again as he fired before being fired upon. Another guard sprayed blood on someone and then fell dead.

It was madness. Bodie was at the centre of it, spinning and shooting and lashing out. Close by, Lucie and Cassidy were working in tandem, the latter looking after the former. They dragged guards down off their bunks or met them head on when they jumped down, or barged right into them, knocking them off balance. Beyond them fought Heidi and Yasmine, also working together and watching each other's backs. Jemma was further back, mopping up behind Bodie. She moved faster than anyone. Between them, and around them, were dozens of prisoners, all hell-bent on defeating the guards and securing their freedom.

Bodie could barely think straight. He didn't dare rest for fear of missing the attack of a guard. His eyes were constantly seeking opponents, looking for the barrel of a gun. He tried to keep himself small. Already he'd felt the whistle of a bullet slicing by.

The pandemonium continued. Bodie saw the other aisles now, filled with fighters. Guards were being thrown left and right, knocked unconscious. When one guard escaped and started firing on the prisoners, he was mowed down.

Gradually, the sounds of shooting died down. The prisoners had overwhelmed the guards. Looking back along the aisle, Bodie saw a huddle of bodies, some still alive and wounded, and ran to one man, staunched the bleeding. He looked up, saw his team assembled around him. Reilly came up then too, gripping his weapon and smiling hugely.

'This isn't the only set of guards,' Bodie told him. 'Others are out patrolling the perimeter, or just outside. There will be more in the sovereign's house and maybe some we missed in Phoenix's. We haven't won yet.'

Reilly nodded grimly. He looked around for his team. 'Time to make sure the sovereigns are all rounded up.' He said.

'Trussed up ready for the authorities?' Cassidy asked. She was breathing heavily, spotted with blood.

Reilly nodded. The commotion inside the barracks was dying down even more. Bodie looked back. There was a rear exit to this place, right next to them.

'Come on,' he said.

Together, the two teams exited the barracks and stepped back out into the night. By now, the dawn was coating the horizon, a mix of red, gold and yellow brushstrokes painting the edge of the world. It cast an odd burnished light across the landscape and brought with it a cool breeze.

Bodie stopped and sniffed the air for a moment. This was the first time he'd experienced free air in over a week. It felt good. But they weren't free yet. They still had work to do.

They raced around the building, saw the sovereign's house in front of them, and ran to the front door. Already, other prisoners had entered, and the door stood wide open. There was the sound of a commotion from within. Bodie ran straight inside, found himself in a wide, circular hallway with a polished floor and walls.

It was madness. Sovereigns were being dragged down

the stairs by their hair or ankles. They were screaming; they wore just night clothes – some were even naked – and they struggled in the grips of their captors, but they did not stand up and fight. Their captors were armed with guns and knives and makeshift weapons and weren't shy about using them.

It was a double staircase with two wings. Sovereigns were being dragged down both sides, and some lined the hallway above. One prisoner was threatening to throw a man off the balcony. Bodie saw the man throw up his hands and fall to his knees and then the prisoner rammed his knife through the man's skull. Bodie winced. He understood, but didn't condone. These prisoners had watched the sovereigns clap and cheer and smile at their expense for weeks. They had seen friends die, had been terrorised, all in the name of bloodsport. And the sovereigns had been the architects of that terror.

Men and women were flung down the stairs and lined up along the perimeter of the room. Bodie counted four and then six and, finally, nine. Was that all of them? An opportune night. Bodie wasn't sure, but he thought so. Phoenix made ten, and they already had him. As he watched, he saw Rahim, Phoenix's right-hand man, also dragged down the stairs and thrown headlong across the polished floor. Rahim slid to a stop with his hands held high and was then manhandled to his feet and forced to join the growing line.

Bodie stepped forward. It looked suspiciously like a firing squad. 'What are you doing to these people?'

'They're gonna get what's coming to them,' more than one voice shouted back. 'And this arsehole. This bastard.' They shook Rahim. 'He's doing the gauntlet.'

Bodie looked around, realising he had no authority here, no way of regulating what these former captives did. The sovereigns weren't fighting back – they were meek and cowering and submissive.

But the prisoners were raging.

Bodie walked to where he could be seen and heard. 'Don't do anything rash,' he yelled. 'Anything that might get you thrown into jail. This is a matter for the authorities now. They will handle it.'

Guns were already being lined up on the sovereigns. 'They deserve a bullet,' someone muttered.

'They do,' Bodie yelled. 'But that bullet could land you in jail for years. And there's your freedom gone again. The authorities *will* figure out what happened here. Don't risk losing your freedom... again.'

That sobered a few of them up. Some weapons were lowered. The sovereigns quaked in their shoes, shivering in a line. Bodie saw the light of madness leave some eyes, but common sense didn't touch a few of the others. Their faces were twisted with rage.

'This bastard,' they grabbed Rahim. 'He's going outside.'

Bodie knew Rahim had been a constant at all the contests, always standing and clapping and cheering with Phoenix. He knew how these people felt, and he couldn't stop them from carrying out their devilish plan. They herded Rahim out of the house and started pushing him across the square toward the Gauntlet.

Reilly pulled out a sat phone. Bodie watched him place a call to the authorities and found himself torn. He didn't want to put the men and women who were about to execute Rahim in jeopardy. He knew why they were doing what they were doing. But at the same time, this was not a kangaroo court. They needed specialists and consultants and people used to being in charge. Someone to take hold of Phoenix and the sovereigns and clap on the irons.

The Contest

Through the window, he watched at least a dozen men and women march Rahim off to his fate. A moment later, he saw Phoenix dragged into the square too and forced to his knees. A large man held a gun to Phoenix's head and was mashing the barrel into his ear.

Bodie burst outside. He yelled at the man to stop, saw Phoenix's eyes turn towards him.

'This is not the way!' he yelled.

The man opened fire. Phoenix collapsed into the dust, blood and dirt mingling on the ground.

This was what you ended up with, Bodie thought. This was what you ended up with when you pushed people beyond their limits, made them feel like wild animals, forced them to fight for their lives against all odds. This was what happened when you turned a civilised person the wrong way around. You created murder and death and bedlam and a man or woman who, otherwise passive, would easily condone the killing of the architect of their misery. Bodie looked at Phoenix's dead body and he felt deeply for the people who believed they had to kill him, to extract that final bit of revenge.

Behind him, there came a volley of gunshots. The sovereigns had also been executed.

Bodie let his head drop. Vaguely, he heard someone say, 'They'd have had the power and money to evade prison anyway,' and couldn't let the thought get away. It was true. These days, was justice ever really *just?*

In the distance, he heard the gauntlet starting up. Reilly had finished his phone call. Now all they had to do was wait. He thought about everything they'd experienced during the last week, all the trials they'd endured.

And still they stood in the same dust and dirt, surrounded by blood, but now they were survivors. They had faced the worst type of contests, pitted against evil and innocent human and machine, and they were still standing. He saw team Bill, and the others, saw the familiar faces all turned to the warm light of the rising dawn, saw a new glint in their eyes.

Hope.

It was a hollow victory though, he thought, where they had chosen to execute their captors. He wished it could have been done the correct way. Was it simply savage, or was it savage human nature?

Bodie let all the angst, the internal inspection, the torment just slough away. He hadn't asked for any of this. It had been forced upon him by evil men and women who cared nothing for human existence, for civil liberties and freedoms. Maybe, in the end, they had got what they deserved.

His friends came around him now, first Heidi and then Cassidy and then the others. Reilly came up last, still holding the phone.

'We should stay alert,' Jemma said. 'There are still some guards around.'

'I would say most of the stragglers are making themselves pretty scarce by now,' Cassidy said with a laugh. 'They must be able to see what's happened here.'

Bodie stared at his team, looking from face to face. 'I think that's the hardest thing I've ever done,' he said. 'Surviving this.'

'But we did it with style.' Cassidy tried to lighten the mood, but Bodie's words took them all back to the trauma of their individual trials.

'Pure hell,' Lucie said.

It wasn't something Bodie thought he'd ever fully recover from. He said as much and listened as the others talked about their sufferings. As they talked, other teams

The Contest

joined them and soon there were dozens of them standing around, listening to one or two people speak, shedding themselves of their own burdens or just skimming the surface, some trying not to dip too deeply into the crawling pit of their anxieties, others hoping they could rid themselves of the terrible burdens they had been forced to bear. It was a deep, profound, multilayered discussion, progressing as the exquisite dawn captured the eastern skies and a peace that none of them had experienced for some time spread softly over the landscape.

For Bodie, it was therapeutic. He'd never known so many people come together to talk openly about their recent problems. It both soothed and comforted him and, he hoped, it might allow him – and his team – to move forward.

THE END

Thank you for purchasing and reading the new *Relic Hunters* novel. I really hope you enjoyed it! I'm not yet sure what the next book will be about, but it should be available in April 2024. Thanks for your continued support!

If you enjoyed this book, please leave a review or a rating.

DAVID LEADBEATER

Other Books by David Leadbeater:

The Matt Drake Series

The Alicia Myles Series
Aztec Gold (Alicia Myles #1)
Crusader's Gold (Alicia Myles #2)
Caribbean Gold (Alicia Myles #3)
Chasing Gold (Alicia Myles #4)
Galleon's Gold (Alicia Myles #5)
Hawaiian Gold (Alicia Myles #6)

The Torsten Dahl Thriller Series
Stand Your Ground (Dahl Thriller #1)

The Relic Hunters Series
The Relic Hunters (Relic Hunters #1)
The Atlantis Cipher (Relic Hunters #2)
The Amber Secret (Relic Hunters #3)
The Hostage Diamond (Relic Hunters #4)
The Rocks of Albion (Relic Hunters #5)
The Illuminati Sanctum (Relic Hunters #6)
The Illuminati Endgame (Relic Hunters #7)
The Atlantis Heist (Relic Hunters #8)
The City of a Thousand Ghosts (Relic Hunters #9)
Hierarchy of Madness (Relic Hunters #10)

The Joe Mason Series
The Vatican Secret (Joe Mason #1)
The Demon Code (Joe Mason #2)
The Midnight Conspiracy (Joe Mason #3)
The Babylon Plot (Joe Mason #4)

The Rogue Series
Rogue (Book One)

The Disavowed Series:
The Razor's Edge (Disavowed #1)
In Harm's Way (Disavowed #2)
Threat Level: Red (Disavowed #3)

The Chosen Few Series
Chosen (The Chosen Trilogy #1)
Guardians (The Chosen Trilogy #2)
Heroes (The Chosen Trilogy #3)

THE CONTEST

Short Stories
Walking with Ghosts (A short story)
A Whispering of Ghosts (A short story)

All genuine comments are very welcome at:

davidleadbeater2011@hotmail.co.uk

Twitter: @dleadbeater2011

Visit David's website for the latest news and information:
davidleadbeater.com

Printed in Great Britain
by Amazon